THE TITHING

THE SACRIFICE DUET
BOOK 1

A. ZAVARELLI

NATASHA KNIGHT

Copyright © 2023 by A. Zavarelli & Natasha Knight

All rights reserved.

No part of this book may be reproduced in any form or by any electronic or mechanical means, including information storage and retrieval systems, without written permission from the author, except for the use of brief quotations in a book review.

This is a work of fiction. Names, characters, places and incidents are either the product of the author's imagination or are used fictitiously, and any resemblance to actual persons, living or dead, business establishments, events, or locales is purely coincidental.

Cover by Coverluv

NOTE FROM THE AUTHORS

IVI
Imperium Valens Invictum

The story you are about to enjoy is set in the world of *The Society* created by A. Zavarelli and Natasha Knight. Although you do not need to read any other books to follow this story, here is a brief description of what IVI is and how it operates.

Imperium Valens Invictum, or IVI for short, is Latin for Strong Unconquered Power. The organization is frequently referred to by its members as The Society.

We are a well-established organization rooted in powerful dynasties around the world. Some call us thieves in the night. A criminal syndicate. Mafia. The truth is much more intricate than any of those simplistic terms.

Our ancestors learned long ago there was power in secrecy. The legacy handed down to us was much more evolved than that of the criminals waging war on each other in the streets. We have money. We have power. And we are much more sophisticated than your average knee-breaking Italian mob boss.

IVI holds its members in the highest regard. With that power comes expectation. Education. Professionalism. And above all, discretion. By day, we appear as any other well-bred member of society. They don't and never will know the way our organization operates.

Thirteen families founded the ancient society. These families are held in the highest regard and referred to as the Upper Echelon. These are the Sovereign Sons and Daughters of The Society.

The Society has its own judicial branch, The Tribunal, that operates outside the norms of what is acceptable in the world today. Its laws are the final law for Society members.

The Society will go to great lengths to protect its members from the outside world but their expectations are often higher and sentences handed down from The Tribunal often harsher if even, at times, Medieval.

Welcome to The Society...

PROLOGUE
AZRAEL

The hanging tree is barely visible through the mist that's settled heavily across the land. The sun is a line on the horizon. A man crosses the field. He draws his cloak closer against the morning's chill, his careless steps crushing the frozen ground beneath his boots.

His eyes catch mine, and he grins.

Isaiah Delacroix. The first Penitent.

He wears my face, but there's something wrong with it. Something I can't put my finger on.

My vision blurs and I feel myself tugged, as if hooked like a fish. My head feels as though it's cracking open, being divided in two parts. The pain is agonizing, but it will pass. The worst is yet to come. I know.

And in the next instant, it comes. Oh, how it comes. Always the same, yet always a shock.

Because I *am* him. I am Isaiah Delacroix.

I see through his eyes. I think his thoughts. I feel every evil thing he feels.

"The Tithing time has come," he says.

His words terrify me, but I am trapped and mute, a prisoner to this man whose face I have inherited. I look down at the clothes I'm wearing. I don't recognize them. But the hands, they're mine. The ring on my finger? It's Isaiah's. The ring of The Penitent.

I shove my hands into my pockets so I don't have to see it. There's something in one of them, though, something soft and wet.

"Duty, boy," he says, and I turn to him because his voice is my own.

That head-splitting pain comes again. The scene before me flickers, blurring momentarily as I break free of the tether binding me to him. But I'm powerless to flee, my feet rooted to the spot. We are two men with identical faces standing alongside Proctor's Ledge.

Except my thoughts are not my own. They're still his.

We stand apart from the people of Salem who have all turned out in their Sunday best. They wouldn't miss the execution of the Wildblood witch. They're a bloodthirsty bunch. I find I hate them as much as he does. It's the one thing we have in common apart from our last name. Mothers and fathers point out heavy branches, their children making a game out of guessing which one they'll string her up to.

"I have my money on the highest branch, although

it wouldn't be a fair bet, seeing as how I paid for it," Isaiah says with a laugh.

He, too, wants to see her hang. He's hard at the thought of it. He wants to see her fear as they tighten the noose around her neck and when they pull the cart out from under her, he wants her eyes on him. Isaiah will watch her twist and turn in agony and terror as her life is stolen from her. He has bought and paid for these, her final moments. They will be his morbid keepsake. Because he has won and she has lost and she will finally know it.

Except it hasn't gone quite the way he wanted.

Exhausted, I hear my own ragged breath and feel the bite of this freezing morning with each inhale as if this were real. As if I were truly standing here, on this ledge upon this condemned land watching an execution that took place centuries ago.

The crowd quiets at the sound of horse's hooves approaching, signaling the arrival of the wagon carrying the accused.

Anticipation builds in them.

In me.

Anticipation of something wicked to come.

I watch, riveted, as an unearthly silence settles around us. No one dares to breathe as the carriage cuts a line through the center of the dirt road. People making way, crossing themselves as she passes. A child howls and buries her face in her mother's neck.

She's right to be afraid. After all, her mommy could be next if she isn't careful.

The mist clears unnaturally, as if obeying some command. The wagon slows, and my gaze falls on the condemned woman. I know exactly who she is. The Wildbloods and the Delacroixes have a long history.

This is Elizabeth Wildblood.

She is the first of their line to be sacrificed, the first witch to be hanged.

Beautiful. Even in the filthy remnants of her rags, her finery long taken from her. A mass of the loveliest, reddest hair—a sign of the devil—tumbles thick and long down her back, over a pale, bare shoulder where her dress is torn.

She's thrown off balance when the wagon halts, and an onlooker catches her instinctively to save her from falling. I notice how Isaiah's hands fist at the gesture—or maybe it's seeing the man's hands on her. When she is righted, I see that the hair behind her right ear has been hacked off at the scalp, the skin still bloody, as if someone's crudely taken a lock of it.

The man senses his mistake in touching the witch. He snatches his hand away as if he touched fire. The crowd gasps, each person frantically making the sign of the cross.

But all else falls away when, as her sentence is read aloud, she turns that bewitching gaze toward Isaiah and me and I realize I stand alone. Isaiah has vanished. Or maybe he was never here at all. Maybe it was me all along.

Her gaze makes my heart stop beating. It sends a

The Tithing

shiver so cold along my spine that I wonder if it's all true. If she is a witch after all. If there is such a thing.

The wagon is moving again, the horse carrying the doomed woman up the hill to the hanging tree.

I swallow down bile, my jaw tense, teeth so tightly clenched my face hurts. I watch her, the crowd hurling accusations, condemnations. It's all background noise to me.

Our locked gaze is broken when two men mount the carriage, and I am relieved. They take her bound arms and move her toward the readied noose. She struggles.

It's the first time she betrays her fear, and there is an evil inside me that relishes the sight. It shames me. Maybe I'm no different than Isaiah Delacroix. No less evil. I am, after all, of the bloodline, a direct descendent. The next Penitent.

They turn her so she is facing me again. This is what Isaiah's money has bought.

Her eyes lock on mine once more. Eyes I know. They belong to another Wildblood. One not for this time. One who will be sacrificed to me.

When they fasten the noose around Elizabeth's neck, I feel the rope scrape roughly against my own. My throat closes up as they tighten it.

Always in this nightmare, this time is ours. Her witch's gaze never leaves mine. This is our shared moment. It's seconds away, her execution, and it's then that her lips begin to move, subtly at first.

So subtly I'm the only one to see it.

To *feel* it.

An angry wind icier than the morning air howls in the distance, and the line of the sun darkens, a storm cloud appearing out of nowhere to obscure it.

A woman screams. Another follows. Cries from the crowd quickly grow into a full panic as Elizabeth Wildblood's lips move faster, speaking her silent words. She casts her spell, her curse, as thunder rumbles in the distance, lightning splitting the now near-black sky.

Screams to *hang the witch* abound. Our eyes remain locked even as the men hurry to jump from the carriage, to flee the witch in their panic.

I know the driver wants to crack his whip over the back of his horse and get away from her as fast as he can, but there's money in it for him if he goes slowly. If her neck snaps, he only gets a third of it. It's a mercy Isaiah would not allow her. She will hang. She will feel the rope tighten around her neck, feel it bite into that delicate, alabaster flesh and slowly, ever so slowly, strangle her.

Some darkness inside of me is jealous of that rope, and I know Isaiah hasn't fully left me. He's inside my head, his vile thoughts contaminating mine.

The horse neighs. The animal wants to be away, and in the next instant, the wagon is gone from under her, and she drops. The branch creaks even with her slight weight. But her lips are still moving, and her eyes are still on mine, and I pull my hands out of my pockets because I can't breathe.

But when I see what it was in Isaiah's—my—

pocket, a wave of nausea has me stumbling. I open my hand and watch those wisps of the reddest hair fly into the wind, some sticking to my palm with her wet blood.

The noose is tighter now and I'm choking. I'm fucking choking. Even though she is the one at the end of that rope, it is I who cannot breathe.

Blood vessels burst in Elizabeth's eyes. It's the last thing I see before she stops her twisting, her turning, a stream of urine running down her legs, over her bare feet and into the ground. She swings there in that icy morning, her eyes open, locked on me in death. Accusing me. Cursing me.

My own throat is raw as the dark cloud vanishes back to the hell it came from, and there's one final shift in the scene, this nightmare of mine. One new aspect I haven't seen before.

The woman hanging from the rope, it's no longer Elizabeth. This woman is not yet dead. Her eyes accuse me just as those of her ancestor did only moments earlier.

And I hear Isaiah Delacroix's voice again telling me *it's time, boy.*

The Tithing time.

Time for the next Wildblood witch to be sacrificed.

1

WILLOW

"Blessings!" Cordelia sings as she presents a three-layer chocolate cake onto the table before me.

As the youngest Wildblood sibling, it is her privilege to deliver the cake to the birthday recipient each year, an honor she has always loved and cherished. But this year, even my youngest sister seems to be aware of the dark shadow looming over the festivities. In place of her vibrant smile is a notably tamer one, and the lightness she injected into her tone was forced–much like all the moods around the table this evening.

It is the eve of my twenty-second birthday. The entire family has gathered for the occasion, just as we have every year. My mother and father are opposite me, smiling somberly, while my grandmother Celeste gathers plates for the cake from the kitchen. The rest of the seats at the table are littered with more of the Wildblood spawn—my sisters Raven, Winter, Aurora, and now Cordelia, who quietly slips into her place beside me.

They are all trying very hard to convince themselves this is just another birthday. This morning, I received a large stack of pancakes delivered to me in bed. And this afternoon was spent in the company of the Wildblood women. They painted my nails, braided my hair, and watched all my favorite movies with me. There was tea, fine European chocolates, and gifts aplenty as we all set aside our thoughts and acted as if it was just the mark of another year gone by. But we all know it's not. Tonight, the energy has noticeably shifted as the hour draws nearer.

Tomorrow, I will be chosen.

As if to remind me, the crescent-shaped birthmark on my breast seems to warm with its own energy. It's the same mark every Wildblood woman who's been chosen has carried, an inheritance from my ancestor Elizabeth whose traits have passed down from generation to generation as if by some unwritten decree.

Even after all these years, my sisters and I have the same red hair and blue eyes. The laws of genetics can't alter these traits. Though my father has no trace of red hair in his family, we still inherited. It is believed to be a part of the magic. The lore.

The Wildblood curse and honor.

We will appear in Elizabeth's image as a reminder to the Delacroix family that she can't be killed. She will live on through every Wildblood woman birthed into this world and never be erased.

A shiver moves over me as my grandmother directs us to gather our hands around the table. She's a wise woman—one I admire deeply—and I feel her strength as she sets her eyes upon me.

"Mother Goddess, may you protect and watch over our beloved Willow in the coming year. Bless her with courage, honor, and wisdom. And above all, please bless her with strength and protect her from evil."

At the conclusion of the last sentence, my mother promptly bursts into tears and shakes her head as all of our gazes fall upon her. "I'm sorry," she murmurs. "It's just the emotions of the day. Please give me a few moments to compose myself. But do enjoy your cake, Willow, and don't wait for me."

She excuses herself and retreats to the second floor while my grandmother offers me a reassuring smile and serves up the cake. Nobody speaks while we eat. I chew, not really tasting anything as numbness takes over. Every bite I swallow seems to sour in my stomach, and honestly, I'll be glad when the festivities are over.

"Want me to read to you, Willow?" Cordelia asks as my grandmother clears the plates.

"Or perhaps you'd like to sit beneath the moon," Raven offers. "It's beautiful tonight."

"Thank you, but I'm tired." I offer them a smile for their benefit. "I think I'd like to rest now."

My grandmother nods at me in approval, and silence settles over the room as I make my way to the stairs. I can feel their gazes on me as I ascend, and guilt weighs heavy on me for not being able to set my emotions aside any longer. They are only trying to help, but nothing can be done. I know what awaits me tomorrow, and there's no use in pretending otherwise.

When I open the door to my bedroom, I'm not surprised to find my mother waiting for me at the end of my bed. She's still weeping, and she doesn't try to hide it any longer.

"Willow." My name leaves her lips on an anguished cry.

I join her, settling onto the bed beside her as she takes my hand.

"Please." A renewed fear alights in her eyes. "I have some distant relatives in Ireland who can take you in. I've packed a bag, some money–"

"You know I can't do that." I reach up to wipe her tears away. "There isn't a place they won't find me. And if I weren't here, they would likely take one of my sisters anyway. I could never live with myself if I let that happen."

"And I can't live with myself if I let them take you." My mother sobs. "The others don't have the mark. Maybe they won't take them. Maybe they will believe the curse to be broken–"

She's grasping at a fantasy we both know can't be real. But I let her have it, at least long enough to compose herself.

"It will be okay," I assure her. "I'm strong. A Wildblood woman, remember? There's nothing we can't do."

Her eyes soften as she shakes her head. "You've been through too much. I know you're strong, but–"

"It is done." I settle my hand over hers. "This is my fate, and I accept it."

"Willow." My name comes out as a whisper and a plea.

She wants me to run away. She wants me to escape, but I can't. So, I tell her the same thing I've told myself my entire life, despite knowing this day would come. I've always been aware that my destiny had already been written, and I would be sacrificed to a Delacroix as his wife—knowing all the same that it will end in tragedy.

"It will be okay, Mama. It's all going to be okay."

2

AZRAEL

It's time, boy.

I open my eyes. Sweat drenches me. My heart is racing as if I've been running a marathon. But I know I'm in my bed, and from the cast of moonlight in the room, I can see it's not quite morning yet.

Benedict whines, nudging me with his cold, wet nose. I glance at the huge German Shepherd sitting beside my bed, his wide, anxious eyes on me. I wonder if he'd been trying to wake me.

"It's okay, boy," I say, petting him. "It's fine."

I rub my face and instantly draw my hand away. Because there, just like in the fucking dream, is the ring. I sit up, tug it off, and hurl it across the room. I should fucking bury it.

I take a deep breath in. It's not the first time this dream has come, this fucking nightmare. That's what this is, what all of this is. It's not the first time I've woken up with that thing on my finger.

Scrubbing at my face, I look at the ring in the corner and shake my head at my own idiotic panic. There's nothing uncanny about it, I tell myself. Nothing supernatural. I must slip it on in my sleep. That's all.

I get up, pick up the ring, and drop it into the nightstand drawer. Exhausted, I lay back down to stare up at the ceiling, the wood carving there a larger-than-life copy of the one on the ring face. It is the Delacroix insignia, the triangle containing Shemhazai's sword with wings of fire breaking the crescent moon in two.

That moon was added a few hundred years ago. It wasn't always part of our insignia. Originally it symbolized the witch's mark, or, as it was known back in that time, the devil's seal upon his initiate pledging her into service. Elizabeth Wildblood was born with the crescent moon upon her breast and with every generation, a Wildblood girl is born bearing that same mark. Since the fate of the Delacroixes and the Wildbloods is inexorably linked, I suppose it seemed right to Isaiah to incorporate the mark into our insignia.

There's a deep crack in the carving. If only it would crash down on me and kill me in my sleep.

But then what?

The curse would pass to Emmanuel. We've lost one man this generation. We'll lose another in time. It's how this goes, how it's always been. I won't let my brother pay that price. That would be cowardice.

The instant I think the words, I regret them.

Fuck.

I sit up and push the damp sheet off, my head pounding already with the fucking migraine that hasn't abated in three weeks. I glance at my watch, an antique that belonged to my father. It's barely five o'clock. I take in the light coming from the arched windows. The fading night will give way to day soon.

It's going to be a long one.

I get up, pull on my running clothes and shoes, and slip out of the bedroom. Benedict follows, tail wagging, excited for this unexpected outing. The house is quiet as I walk down the hall, passing my brother's and sister's rooms. I glance at the double doors at the far end of the corridor, the room that mirrors my own. It's my grandmother, Salomé's. There's a line of light beneath it. I sometimes wonder if she sleeps at all.

I walk as quietly as I can to the staircase, although I'm sure she knows I'm up. But she won't bother me. Not yet.

As anxious as she is about what is to come, she knows to give me space. She knows my temper as well as I know hers. Hell, I inherited it from her.

Benedict's nails click along the ancient hardwood floors as we make our way down the stairs. The house is dark, only the dim light of the outdoor lamps that always remain lit to guide me. It shines through the iron clad window above the double front doors, casting its shadow onto the floor. It is the original Delacroix insignia, minus the crescent moon.

I pass through the hall toward the living room, which is the center of the house. Two wings extend from it like arms, one in use by my family, the other locked up. Using one of the French doors at the back, I exit into the cool morning and set off on a run—no warm up, no stretch. My pace is fast and, tall as I am, my stride is long.

My brother, Emmanuel, is almost as tall as me. I've got an inch on him. Most of the men of my family are tall and strongly built. According to Grandmother, it's our inheritance, and, with pride upon her face, she reminds us as often as she can of it.

Weaving around the manicured garden with Benedict at my side, I glance at the pool house with its glass walls. Water shimmers in the lamplight. I move quickly out of sight of the house and into the woods, trees growing denser as I run deeper under their cover.

The Delacroix mansion is surrounded by more than fifteen acres of land, most of it unused and untouched by man. There is a cleared path to my destination, but I bypass it, choosing to run through the trees. I'd prefer to have gone into the dark wing of the house to my piano than run, but I need to burn off this energy.

The dark wing is technically the east wing, but Mom started calling it the dark wing back when it was just Abacus, Emmanuel, and me to scare us from going into the maze of rooms that had yet to be renovated. It was too dangerous. She was right. It still is because we never did get around to renovating, even after Abacus and I came of age. By then it was too late. Grandmother had the wing sealed off.

I wonder if she knows I have been visiting it again since Abacus's death. If I had to guess, I'd say yes. Her hearing is almost inhuman, even at her age. She can hear a mouse in the cellar. She claims it's her gift from above, just as ours is our height and strength.

My teeth clench together at the thought of it all.

Just one week after our parents disappeared—yacht and all—on what was meant to be a relaxing week in a calm sea, Grandmother had arrived at our house. We were only children then, Rébecca, my sister, barely a year old, my brother, Emmanuel a year younger than my twin, Abacus and I who had been eleven at the time. She was a formidable woman. My brothers and I made fun of her strange ways at first. It was one of the few things that made us laugh, even if there wasn't anything funny about it. We missed our parents, and Grandmother has always been a cold substitute. She heard our mocking laughter, but she was patient.

Over time, over years and years of hearing something, you almost start to believe it, no matter how preposterous, how unbelievable. You start to believe the texts she carried with her from her home in the suburbs of Paris telling the history of our family.

Rébecca has no memory of our parents. In their place, she had Grandmother and her strange stories. I'd worried about Rébecca then and I still do now, but it turned out Abacus had been the one to watch.

At the memory of him, my chest tightens. We were as tight as twins could be. But during the last year of his life, everything had changed. Every single thing.

Fuck.

Now I wish I'd brought my phone. At least I could blare music to drown out my thoughts—not that I could bear it with this fucking migraine.

This is why I prefer going into the dark wing on nights like this. The piano is there. There, I can hammer at the keys and drown out every other sound. Grandmother had it put away when she moved in, calling it an unnecessary distraction. When I play there, no one hears it; it's too far from the west wing of the house.

Well, no one but my grandmother, but I'm too old to be chastised by her. Besides, as the rules go within The Society we are a part of, I am the head of this household, not her. No matter how much she'd like it to be otherwise.

As if taking pity on me, birds begin waking as the sky ahead glows a deep crimson with the first light of day. I stop, barely out of breath, to take in the beauty of it, but it triggers a memory of the dream I am running from: the sun breaking the horizon as Elizabeth Wildblood is carted out to Proctor's Ledge. To the hanging tree.

Jesus Fucking Christ.

I charge on faster than ever, twenty more minutes of single-minded focus as I run the length of the property and circle back, only hearing the chirping of birds and the crunching of branches underfoot. Twenty more minutes pass before I just make out the red glow of the Tabernacle lamp in the distance. It burns in the small chapel on the property and is visible through one of the narrow windows.

It's only then that I slow my pace, as the forest grows thinner and I get my first glimpse of the angel Shemhazai standing tall and proud.

Benedict stops altogether, whining at the border of hallowed ground. As if there's a barrier only he sees, he never enters this place. He just whimpers until I or my siblings are safely out of it.

"It's all right," I tell him as I walk onto the burial grounds and meet the eyes of Shemhazai, who is ever-angry, as if he was frozen in a moment of utter fury. Maybe he was. What do I know? The statue stands ten feet tall in the very center of the cemetery, with the chapel itself set to the side. His wings are spread wide; one knee is bent, the other leg straight as if he was frozen in time the moment he landed upon this earth. His powerful chest, shoulders, and forearms are armored ornately as if ready for war. A hood over his head sets his face in shadow for most of the day. I wish it would cast it into obscurity, but it does not. He's missing part of one arm—sadly not his sword arm. No, that is intact, with his hand wrapped around the hilt of his sword that has pierced the crescent moon through.

I know every detail of this statue too well. Shemhazai is inked into my skin as if my arm and hand were an extension of his. I wear tattoos of his armor on my forearm, a part of my chest, and my back in brilliant colors.

I meet the statue's eyes now. I do not bow my head. Grandmother was quick with a smack to the backs of our heads when we were younger and refused to acknowledge the angel. I have no doubt it was she who laid the fresh lilies upon his altar. I hate the smell of them.

Well, it was either her or Rébecca. She has twisted my sister's mind, terrorized her into near paralysis.

No, I don't bow. Instead, I walk straight to the altar.

Shemhazai supposedly led the angels sent by God to watch over the humans. They became known as the Watchers, but their story turned into an ugly one—a story where those chosen by God defied him and fell from grace.

With one sweep of my arm, I wipe away every single one of those fucking flowers. Offerings to a demon-angel, a hateful one who has become a god in his own right, at least to Grandmother.

But once the altar is cleared, I spot the dark stain on Shemhazai's feet. I know what that stain is, and my mind conjures up the image of Elizabeth Wildblood again.

Hanging.

Dying.

Dead.

Then I see the other face, the one that has me out here running from the hell that awaits me.

The face of The Sacrifice to come.

A breaking branch alerts me to the fact that I am not alone. I don't move. Whoever it is isn't close yet. Grandmother would say it's my preternatural hearing, similar to her own, another gift and a sign of our greatness. She believes we are descended from Shemhazai himself.

"Az?" comes the sweet voice that has me smiling even as my heart twists. "What are you doing out here?"

I turn to find Rébecca emerging from the woods, and that smile fades fast. "Bec? What are you... Why are you soaking wet?"

"I'm not," she says with a shudder, long hair slick down her back and sticking to her face. She hugs the terrycloth robe tighter. Benedict wags his tail, and she bends to pet him.

I rush to her, wrap my arms around her to warm her. "Christ. It's freezing out here." I lift her off her feet and carry her toward the chapel door. There are always a few blankets in the pews. There's no modern heating system in place, so unless someone starts a fire in the grate, it's usually cold.

"I'm fine. Put me down, Az." She twists, and a flip flop drops to the floor. At least she's not barefoot, although with flip flops, she may as well be.

I set her down once we're inside, and then only so I can wrap one of the wool throws around her shoulders. I get a proper look at her. Her nearly waist-length white-blond hair seems to grow finer and finer by the day. Both skin and hair have lost more of their luster in the last months. Her face is more gaunt than ever, and the shadows beneath her pale green eyes look like bruises.

"What were you doing, Bec?" I ask, trying not to show how worried I am about her.

She looks guiltily away, biting her lip. My sister, who is almost sixteen, looks more like she's twelve. She is barely five feet tall and so thin, I can see the outline of her bones across her chest. She seems to have less and less of an appetite these days, and no matter what, the doctors can't figure out what the hell is going on. Why she isn't growing, developing. Why she seems to be doing the opposite.

"Rébecca?" I tilt her chin up.

"Swimming."

"You were swimming?" I drop my arms to my sides. "This time of the morning? Hell, it's barely morning."

"Grandmother says my muscles are wasting away. I need exercise."

I grit my jaw, my hands balling into fists. "If you want to swim, I'll swim with you. You can't be alone in the pool."

She snorts, turns stubbornly away, and folds her arms across her chest. Well, she does act like a teenager even if she doesn't look like one. I'm glad for it.

"I'm almost sixteen years old, Azrael. I think I can be alone in a pool."

"It's not that. You know that. If something happened—"

Rébecca shrugs, jaw setting even as her eyes grow shiny with tears she won't allow to fall. "Grandmother would be happy then."

"No, she wouldn't. And don't ever say that again," I tell her, pulling her in hard to hug her. "You have your appointments with the therapist. You're getting the exercise your body can handle. She's not a fucking doctor."

She pulls back, looks up at me. She studies me with eyes much keener than anyone gives her credit for. Although I've been shielding her from what is coming for so many reasons, I know she knows at least a part of it.

"Are you going to do it?"

It's me who looks away this time.

"Az. Tell me. Are you going to do it?"

"Let's go back. I'll make you French toast." I take a step toward the door.

She tugs my sleeve. "I'll eat it if you answer me first."

I sigh.

Rébecca remains silent, watching me with an intensity in her gaze similar to that of the marble statue of Shemhazai.

"I don't have a choice." I open the door.

"Maybe it'll be different than you think. Maybe she'll—"

"Let's go. I answered your question. Let's go in and eat."

"It's tonight."

I don't quite look at her. I can't. Instead, I nod once.

"Maybe that's why your head hurts," she says, reaching up with both hands to brush the hair at my temples back, her fingers coming to rest on exactly the spots where my head is going to fucking explode.

I close my hands over her tiny ones and draw them away. "Maybe."

Rébecca is gentle and kind. She is innocent. All things opposite of me. She should hate me for what I will do, but when she wraps her arms around my waist and presses her cheek to me, I find myself taken aback. I rub her back, feeling again how small she is.

"You're good, Az. You can't do anything bad. It's not in you."

I stiffen at her words as the memory of the dream replays, visions of Elizabeth Wildblood. Of what the sight of her at the very end did to me, that her fear and her terror didn't sicken me. That's not exactly a sign of someone who is good.

Ashamed, I push the thoughts aside, afraid she'll see even those.

"I know you won't hurt her." She hugs me again. "Think I can have bacon too?" she asks, drawing back.

I smile down at her, grateful for this change in subject. "You can have all the bacon in the world if that's what you want. Let's go, little sis. And no more swimming on your own at the ass crack of dawn, okay?"

"Fine." She chuckles and takes my hand as we walk out of the chapel.

3

AZRAEL

I was right about it being a long day. It has been. And it will be a longer night.

I stand in the vast library that takes up two floors. It is the space that divides the west wing from the dark wing. My way to the dark wing is through a hidden door, probably something that was created when the house was originally built for servants to come and go unseen. The shelves that line three of the four walls are stacked with leather-bound tomes, some centuries old. Ladders slide along to grant the reader access to the books on the upper shelves.

One wall is a stained-glass masterpiece. Apart from fairly minor repairs my parents made to the window, it is original to the house. As I sip my whiskey and gaze upon the image now, I wonder at the implausibility of such a thing. Even as walls crumbled, this glass somehow survived the ravages of time.

I take in the image as the full moon casts its light

through the array of colors. The spotlight is on the beast. Well, beast or angel, depending on who you ask. The beast's black wings are stretched wide but curve in around the edges almost protectively as he gazes upon what? His prey? Victim? Sacrifice?

If you ask Rébecca, she is his fallen beloved. Only Bec can tell the story in a way that romanticizes an image such as this.

It is that fallen woman I study now, taking in the vibrance of the red hair that spills in a mass of waves through the beast's fingers. At least her eyes are closed. I don't think I could stand it if they weren't. The shades of color in the rest of the glass are dark grays and blues so deep they could be black. Shards of lightning break up the monotony, and although each color is represented, it all fades in the brilliance of the red hair of the woman.

The door opens. I turn to find my brother, Emmanuel, entering.

"Thought I'd find you here."

Tonight, it begins. Tonight is the ceremony of the Tithing where the chosen Wildblood girl, the one wearing the witch's mark, will be sacrificed to me. She would have been Abacus's if he'd lived.

Since he did not, the task of accepting The Sacrifice and doing what has to be done has fallen to me. She'll have red hair and the birthmark. That's all I know. All these years later, the Wildblood women arrive into the world with red hair in defiance of science or logic. The gene should have died out centuries ago, yet they just keep being born with it.

"How the hell has this thing survived so fucking long?" I ask him, my gaze on the image of the beast looming over the unconscious woman.

"Grandmother's backwards fairy tale version or reality?" Emmanuel asks.

One corner of my mouth curves up into a grin. "Not sure I'd call her version a fairy tale."

"No, you're right." He comes to stand beside me after pouring himself a drink. "You ready for tonight?"

"Not really." I turn to study him as he studies the stained glass. Emmanuel and I are very similar in appearance. In height and build, we're well matched. Our hair is dark, although I wear mine to my shoulders and his is to his chin. When we go into town together, not a single person doesn't do a double take. We're like twin marble statues brought to life, almost inhuman in appearance with our great height, powerful build, and bone structure any supermodel would envy.

Ironically, my twin Abacus had looked nothing like me. He was shorter, stockier, more common in appearance–as Grandmother had liked to emphasize with disdain.

Emmanuel and I, though, could be twins. The one thing that distinctly differentiates us is the color of our eyes. Mine are a fiery gold, not brown, not hazel. Gold. Not quite natural in moments, especially when I'm angry. Emmanuel's are a cool, icy silver that look as if backlit by some otherworldly light.

In dress, we are distinct. He has always preferred more casual clothing, lightweight cashmere sweaters, tailored pants and suits, with his tastes being expensive. Not that mine are any less so, but I prefer an older style of dress. My favorite coat in fact is one from my father's closet, a lightweight, well-worn leather coat with wide lapels detailed with fine gold thread. The brass buttons, which are antiques themselves, gleam even in the dim light of the library. I remember my father wearing it. It was his favorite.

Where Emmanuel and I are exactly similar is that we both prefer black or gray clothing for the most part. Perhaps it's just part of our dark nature.

"I checked in on Rébecca on the way down," Emmanuel says. "She told me to remind you what she said?" he says it like a question, one eyebrow raised.

"Why isn't she asleep? It's almost midnight."

"She's almost sixteen, even if she doesn't look it. It'd be weirder if she didn't stay up until midnight."

"Is Benedict with her?"

"Yeah." Emmanuel smiles, and so do I. Grandmother doesn't like *that animal* upstairs or in the house at all. If she had it her way, she'd leave him out on the street. Hell, she'd probably try to have the driver run him over. I wonder if she isn't afraid of the oversized German Shepherd. He certainly has no love for her. "Saw Gran in your room by the way."

My face tightens. "What was she doing?"

The door opens then, and Grandmother enters, followed by two servants. One carries our cloaks over his arm, while the other holds a tray with our masks and, fuck me, that ring.

"What I was doing was making sure you followed protocol," Salomé Delacroix says in the tone of one in command. She turns to the man carrying the cloaks. "Wait here. You!" She snaps to the woman with the tray. "Come with me."

The woman cowers behind my grandmother, who looks like no one's grandma that I know. First, she is tall and broadly built, and her wavy gray hair is pulled tightly back into a bun at her nape. Her face is, as usual, scrubbed clean. She's never worn makeup that I can remember, not for any occasion. Her cold eyes, a watery blue so pale they're almost colorless, miss nothing although I do notice the shadows beneath them. I wonder if she's dreading what is to come, but somehow, I doubt it.

There is nothing soft about my grandmother. Nothing warm.

"Grandmother. Do I need to put a lock on my door?" I ask her as my gaze falls upon the ring on the tray.

"What have you got to hide from me, Azrael?" she asks, adjusting the lapel of my jacket before taking the ring from the tray and holding it out to me. "You should wear it always. Be proud of it."

I look down at the ring, wondering how something so insignificant can feel so evil.

"It's a fucking ring, Gran," Emmanuel says to her utter annoyance. She has forbidden the use of foul language in the house, and I'm sure my brother takes pleasure in using it so openly.

But mostly, she hates being called anything but Grandmother.

Slowly, she turns a calculated gaze to Emmanuel and the instinct to protect my younger brother kicks in as she sets him in her sights. He can handle her, mostly. He likes messing with her, but it's dangerous.

"You, Emmanuel," she starts, stepping toward him to brush imaginary dust from his shoulders. "Should be prepared. Should anything befall your brother, you will be our last hope."

"Well, let's make sure nothing befalls my brother then," Emmanuel says with a snort.

"Disrespectful—"

"Enough. I'll wear the goddamned ring." I put it on without allowing myself to think about it and check my watch. "We need to go," I tell Emmanuel and step past my grandmother.

"Cloaks and masks. It is tradition," she says, closing her hand over my arm to stop me.

I turn to find her holding up one of the masks. These are not specific to our family. They're masks of The Society, the secret organization our family has been a part of since the very beginning. A founding family of IVI, the Delacroixes are powerful both here in New Orleans and in France, where our family originates.

Emmanuel and I have minimal interaction with The Society. My father had been shunned because he married outside of IVI. It's at least one of the reasons Grandmother hated our mother.

For my part, as head of this household, I will do what I need to do to maintain our standing within The Society. They are, after all, a necessary part of our lives, although by taking the Wildblood sacrifice as my bride, I'll be following in my father's footsteps and marrying outside of The Society. That is as it needs to be. When it comes time for Emmanuel or Rébecca to marry, expectations will be very different.

But I can't think about that right now.

I take the mask and look at it, my gaze catching on that ring on my finger.

My grandmother gives me a victorious grin. "The girl, I've prepared a room for her," she says.

"Have you?" I ask, meeting her gaze. It irks her to have to look up at me even though she is almost six feet tall herself, but I have six inches on her. "Where exactly did you prepare a room?"

"In the servants' quarters, of course. You won't want that witch in your bed any longer than necessary."

"They are staff, not servants."

She chuckles.

"And besides, what if I like her in my bed?" I ask, cocking my head.

She stiffens, narrowing her eyes but clearly uncomfortable. "You'll claim her once. Consummate. It's the rule. After that, there is no need. You can have any woman from the Cat House or anywhere else. God knows the city is full of whores."

"But she'll be my wife, Grandmother. It would go against the God you claim to love to find pleasure elsewhere. Thou shalt not commit adultery. Which commandment is it?"

Emmanuel snorts.

Grandmother sends an evil glare his way but focuses her attention on me. "You've forgotten your lessons, have you?"

"I haven't forgotten the beatings."

"Speaking of lessons, I have one with Rébecca tomorrow," she says as if I didn't say what I'd just said, eyes narrowing because she knows my sister is one way to control me. "She hardly pays attention anymore. Always distracted, that one. A replica of your mother. I may have to reintroduce incentive learning."

Incentive learning. The incentive being not to take a beating. I will never forget the bite of her favorite cane or strap. I still remember the day I saw my father's back, the years-old scars that criss-crossed the expanse of it. He was as gentle as my grandmother is not.

I grit my jaw and close the space between us, hands fisting, crushing the mask. "If you ever lay a finger on Rébecca again, you will deal with me. Am I perfectly clear?"

She stares up at me, a sheen to her dark eyes I hadn't noticed before. "I understand consequences, Azrael. Do you?"

"Am I fucking clear?"

A heavy moment hangs between us, and I know she wants to reprimand me for my language, but she's cleverer than that. She takes a step backward. She is afraid of me as much as she wishes she weren't.

"You're right. She's so sickly as it is. I wonder if incentive learning wouldn't push her body further than it can handle. Abacus couldn't handle any of it. He was weak. A coward. And she's more like him than us, isn't she?"

My vision blurs, blackening along the edges as red-hot rage burns from my very core through my extremities. If Emmanuel hadn't put his hand on my shoulder in that moment, if he hadn't stopped me, I think I would have hurt the old woman.

"Az. Let's go."

It takes a long, long moment but he manages to turn me away. We walk toward the door, bypassing the man holding out the cloaks.

"Masks and cloaks!" Grandmother calls out, running after us.

"Keep walking," Emmanuel tells me, one hand firmly around my arm to keep me from turning on her. "She's an old woman. Just keep fucking walking."

"There will be consequences!" she yells once we've reached the front doors.

There, I do stop and turn back to face her. "There are always fucking consequences! To hell with them!" I bark back, throwing the mask at her or at the wall, I'm not really sure which. "And with you."

4

WILLOW

"Willow?"

Raven's voice breaks me from my thoughts, but I can't seem to drag my gaze from my reflection in the mirror. I feel numb. Hollow. I barely recognize the woman staring back at me.

The black silk robe draped over my skin, covering the chemise beneath, was meant to be a statement—an act of rebellion against the decree that we should be dressed in white. A representation of purity.

There is nothing pure about what's to take place, but while we may not be able to alter the outcome of this curse, we are clutching to the smallest details we can control.

My sisters and I have all worn our hair down this evening, wild and free like our spirits. Another broken rule. While our faces are meant to be free of makeup, we have no intentions of bowing to that indignation either.

If I shall go, it will be on my own terms. While I still have a voice. While my heart still beats, and blood runs wild in my veins, as wild as our heritage.

"Are you ready for your makeup?" Raven asks gently.

She doesn't ask if I'm okay, and I'm glad for it. I don't want to lie to her, and she doesn't want to acknowledge that I never will be.

"Come." She gently pulls me away from the mirror, turning me and directing me to sit on the velvet vanity stool before her.

I watch her silently as she retrieves an assortment of items from my drawer, taking care to do my makeup exactly how I like it. She dusts my face with a thin veil of near-translucent powder as pale as my skin. Raven has perfected the art of winged eyeliner, and she draws it steady and sure even as her hand trembles with nerves. When it's time for our signature blood-red lipstick, she applies two coats for extra boldness before offering me a shaky smile.

"Beautiful," she murmurs.

"Just like you." I manage to find my voice to utter the familiar retort.

It's always been a joke in our house. All of the Wildblood girls are so similar in appearance that there are only minor differences to set us apart. Since Raven and I have only two years between us, we look as if we could almost be twins. The most notable differences are a couple inches of height and her curlier, slightly shorter hair. It wasn't uncommon for people to mix us up when we were younger, but now our personalities differentiate us.

She's the lighter half of me: the confident, social, unshakable one. I'm the locked vault–the one who never lets her guard down, the one who knows all too well the evils in this world.

I used to smile like her. I used to trust like her.

Sometimes, when I look at her, I find myself grieving the loss of that innocence. She's beautiful in a way I can never be because she hasn't been touched by evil. She hasn't had its shadow following her, waiting to wrap its ugly claws around her and pull her into the darkness. But I've never begrudged her for that. Raven has always been my biggest defender and the light in my world when I thought none could exist. I would never want her to feel the way that I do.

After what we refer to as the 'incident,' I retreated within and cut myself off from most of the outside world. I let go of friendships. Goals. The foolish idea of happiness. But my sister has never let me push her away, even at my lowest. She has always been there for me, as she is now, and I know she will continue to be that steady, reassuring presence in my life for as long as I'm alive.

I don't doubt that tonight, the moment I'm gone, she'll be nose-deep in the family spell-book, searching for ways to curse the Delacroix name anew.

"You can still run," Raven whispers, her eyes

moving over my face. "We can go together. Start a new life. We can take Cordelia, Winter, and Aurora too. Then they will have no choice but to leave us alone."

I force a smile that feels exhausting, shaking my head. "You know we can't do that. They would find us. And I won't let the rest of you suffer over my fate."

"But we will suffer." Emotion cripples her voice. "We will suffer without you here, regardless. If I die, I want it to be by your side."

Despite the heaviness in my bones, I find it in me to rise to my feet and pull her in for a rare hug. It's something I seldom offer these days but something I want to give her now.

"I love you," I whisper. "But you know I can't let you do that. I can't let any of you do that. This is my fate, and I can't and won't try to escape it."

She releases a shuddering breath and nods, too choked up to speak. We always knew it would come to this, and entertaining any other notions is just a fantasy. I learned the hard way not to indulge in such girlish dreams. I live in the real world, and there are no escapes from this reality.

A knock on the bedroom door separates us just as Cordelia's voice rings out from the other side.

"Can I come in?" she asks.

Raven opens her mouth to reply, but I stop her with a hand around her wrist. She glances back at me with wide, curious eyes.

"Promise me if anything ever happens to me, you'll get Fiona and bring her back home."

Raven's eyes settle on the black cat curled up at the end of my bed, determination steeling her voice as she responds, "An army couldn't stop me."

Cordelia knocks again, calling out one more time. "Hello? Willow?"

"Come in," Raven and I call out in unison.

My little sister enters the room with a somber expression on her face, trying for my sake to hold back tears, and I'm glad for it. I don't want to cry anymore.

"How is Mom?" I ask.

"She was resting," she answers quietly. "Nan gave her more special tea to calm her."

I nod, relieved, until Cordelia swallows and squares her shoulders. "The assholes have arrived."

"Cordelia!" Raven tries to scold her for the language, but it comes out more like a laugh, and I start laughing too.

"What?" Cordelia shrugs innocently. "That's what you always call them."

Raven looks at me and smiles, and I can't help smiling too. Leave it to Cordelia to inadvertently lighten the moment.

"Well?" Raven asks. "What do they look like?"

"Huge." Cordelia's eyes flare as she lowers her voice. "They're like... trees."

I swallow and nod, not in the least surprised. The legends of their height have long since echoed through my mind. I've often heard it said the Delacroix spawn look like gods among men, although, if it were up to me, I'd use a different term.

"I could probably kick him in the knee," Cordelia says thoughtfully. "When he comes to inspect us."

"Don't you dare." Raven snorts. "Remember what we've told you."

Cordelia sighs in annoyance. "That would make me as bad as them. We don't use violence. We use magic."

"Exactly." I tap her on her freckled nose. "Now, let's get this over with before their energy stains this house."

Raven and I move to go, but Cordelia steps in front of us, whisper-hissing a command for us to wait.

"What is it?" I ask.

She glances between us nervously before removing an envelope from her pocket. It's a cream-colored missive with familiar black handwriting.

Dread curdles my stomach, and the energy shifts as Raven reaches for my hand.

"I didn't want to say anything with Mom already upset," Cordelia explains. "And you said to always bring them to you if I found them in the yard."

I nod, reaching out with stiff fingers to grasp the envelope. My sisters watch me carefully as I open it, eyes moving over the message before my hand falls limp to my side and the paper flutters to the floor.

"What does it say?" Raven asks.

I open my lips to respond, but nothing comes out. I can't give voice to the words. I can't repeat them, even though they are burned into my brain. The threat is as clear as any other my attacker has sent.

On this day, the day of the Tithing, without even knowing it, he has proven that Azrael Delacroix isn't the only devil I have to contend with. Because Caleb Church still lives and breathes, biding his time in a prison cell, waiting for the day he gets out.

The day he can come back for me.

These eight words confirm it.

Watch your back, witch. Your days are numbered.

5

AZRAEL

She's more like him than us, isn't she?

I'm not sure which part of that statement is worse, the part that she is calling both my sister and my dead brother weak or that she has put me in the same category as herself.

It's not that I want to deny the fact that she and I are similar. That's not the issue. That part is true. I am more like my grandmother than I like. Emmanuel is, too.

But calling Rébecca and Abacus weak? I can't stand it.

"Let it go," Emmanuel tells me as we're driven to the Wildblood house. It's about a half-hour ride from our house in Eden's Crossing. "She won't touch Rébecca. She knows what you'll do to her if she does. It's an empty threat. Don't let her use it to get to you. She wins if you do."

I nod. It's true. She won't touch our little sister

again. She did, a few years ago, leaving marks crisscrossing the length of her back. I admit part of that night is absent from my memory, but when I came home and saw Rébecca and what Grandmother had done to her, I saw red. All I know is if it hadn't been for Emmanuel, I might have killed the old woman. Like I said, I have her temper.

But I recall how Rébecca had cowered from me that night, the days that followed. I never intended for her to see me in that state, where my control snaps. When I lose my mind and my self.

For Grandmother to have threatened to hurt Rébecca again, though, reveals how important the Tithing is to her, how wholly she believes in the curse —in what needs to be done.

"She's insane, you know that," Emmanuel says, as if having read my mind.

I turn to glance at him. "If she's the one who's insane, why are we doing this? Why are we going to their house? Aren't we as insane?"

His expression falters, darkens. He shifts his gaze away momentarily, lips tightening. "What happened to Mom and Dad. To Abacus. Are you willing to take the chance?"

He's talking about the curse Elizabeth Wildblood placed on our family centuries ago. He's talking about the words she whispered as they tightened the noose around her neck.

I recall how lightning had splintered the sky in my dream, and I touch my neck as I remember the very real feeling of the rope biting into it, the sensation of suffocating. This all began when our ancestor, Isaiah Delacroix—with the backing of IVI—was able to accuse and condemn a woman to death. I can guess at his reasons, knowing the petty, sadistic man he was, because I do know him. Not only from the tomes containing the Delacroix history, but from our time on Proctor's Ledge.

That knowledge may come in the form of dreams, but it's no less real than my brother sitting beside me now. No less real than the moon shining in through the tinted windows of the Rolls Royce.

I draw a tight breath in, steel myself. "No, I'm not."

He pats my arm as the driver pulls up to the gates of Briar Rose, the Wildblood home. It has been for centuries now, ever since Elizabeth's descendants settled in New Orleans several decades after her execution.

The car comes to a stop. Emmanuel and I open our doors and step out. I button my coat as I stand on the curb, taking in the gated property. The house, which is set back a little, is still visible from the street. It's a typical Garden District home: well-maintained, sizable with a good plot of land around it. The porch, which wraps around it, is dotted with furniture, a swing, and hanging plants. The vivid blue is a stark difference to the darkness of the Delacroix mansion.

Here, there is light. There, there is only darkness.

Here, there is life. There, well... there, there is death.

But that's the point of tonight, I remind myself, to take the Wildblood woman and make the sacrifice. Then balance will be restored, and my family will be safe.

What's left of them.

If it isn't to be, if it isn't what is destined, then none of them will be marked. But in the long history of the Tithing, every single time, the fate of the chosen one has been decided before any Delacroix even enters their lives. Tonight, just as on every other night of a Tithing ceremony, one of the Wildblood women will bear the mark of the crescent moon. When I see it, I will know she is The Sacrifice chosen by powers higher than myself or her. If it wasn't meant to be, she wouldn't be marked. None of them would have ever been marked.

The second Rolls Royce pulls up to park behind ours. Emmanuel turns from the house to me. I nod and step toward the gate, noticing the salt along the border, some protection spell no doubt, and trample right through it.

In order to save my family, to save Rébecca and Emmanuel and even my grandmother, I cannot care about the Wildblood Sacrifice. I cannot allow myself to see her as human. Her safety won't matter. It doesn't matter. She will pay The Tithe—and so will I, ultimately. It's not as though she'll be the only one making a sacrifice.

Something flickers in one of the windows upstairs. I look up as the curtain falls closed. A glance at

The Tithing

Emmanuel tells me he has also seen the infinitesimal movement. He raises his eyebrows and one corner of my mouth curves upward. We're being watched. By the sisters? By her? They know which of them will be taken tonight. They know which witch bears the mark.

"Let's go," I tell Emmanuel.

My brother walks at my side, our shoes loud on the white-painted wooden stairs leading to the porch. The light goes out upstairs as the front door is opened. I don't acknowledge the man standing there but stride into the house as if it were my own.

I take a look around at the space. Cozy, as I expected, with lamps lit in both living and dining rooms. Books are piled along a bay window with a half-moon cushioned seat that looks out over the backyard. Moonlight glints off the water of a swimming pool in the garden. It is a tidy, lived-in and loved house. A home.

"This way," the man who opened the door says.

I follow him to where I assume the sisters will be waiting. For a moment, I wonder if they'll try to ambush us. Kill us. End the curse. The thought, as dark as it is, makes me chuckle, and Emmanuel glances at me. I slow down to take in the prints hanging along the walls, family photos documenting lives lived–commemorating them, immortalizing them. They're artfully done, mostly black and white with only the red of the Wildblood hair standing out. Five girls who look very much like their mother. Five children, four of whom are now women.

Cordelia is the youngest. Winter and Aurora are closer in age to Raven and Willow, but still distinctly younger. The oldest two I can't tell apart just yet, but there's one particular photograph that makes me stop. It's the two of them, arms around each other. One is laughing; the other is pretending to. I lean in for a closer look.

There's something dark in the eyes of the sister who is attempting to smile that her sister does not share. Something that seems to carry centuries within itself. This is the difference between them, and this, I know, is the Wildblood from my dream. The one whose face replaces Elizabeth's at the end.

My throat tightens. I rest my hands against it, but when I realize what I'm doing, I draw them away. I almost push them into my pockets but stop when I remember what I found in the pocket of my dream self. I look at the girl again. All that hair, just like Elizabeth's. It'll be her. She'll be the one to bear the mark.

I know it, and it's suddenly hard to swallow.

"You're good, Az. You can't do anything bad. It's not in you."

Rébecca's words play in my head. Was she trying to convince herself or me?

"You okay?" Emmanuel asks, rescuing me from the moment.

I draw a tight breath in and remember Grandmother's words. "She was right about one thing," I say, trying not to look at the girl in the photograph.

"Abacus couldn't do what I'm about to do. Not because he was a coward or weak. Because he was good."

I miss my brother. Losing a twin, one I was so close to and especially given how it happened, it was like I lost a piece of myself. I still feel the empty space. I think I always will.

"He was born into the wrong family," Emmanuel says.

Footsteps have us turning, and we watch Clara and Barrett, the parents of the sisters, enter. They stop when they see us, a sob breaking from the woman when she lays her eyes on me as if, out of the two of us, she knows it is me who is here to take her daughter. Not my brother.

Her husband draws her closer, his embrace practically holding her up.

I don't speak but instead turn away from the couple and gesture to the man standing at the door that divides me from the sisters to open it. He does, and I straighten up to my full height and enter. Now is not the time for sentiment, for conscience. Neither has helped us in the past.

Now is the time to take what is owed.

6

AZRAEL

The sight that greets me is not what I expect.

There are five girls, almost identical in appearance.

But where they should be presented in white, these sisters are wearing black silk. Where their hair should be tied back in a neat, respectable style, it is loose and wild down their backs. Their faces, which should be scrubbed clean, are not; their eyes are accentuated dramatically with dark liner and their lips are painted a red that would rival the red of their hair.

I almost laugh, and that is what it takes to break the spell of whatever the fuck was happening out there. If I have any hope of saving Rébecca, of ensuring nothing happens to my brother, then I must follow the course laid out for me. This curse, the tragedy upon tragedy that marks the passing of time for my family... It has been proven over centuries that taking the chosen

The Tithing

Wildblood girl and making the sacrifice is the only way to end it.

I can't simply choose not to do it. I saw what happened to Abacus. What did we gain? What did his unwillingness or inability to carry out this evil get us but one dead brother? I won't risk another.

I step toward the sisters, barely taking in the room. My attention is fully on them. To see them in person like this, all so similar but distinct, is strange–or maybe that's their witchy power. Discomfort or not, I will take the Wildblood owed me, and The Tithe will be paid.

Isaiah was right. It is my duty.

The five of them stand with their backs straight, but I see how their hands tighten around each other's, see how their knuckles whiten as they take in the Delacroix brothers. The tallest of them can't be more than 5'4." We tower over them, not only in height but in build as well.

My brother makes a sound not unlike the rattle of a snake. I glance at him, but his eyes are locked on one of the Wildbloods. I'm not sure which. He's affected by them too—or by one in particular. I hope for his sake it's not my witch.

They're lined up by age. Cordelia is first, but she is too young to be The Sacrifice. I step past her to her sister, Aurora. Young, but old enough. She swallows, the beads of sweat along her forehead betraying her fear. I meet her blue eyes and lift one wrist, drawing the sleeve of her robe back to look for the mark. It will be on the inside of her wrist, her elbow, or the swell of her breast. Always.

Her arms are unmarked. I meet her eyes as I untie the knot of her robe, beneath which she's wearing a chemise, also black. She gasps, drawing back when my knuckle brushes her skin, but her sisters have her and she doesn't back away. Good. I don't want to make her. Not this one.

I take in the small swells of her breasts. Perfect, unmarred skin so white it's nearly translucent.

Relieved, I move to the next. Winter. Much the same as Aurora, I look her over, but find, as I guessed, she is unmarked.

I stand before Raven Wildblood. My brother's eyes bore into my back, and I know at that moment that she was the one who caused that rattle in his chest.

Raven is the laughing girl in the photograph. She won't be marked. I know it. But ceremony is ceremony, and I will play out my role in this archaic ritual.

Raven Wildblood doesn't meet my eyes as I take her wrists and inspect them for the mark. When I open her robe and push down the top of her chemise, I can feel Emmanuel's eyes burning into me.

Well, this is interesting. I can't help a small grin. My brother likes women. He enjoys them at every opportunity. And never have I seen him affected by one.

She's unmarked, as I knew she would be, and when I step to the last Wildblood, *my* Wildblood witch, I feel my brother's relief.

This one meets my eyes squarely, and the temperature in the room seems to drop. I take my time, my gaze locked on those icy eyes, the blue clear and vibrant. I'm trying to find what I saw in the photograph. The past. History. There's defiance in her gaze, fear just beneath it.

When I take her left arm and turn her delicate wrist to my gaze, she shudders. That shudder moves through me as I slide my fingers up along the inside of her arm to expose flesh that is unmarked.

I set her arm at her side and lift the right one. A tattoo on her ring finger captures my attention and I slip my hand to hers, inspecting the inked dagger there. I glance at her face and she tilts her chin upward. More defiance. I exhale, entertained, and return to the task of inspecting her for the mark. Her eyes bore into me and I can't deny the stirring of something dark at my core much like what I felt in the dream. It is the very same thing I condemned my ancestor for, a thing I tried to deny in myself.

Arousal.

When I untie her robe, I meet her eyes and hear her sharp intake of breath as it falls open to expose her chemise. In my periphery, I see her sisters' gazes on me. They know what I'll find. They all know.

Her mother's sob breaks the silence, but it does not interrupt us.

I draw my knuckle down along the alabaster of her chest. Her skin is soft, so soft. Slowly, I expose the swell of her breasts until I see it. The crescent birthmark that promises her to me. When I do, there is a strange sense of something, of a circle closing, a duty and a certainty of what will come to pass at my hands.

As I draw the chemise lower, I let my knuckle brush the stiff peak of her nipple and when I do, I feel a hunger so raw, so feral, that when I turn my gaze back to hers, she gasps audibly. I am certain it takes all her strength to not step backward. To not try to run from me.

But it doesn't matter. There's nowhere for her to go.

Because I am the beast in the stained-glass window of the library.

I am the monster who will loom over her when I've taken what I must. When she's paid what she must.

She is the sacrifice.

And she is mine.

7

WILLOW

The ride to Saint Trinity's Cathedral in the Garden District of New Orleans is tainted with silence. After an emotional goodbye with my family, I'd been ushered into a Rolls Royce with Azrael while another driver delivered my belongings and Fiona to his house where I will live for whatever remainder of time I have left upon this earth.

Azrael sits beside me in the back seat, his presence looming almost larger than life. The car is roomy and comfortable, but it's dwarfed by his imposing frame. He takes up so much space that it feels like his energy might suck me into an abyss I'll never escape from.

He's quiet, his gaze unfocused out the window, as we travel together toward our inevitable doom. I don't know why the silence throws me off balance, but it does. In my mind, I had conjured up many different expectations of this man, but none of them could prepare me for the reality.

His strange gold eyes were the first thing to grab hold of me, like they didn't want to let me go. The moment our gazes had clashed, I felt like I was drowning, yet I couldn't look away. There was an ache in my chest I didn't recognize, a sense of agony so profound it paralyzed me at that moment.

I knew without question it was his, something he carried with him. Something unsettling. The longer I watched him, the more I realized it wasn't any of the things I'd been warned about.

His spirit is restless, his energy dark and mercurial. He's tormented in a way I didn't expect. I wonder if anyone else can see it or if it's just me—something I feel, in the same way I've felt things long before others can see them.

Nanna always told me intuition was my gift, and I can feel it now, caressing the nape of my neck like a presence I can't shake. If I stop to listen closely, I can hear a familiar voice whispering through my mind. It's the same voice that has haunted my dreams and waking moments from the time I was a young girl.

A voice from the past. An ancestor I never met but whose blood still runs through my veins.

Right now, Elizabeth is telling me something about Azrael.

The chosen one.

The words rattle around my brain like an echo chamber, setting me on edge. I don't know what she means, but I seldom do. Her words often come in riddles, forcing me to seek the answers myself. As I glance at the man beside me, I wonder what he'd think if he knew what was happening inside my head.

My mind supplies an answer readily. He'd probably wish they could still hang witches freely.

But that thought is at odds with what I feel when I look at him. Despite what I had predicted, he doesn't seem to be savoring this moment as I was assured he would. After all, the Delacroixes are known for their sadistic enjoyment of claiming the Wildblood women. As he sits beside me like a statue, though, unnaturally still and quiet, I can't help but feel a sense of conflict from him.

Or maybe that's just what I want to believe.

The car pulls to a stop, and I swallow as I wait for him to look at me again. It takes him three full seconds, and if I didn't know any better, I'd swear I saw him drag in a ragged breath before he does.

"It's time," he utters the words without emotion as the driver opens the door for us.

I don't reply. What is there to say? I'm about to marry my family's sworn enemy and live beneath his rule until tragedy inevitably snatches me away. It's the die that's been cast for me. The history between our families has dictated as much, and there is no altering that.

Azrael unfolds his large body from the car and stands up, spine rigid as he holds his hand out for me. It isn't a gesture of kindness. It feels more like an ingrained habit, as if he were raised to be respectful of women, which is almost laughable.

Despite the somber mood, I find myself quietly amused by the idea as I reluctantly settle my hand in his. This time, I know I'm not imagining the shock that travels through my body. My lips part in a silent gasp, and when I'm pulled from the car and our eyes meet again, his narrow on me. He's casting an accusatory glance as if I'm responsible for this strange, chaotic energy between us. As if my witchy senses conjured it up just to trick him.

Of course, he would think that.

I snatch my hand back and square my shoulders as the driver retrieves my bags and delivers them somewhere out of view. Reluctantly, I glance up at Saint Trinity Cathedral, the gothic architecture of the old building looming over me like a dark shadow. Moonlight dances between the towers and spires, highlighting the details of the structure. I'm not religious, but I can admit it's beautiful in a morbid sort of way–though I'm still not certain I won't burst into flames upon entering the doors.

I knew this was where we'd be married. My sisters and I drove by the place several times out of curiosity after we received the contract from the Delacroix family that would dictate my future. It has been the same since the treaty was struck between us. The chosen Wildblood woman is dragged from her home and her life and brought to this place to perform a ceremony that makes little sense, considering the lingering hatred between our families. The Delacroixes believe it will save them from further tragedy, and the Wildbloods participate only to prevent further bloodshed at the hands of our centuries-old enemies.

The ceremonies that take place between our families aren't marriages, despite what they may look like. They are Sacrifices.

I'm all too aware of what the night will entail. I will be claimed, first in name, then marked as property of Azrael with his brand inked into my skin. Before the night is through, he will lay claim to my body as a final mark of his ownership.

A shiver runs down my spine as I dare a glance at the enormous size of him. I'd be lying if I said I wasn't nervous. I've remained a virgin as was decreed, but I'm not completely naïve to the act. My curiosity over the years has been sated by reading bodice rippers and, more recently, sneaking a few previews of videos online for glimpses of the real thing. I wanted to be prepared for tonight, but something in my gut tells me there was nothing that could prepare me for Azrael.

I'm not even certain he's fully human, and as my eyes wander down between his thighs, a small moment of panic moves through me. Oh God, he's probably going to split me in half.

He clears his throat, drawing my attention back to his face as he arches a brow at me. A flush creeps over my cheeks as he watches me as if he knows exactly what I'm thinking. But he doesn't offer me any reassurances.

Needing space, I glance around in question,

wondering where I'll get ready. Before I can ask, a woman in a professional gray dress appears, eyeing me curiously. She's beautiful and elegant, her hair styled neatly into a chignon and her makeup simple and classic. I have no doubt she's part of The Society.

"Miss Wildblood, I presume?"

"Yes," I answer reluctantly.

"My name is Nina. I'll show you to the dressing area." Her tone is polite, but I'm not fooled into believing for one second she's an ally. She's been sent here to watch over me, to make sure I don't run before the ceremony.

I don't meet Azrael's gaze, though I can feel his on the side of my face. Right now, I'd give anything to know what he was thinking, if the conflict I felt from him in the car was real or just my imagination. As we part ways and I follow Nina around the cathedral, a fleeting thought passes through my mind that perhaps he wanted to marry someone else.

It would make sense. He's older than me by four years and undoubtedly has had more freedom since he wasn't bound to the same rules of celibacy as I was. I can begrudgingly admit the man is stupidly handsome. If I didn't know he was a Delacroix, and my heart wasn't encased in ice, I may have been captivated by his striking features. He's not like any man I've ever seen before. He's stronger. Taller. Genetically gifted in every way.

I didn't want to give credence to the legends, but I think perhaps there is a part of them that rings true.

There's something about Azrael that's otherworldly. I can see how he might be mistaken for something other than a mere mortal. I can also see how a woman who wasn't cursed to marry him might even fall into the trap of succumbing to that hypnotic gaze that challenges you to submit without saying a word. That commands your attention without even trying.

The more I consider it, the more I think it's the only thing that makes sense. There must be someone else. Perhaps there were many before me. I'm not sure why that thought leaves a sour taste in my mouth, but I chalk it up to the fact that I was constrained by the rules while he was free to do as he pleased.

Nina leads me around the back of the cathedral to a smaller building, seemingly unaware of the turmoil in my mind. "This is where you'll prepare yourself," she explains as she opens the door and gestures me into the room.

I glance around the small space as I step inside, my eyes falling on the dress already hung and waiting for me. It's white, of course, a mermaid cut with a sweetheart neckline. Delicate beading and floral appliques adorn the silhouette, and admittedly, it is beautiful. Probably even designer. But I have no intention of wearing it.

"You'll need to get ready now," Nina says. "You only have about fifteen minutes."

Of course there's a schedule to keep. It's not as if any of this is even necessary. It seems like a waste to go through the motions of a church wedding, particularly when Azrael seems to believe Wildbloods are evil incarnate. But this is the way of The Society, and there is no deviating, even for perfunctory arrangements such as ours.

"Can I have some privacy, please?" I turn to Nina and force a smile.

She frowns. "But you'll need my help getting into the dress."

"I'll call for you when I need you."

She hesitates but resigns herself to the fact that I'm going to be difficult. When she steps outside and closes the door, I breathe a sigh of relief and touch the moonstone pendant around my neck. It grounds me and makes me feel close to my mother. I miss her already. I miss all of my family, but I'm also glad they aren't here for the ceremony. They wouldn't be able to sit quietly while I sacrifice myself to Azrael.

They are my reason for existing, and I won't allow any harm to come to them. So, I will do this on my own, and I will do it without protest. Abiding by the treaty is the only way to maintain peace between us.

I glance around the space, taking in the antique furniture and grandfather clock. The bags I brought with me are already waiting for me on a small wooden table on one side of the room. I doubt they'd have brought them at all if they knew what was in them.

I unzip the largest bag, retrieving the dress I chose myself. It's a black floor-length gown with a corseted bodice and a layered tulle skirt. It's not even close to a traditional wedding dress, but I like it. If there's one thing I need Azrael to know, it's that he won't strip away who I am. No matter how many rules he imposes on my life as he locks me in his gilded cage, I will cling to the choices I can control. He will have to learn to pick his battles.

If I am to be married, I will do it my way.

After getting myself into the dress, which is quite the chore on my own, I glance at the clock and realize I've already wasted ten minutes. I'm not worried about my makeup, as it's held up quite well, but I apply another coat of red lipstick anyway.

I'm just pulling out my red velvet heels when Nina knocks on the door and calls out, "We need to get you into your dress now."

"Just a minute," I grumble, slipping into my heels quickly as awareness prickles my spine.

I was feeling quite confident with my choices, but as the minutes draw nearer, I can't help wondering what consequences my actions will have. Tonight, Azrael will claim me as his wife, and I'm starting to second-guess my decision to test his wrath by disobeying him this way. But it's already done, and I won't back down now.

Butterflies erupt in my belly as I examine myself in the mirror. I look different somehow, but I can't identify the reason. I tried the dress on several times in preparation. It's exactly as I remember it. I still love it just as much, but now the sheer material exposing the full length of my back seems less like a bold choice and more like a stupid one because I know Azrael will be touching that part of me tonight at the marking ceremony. He will have an unobstructed view and complete access to one of the most vulnerable parts of me—and he will have it in front of his witnesses.

A knock rattles the door again, jarring me from my thoughts, and this time Nina doesn't wait for a response. She steps inside, her mouth twisting in disapproval as her eyes move over me. "That isn't your dress," she argues.

"Actually, it is," I tell her. Before she can protest further, I brush past her, taking note of the time. "Are you going to escort me to the cathedral, or shall I go alone?"

"He won't be happy," she calls after me.

"Good," I mutter under my breath. "I had no intentions of making him happy."

Nina's heels clip along behind me as I head for the entrance of the cathedral. We still have a few minutes, but I figure I may as well get it over with. I'm sure Azrael expects me to make an attempt at fleeing, or to show up late. But I very much doubt he expects me to be early.

It's apparent the other Society members aren't expecting it either, judging by the surprise on the doorman's face as I approach.

"Miss." He nearly chokes on the word. "It isn't quite time—"

I offer him a reassuring smile and open the door myself. It's huge and heavy, and it nearly takes my whole body with it. But I manage, as I always do, and when I step onto the threshold, there are collective murmurs of confusion from the witnesses already sitting in the ancient pews.

The men don their black cloaks and white and black Society masks, so I can't see their faces, but I feel all of their gazes upon me. There must be at least twenty of them.

Flickering candles illuminate the space, casting a warmth to the ceremony that I didn't expect. I also can't help noticing I didn't burst into flames upon entering, so I suppose that's a bonus.

I draw in a staggering breath as I lift my chin and meet my groom's gaze at the end of the aisle. He's already there, waiting for me, his eyebrow arching in challenge before his eyes coast over me. He's in a three-piece charcoal suit with a dark shirt and red tie. He looks... handsome, admittedly.

Before I lose my nerve, I take my first step down the aisle. The organist fumbles to catch up as the witnesses glance at each other, whispering their disapproval. Ignoring them, I focus on putting one foot in front of the other for the longest walk I've ever taken. I feel like I'm holding it together pretty well, considering the jitters.

I wonder if Azrael can see that fear in my eyes, the tremor in my body hiding beneath my veil of armor. I want to pretend it isn't there, but the closer I get to him, the more it sinks in.

Tonight, I will be his wife.

I swallow as the aisle inevitably runs out, and I'm

forced to stop before him. His gaze lingers on my face for a long moment before drifting down my body. He doesn't say a word. He shows no hint of emotion one way or the other, so I can't tell what he's thinking. But I can see the way his eyes darken momentarily before returning to mine.

There isn't time to consider what that might mean because the priest directs us to sit in the chairs on the platform as he opens up the ceremony. I hear very little of it and understand even less. I'm not Catholic, but I know enough to realize he's reading passages from the Old Testament and the New.

It's entirely too long, and I find that the only thing I can do is stare at Azrael. I wait with bated breath, thinking about things I definitely shouldn't be thinking about in a holy place. It isn't just his frame that's massive. His hands are too. I think he could crush my throat with just a few fingers, should he really want to.

But that isn't really what's lingering in my distracted mind. It's the question of where I will feel those hands on my body tonight. If he'll make me shiver with every touch, the way he did when he brushed my nipple. My gaze roams over his gold cufflinks, noting that they appear to be antiques before my attention catches on the strange ring on his finger.

I'm in the middle of trying to examine the details of it when he moves to stand, and I blink up at him in confusion when annoyance flickers across his face. It's obvious I haven't been paying attention, and he knows it. He extends the hand I was just hyper-focused on and escorts me to the altar, where we join both hands.

Now comes the vow ceremony, and this time, I do pay attention. Because I understand the importance of these words. The weight of them. They are promises that can't be broken. Promises that can't be undone. We are bound together by these words, and I feel the stranglehold of that reality with every phrase I repeat.

Unlike me, Azrael doesn't falter in his promises. He repeats them assuredly, as if he might actually mean them. But even though his voice remains steady and calm, I catch a glimpse of something in his eyes again—something that feels like remorse, or even deception. And I can't help the foreboding feeling that creeps over my skin as I consider what that might mean for me.

There isn't time to dwell on it. The vow ceremony ends as the priest directs us to exchange rings, and it's only once the band is on my finger that I realize how much I like it. I didn't expect to. I was quite certain it would feel like a noose around my neck. But the garnet surrounded by a halo of diamonds suits me more than I ever would have anticipated.

Red, like half of my wardrobe. Red like my hair. A deep, rich burgundy like the very shoes on my feet. I wonder if it was intentional on his part, like, somehow, he knew. But how could he?

My eyes move over his face in question just as the priest pronounces us man and wife. The room spins around me, and before I can process that reality, he tells Azrael to kiss his bride. It still feels almost like a dream, everything blurring at the edges when he steps closer and tilts my chin up.

I suck in a sharp breath, but it doesn't help. I'm convinced all the oxygen has disappeared from the room as he bends to meet me at my level, his thumb skating over my jaw as his lips brush against mine.

The contact sends a shockwave through my body, more intense than the first two I've already felt from him. It isn't at all what I expected. There's nothing cruel or rough about it, and as that sinks in, I find myself leaning into him. I don't know how it happens that my hands come to rest on his arms and he's steadying me, or worse, that my lips seem to have developed a mind of their own as they part for him. The smallest sound of satisfaction echoes between us, and I can't decipher if it came from me or him. But I know I'm not imagining it when his thumb drifts to my pulse, and he inhales the air I breathe into his lungs.

Goosebumps break out along my flesh, and I feel slightly drunk as he pulls away with a strange expression on his face. Again, it feels like a silent accusation, as if I'm tricking him somehow. As if I cast a spell on him that made him kiss me that way at a wedding neither of us wanted.

He doesn't give voice to his thoughts, and I'm grateful for the interruption when the witnesses come to greet Azrael. I stay silent at his side, observing as they regard him with respect and admiration. Strangely enough, it feels as though he's on display, too, right now. It's like the sight of him here is such a rare occurrence, they aren't quite sure what to make of it. It only leaves me with more questions as the priest finally dismisses us with a final nuptial blessing and sends us on our way.

The night is far from over. When I sneak a glance at my new husband and the dark hunger pooling in the depths of his eyes, I know it's only just beginning.

8

AZRAEL

One of Councilor Hildebrand's men greets us as we exit the Rolls Royce at the compound gates of The Society's headquarters in New Orleans.

"This way, sir," he says.

I nod, and we follow him. The wide expanse of the courtyard is nearly empty, only a few of the staff working to prepare for the marking ceremony. The men who will stand witness have not yet arrived.

Willow slows her step as she takes in the courtyard. Her gaze moves over the fountain with its gently spilling water to the lampposts and flickering candles that light the way to the ivy and rose draped canopy. Abruptly, she comes to a stop and gasps.

I follow her gaze to the man at the firepit as he sets the iron inside it.

"Let's go. You'll see it soon enough," I tell her.

She glances up at me, wide eyes searching mine,

but her gaze is inevitably drawn back to that fire. The iron.

"What is that?" she asks, and for the first time tonight, I tighten my grip on her hand as she tries to pull free. She looks up at me again, and I see her trying to muster her courage.

"Branding iron," I tell her, my head pounding. "Let's go." I shift my hold to her arm and turn her toward the building where Hildebrand's man waits impatiently. It's the Tribunal building, which houses The Councilor's office.

"Wait. What?" Willow digs her heels in.

I close my eyes, press my fingers into my temple to try to ease the pain of this monstrous headache—not that it does anything. Two cloaked, masked men walk in through the gates.

"The witnesses are arriving. Let's go."

"Branding?" She shakes her head. "Branding... me?"

"I will only use it if you force my hand," I tell her, irritation clear in my tone as more members of IVI enter, their curious gazes falling on us. "Let's go."

"Wait—"

I tug her along and she follows. She has no choice. When we near the man at the door, he opens it and gestures for us to enter. Another one of The Councilor's men is waiting inside to take us where we need to be.

I haven't been in the Tribunal building before. I've never needed to be and don't really want to be now. But the Wildbloods are not members of The Society so, as ever, there is paperwork on this night of nights. I would have preferred to do this another time, but Councilor Hildebrand is not one to budge on the rules, so here we are.

We follow the man, who leads us up a wide, winding stone staircase as if we're heading up to the tower with all the meaning that holds, especially in a place such as IVI. The Society holds its members accountable to their own rules, in their own court of law. When a member is found as guilty of some offense, they carry out their own ritualistic and often archaic punishments here, within the high walls of the Tribunal building.

Willow's heels click on the stairs. She has to hurry to keep up, and she keeps glancing at the man behind us. As we reach the landing where Hildebrand's office must be, her shoe catches on the dress and she trips on the final step, gasping, and instinctively reaches for me.

I catch her before she falls, and for a moment we stand on that last step, her hands on my biceps, mine around her elbows. Her face is flushed, and she's out of breath-probably both from our pace and her near fall. My gaze moves over her hands, to my ring on her finger with its manicured nails that match the garnet. Is it strange that she reached for me when she nearly fell? No. Instinct. Like one would grab a nearby chair. This Wildblood hates me. As she should.

My gaze falls to the swell of her breasts above the bodice of her dress, and I remember how she trembled at my touch during the Tithing ceremony, how her nipple tightened. She takes a shuddering breath and draws away as if she, too, just realized she's holding on to me. She pushes a lock of hair behind her shoulder, and I catch a glimpse of the crescent moon.

"You should have worn the dress I ordered for you," I say, irritable as I release her and she takes a full step away from me.

"Why? So you can hide from what I am? Or maybe you want to hide it from your friends."

I grin, walk toward her so she takes another, final step away. The wall at her back stops her. "Friends?" I ask, eyebrows rising.

She looks anxiously away and waves her arm in the direction of the courtyard. "Your little friends playing dress up out there."

"They're not my friends. I have no friends."

"I'm not surprised."

Now I'm entertained. I am close enough to feel the warmth of her, to remember the taste of her lips and how they parted for me when I kissed her at the church. I lean one hand against the wall and brush the knuckle of my other hand over the crescent moon birthmark.

"And no, it's not to hide from what you are." I lean toward her ear to whisper the rest, watching goosebumps rise where my breath brushes her skin. "But this little witch's mark along with the rest of you are for my eyes only." I inhale her scent, savoring it before I draw back to watch the flush that creeps up her neck.

Someone clears their throat, and Willow startles.

"Councilor," I say without turning. I take my bride by the elbow and move her along toward him. "I hope we haven't kept you waiting." I don't actually give a shit, but Hildebrand is powerful within The Society. There's no need to make an enemy of him.

Councilor Hildebrand's gaze moves disdainfully over Willow before shifting to me. He smiles, steps forward to offer his hand. "Of course not, Azrael. It's always good to see you at the compound and on such an occasion. Congratulations to you both."

Willow snorts.

I slide my hand under her mass of hair and grip the back of her neck in warning.

"Thank you, Councilor. If we can get this finished? I'm anxious to take my bride home," I say, giving Willow my best cat-like grin that I can muster even as my head resumes its pounding. I hadn't realized it had stopped briefly in a small reprieve.

"I'm sure you are, but there are protocols considering the Wildbloods are not members of our Society."

"And I don't need to be," Willow says.

I squeeze a little, but I don't mind her mouthing off to this man I don't much like.

Hildebrand takes in her dress but addresses me when he speaks. "White is customary. I thought I'd glimpsed a proper wedding dress, actually."

"You had. My bride is… creative."

"Well, I'm sure you'll address her *creativity* this evening. She is new to our ways, but young wives, like children... you know what they say." He turns his back and walks toward his desk.

"What do they say?" Willow asks.

He doesn't stop as he answers, "Well, in this case, spare the rod, spoil the wife."

Willow's hands fist and I feel her gearing up for a fight. "Easy," I lean down to whisper so the old man doesn't hear. "Don't give him what he wants."

She looks up at me, but before she can say another word, we're inside The Councilor's office and the door is closed behind us. I guide Willow to a seat and remove my hand from her neck to reach into my pocket for the small bottle of painkillers. I've already had too many, but they're not doing enough so I pop the lid and take two more. Hildebrand sees and gestures to one of his men to pour me a drink, which I take and swallow in one gulp.

"This will only take a few minutes," Hildebrand says, moving behind his desk where he has already prepared the document that needs to be signed by both Willow and myself. "Then we can get on to the marking ceremony. I'm told all the witnesses have already assembled."

I skim the document. I've already read a copy. It's basically a contract stating that as my wife, Willow is now a member of The Society and as such subject to its laws. It emphasizes the importance of confidentiality.

"Your father... well, let's not rehash history but leave it at I'm glad to see you will not shun us, Azrael."

I am tempted to tell him it was the other way around, not that either my father or mother cared. "The Delacroix family is an important pillar of The Society."

I force something resembling a smile. "Pen?"

He does the same. "Of course." He twists the lid off a fountain pen and hands it to me. I sign where I am required to sign, then hand the pen to Willow.

"What is this?"

"It says you will not discuss Society matters outside of The Society, basically," I tell her.

"And that you will conform to our rules," Hildebrand adds.

"I'm not signing that without reading it."

"Would you excuse us, Councilor?" I say, not taking my eyes off my bride.

"Of course." He expected this, I'm sure, and he leaves Willow and I alone in his office.

"I'm not signing anything like that," Willow tells me.

"It's a formality, and it is part of the contract your family signed." I hold the pen out to her. She looks at it, then down at the document, and I can see how out of her element she is here. See she feels it. "He can't touch you without my permission, and I have no intention of giving it. Sign it so we can go."

She looks up at me. "So I'm property now."

"Just sign it."

"Your property."

"Who else's? Don't make this difficult."

"Or you'll use the branding iron?" She folds her

arms across her chest but her eyes water, betraying her discomfort, her fear.

"You belong to me. You know that."

"I'm not—"

"You know the rules as well as I. Your sisters, your parents, they are safe for our sacrifice."

"Our?" Willow snorts, quickly swiping away a traitorous tear. "What sacrifice are you making exactly?"

I press my hands into my temples and close my eyes, but it does nothing to relieve the pain.

"It's not you who has to face a courtyard of strangers where you'll possibly be fucking branded. It's not you who will have to submit herself to a man so he can take his pleasure no matter the cost. It's not you who lost her family—"

"Enough!"

Willow jumps.

I grip her wrist and tug her to me. "It was your ancestor who cursed us both. Yours! You think I haven't lost? I have lost more than you. At least your family is still safe and sound and alive. Now fucking sign or I will use the branding iron, and I will relish your screams."

She stares up at me, her mouth opening as a crease forms between her brows but the instant I see what I read as pity, I slam my fist on the table.

"Fucking sign! Now!"

Anything kind or pitying vanishes. Willow sets her mouth and her blue eyes turn to ice. When her lips start moving, I have a vision of Elizabeth again in her final moments cursing us, cursing me. "May the blood of all the Wildblood women your family has killed forever torment you, Azrael Delacroix."

"Are you cursing me, Little Witch?" I ask with a sneer.

"Little Witch?"

"It fits, don't you think?"

"Fuck you!" She tugs free of my grip and scribbles her name on the document then tosses the pen down. "You want to go? Let's go!"

I make to grab for her, but the door is opened and Hildebrand, with a big smile on his face, reenters followed by his two men.

He walks around the desk and gathers up the pages. "Please, take your bride and prepare her for the marking. I look forward to bearing witness."

I grip Willow's arm and walk her toward the door.

"Tell me, Azrael," Hildebrand starts, making us pause and turn back to him. His arrogant tone making me remember why I don't interact any more than necessary with The Society and its members. "Will you keep up the Delacroix tradition and use the iron? Salomé mentioned you might. And I suppose given the circumstances…" He trails off, every breath calculated, and turns to Willow. "Do you know, young lady, that in Europe witches were burned at the stake? The colonies were… gentler."

"Gentler?" Willow goes to take a step toward the old man, but I hold her back.

The Tithing

"Your ancestor was hanged for witchcraft, was she not? On Proctor's Ledge, I believe. A mercy."

Willow's face is stone, her eyes bright and glistening to overflowing.

"So, Azrael, will it be fire tonight?" The Councilor asks, almost unable to hide his excitement at the prospect of a branding.

Willow looks up at me, and it's neither defiance nor fear I see. It's pain.

I look at the old man. "I'll thank you to keep your comments about my wife's family to yourself in the future, Councilor. In fact, going forward, you will address only me, not my wife. And no, I won't use the iron. I suppose I will disappoint both you and my grandmother tonight."

9

AZRAEL

I keep hold of her as we walk in silence down the stairs of the Tribunal building and out into the courtyard. The witnesses are gathered at the far end, near the canopy. I stop and turn Willow toward me.

"Do you need a minute?"

She glares up at me. Her eyeliner is smeared where she wiped it with the backs of her hands and her skin is flushed.

"I don't need you to stand up for me. I can take care of myself. You're not some fucking hero for telling that asshole off on my behalf, if that's what you think."

"Hero?" I'm taken aback.

"I neither need nor want anything from you, Azrael Delacroix. I may be your wife, but it's only because I had no choice. Remember that. Remember that if I had any choice at all, if my family's safety didn't depend wholly on my submitting to you, I wouldn't be here. I would never choose this. And I certainly would never choose you!"

I feel my expression hardening along with my hand on her arm. She winces and tries to tug free. I loosen my grip. Her words cut in a way that is unexpected, although why would it be? She's only telling the truth.

"But I do agree with you on one thing," she continues. "Let's get this over and done with. So go ahead and put your fucking mark on me. Do your worst. You've already taken everything from me. What more can you do? What more can you take?"

At that, I laugh outright. "What more?" I pull her to me, our bodies touching, and bend down so my face is an inch from hers. "You should be very careful what you say because there is always more that can be done. More that can be taken." She tries to tug free, but I keep her close. "Now here's what's going to happen next. I'm going to give you some choices since you seem to want those. Ready?"

"Fuck you."

"You're going to choose to keep your eyes on the ground and walk at my side to the canopy there, and when I say kneel, you are going to choose to kneel."

"Never!"

"Then you're going to choose to submit to having your wrists bound. Hell, maybe I'll even collar you, and you're going to choose to bow your head low when I do."

"I will never bow to you!"

"I'm going to take my time putting my mark on

your pretty little neck, and when I'm finished, you're going to choose to thank me, your Lord and your God."

She snorts.

"And if you don't choose to do all of those things, well, then I'm going to assume you've chosen to take the consequences instead."

"What consequences?" she spits at me. She sounds defiant as hell, but I hear the sliver of fear there too.

"I'll surprise you. I can be creative too. Now let's go. Get this done, like you said. It's time to make your choices."

A hush falls over the crowd as we cross the courtyard. I'm sure the men gathered are hard at the thought of what they get to witness tonight. I get it. The thought of Willow Wildblood on her knees before me gets me hard, too. Even knowing the little I know of her, I have a feeling she'll make poor choices tonight, so I'm not surprised when she gives every man we pass a glare as we take our place beneath the canopy.

I leave my wife to face the witnesses and move behind her. On the small table beside the tattoo equipment is a pair of leather cuffs. I take them. Apart from making fists of her hands, she doesn't resist as I bind her wrists together. I take the second set of cuffs, and when I draw her elbows together and wrap the leather restraints around them, she turns her head to look back at me. Her breath is ragged, and her eyes are wide as I lock her arms behind her back. The position forces her tits out.

Lifting her hair, I set it over one shoulder and pick

The Tithing

up the collar next. It's a thin, silver collar with a fine chain hanging from the small loop at the front. She gasps when I set it against her throat and trembles as I close the clasp before moving to stand in front of her.

I take my time to look at the sight. She is fucking beautiful. Hell, maybe I'll keep her bound and collared all night long.

I meet her gaze and, true to her word, I can read her curses in her eyes.

"Kneel," I say, my back to the witnesses.

"Never," she says only for my ears.

I grin and lean closer. "Are you sure about that?"

"As sure as a heart attack."

I get the feeling she's wishing one on me now. I set my hands on her shoulders to lower her to her knees, crouching with her. Taking hold of the chain dangling from her collar, I draw her down, down, down until I can hook it into the ring in the ground. She's bent so low I have to tilt my head down to see her eyes.

"Ready, Little Witch?"

"Fuck you."

"Oh, I will fuck you. But what I meant was, are you ready to take my mark?"

Someone chuckles. I guess I'm not as quiet as I think.

"I hate you."

"How you feel about me makes no difference."

Her eyes betray her fear as she scans the shoes of the men all around us.

I get up to take my place behind her. She kneels

bound before me, her back already bared as if just for this. Just for me.

I touch the vertebrae at the back of her neck. She shivers as I trace the line of her spine to where the corset stops me, and I realize how much I want more. I want to see all of that soft, smooth skin. To touch it. Taste it. Lose myself in her wet heat when I take her. I want to feel her body open for me the way her lips did in the church—because it will. She may want to hate me, but her body will betray her.

And I will relish it.

But first, before we can get to all of that, it's time to place my mark on her skin.

Instead of taking the throne-like seat prepared for me, I push it away and instead, set my knees on either side of my wife to be closer to her, to touch her. I listen to her inhalation of breath as my thighs close around her small frame. I bend my head to the curve of her neck to draw in a deep breath of my own, feeling the quickening of hers when my lips brush skin before my teeth do, my cock hard at her back.

When I draw away to clean the skin where I'll place the tattoo, her body tenses at the touch of the cool cloth, the scent of alcohol sharp. For all her bluster, my wayward bride is readying herself. Once the skin is cleaned, I press the stencil into her skin and peel back the sheet. Already I like the look of my mark on her.

The needle buzzes to life and I begin my work. It takes time but it will be worth it. First, the circle encapsulating a triangle representing strength. Within it is the sword of Shemhazai, flames like the black feathers of the angel's wings pulsing with power. Beneath it is the symbol Isaiah Delacroix added once Elizabeth Wildblood had muttered the words that laid the Wildblood curse upon us: the crescent moon turned upside down and split by the sharp blade of our sword.

At the foot, I place the letters *IVI* as required by The Society and draw back to look at my work. At the seal completed, like that circle, ensnaring her and me both. Branding her as mine.

When it's finished and I draw back, setting the tattoo gun aside, Willow exhales, her muscles relaxing at last. I hear her shaky breath, and I wish I knew the thoughts that went through her mind as the needle bled its ink into her skin.

I undo her bonds and she stretches her arms, turning her hands then rubbing her wrists. I get to my feet and move around her to undo the chain, then the collar. I remain crouched before her, and her eyes meet mine. The skin around them is pink, a little damp. I wipe the residue of tears away, my gaze never leaving hers. The blue hue is so vivid, so full of emotions I can neither put words to nor look away from. This binding ritual has a strange power. I understand better now why this is the custom of IVI.

"All right?" I ask because what I see in her eyes makes me forget what happened before. Forget the words she spoke before the ceremony.

Her eyes narrow, all those emotions sharpening, turning to shards of ice. "Fuck you."

I draw a deep breath in then exhale slowly, feeling weary. My own gaze narrows on her, and I force one corner of my mouth upward. "I suppose I forgot myself."

"I suppose you did."

"You know what comes next. You have one last choice to make."

She leans backward on her heels as I straighten to stand, her eyes never leaving mine. The witnesses come to look at the mark, commenting on this or that. Not a single one of them touches her. They know better.

All the while, my bride and I hold the lock of our gazes.

When the witnesses move away and it's time, I know she won't do it. She won't say the words she must, as required for every bride of The Society.

Dominus et Deus.

My Lord and my God.

Silence descends.

I give her a full minute, but I am tired. Exhausted. So I move behind her once more, covering the tattoo gently. Without another word, I raise her to her feet and lead her out of the compound to take her home.

10

WILLOW

The thirty-minute drive to Eden's Crossing is yet again filled with silence. The dominant side of Azrael, which made an appearance in front of his Society brethren, has seemingly gone dormant again, but I know it won't be long before it resurfaces.

As I watch him in the darkness, his jaw clenched and his thoughts elsewhere, I can't help but wonder if he's actually enjoying this or if it's merely what has to be done. Right now, it feels like I'm just something on a checklist he has to complete before he can go on with his life.

Warmth throbs beneath my freshly inked skin as if to remind me it doesn't matter how he feels. I'm his now until death parts us.

I choose to remain silent, too, allowing it to swallow the space between us until the car finally rolls to a stop.

It's dark outside, the moon barely peeking out from

behind the clouds to illuminate the Delacroix chateau. From my window, I can see that it looms large over the estate. The gothic-style mansion with what appears to be a wing on each side is imposing, with a hint of classic New Orleans style, but unique in its own way.

Though it's my first instinct to want to explore the property, it's late, and I know that's not even an option right now.

The driver opens the door as Azrael comes around to join me. He's still quiet as he glances down, watching me take in my new surroundings. I wonder if he wants me to like them—if he's searching for approval in my eyes, or worse, disdain.

"Come." He settles his palm against my lower back. "James will bring the rest of your bags."

Heat licks along my skin just from the warmth of his fingers pressing into my spine, and as much as I don't want to like it, I have to admit I don't hate it.

I've spent enough time with Azrael tonight to understand three things about him. He's an asshole, albeit a hot one. It's his sense of duty to his family that's driving him, not his own desires. And as much as he's trying to hide it, he's in an enormous amount of pain.

I've noticed it off and on throughout the evening, the way his jaw tenses, his spine goes rigid, and the vein in his temple throbs like an angry beast. If I had to guess, I'd say he suffers from migraines, along with an unfortunate personality and bloodline.

I shouldn't care one way or the other, but admittedly, it's always been my weakness. Despite the armor I've crafted so carefully to protect my emotions, I'm an empath at heart. I hate to see anyone suffering, and it's in my nature to try to fix it somehow.

This is the part of me that tends to get me in trouble. I failed to trust my intuition before, and it didn't end well for me. I didn't set boundaries when I should have. My intentions, however pure, can't protect me from the evils in this world. It's up to me to do that, which is a lesson I've learned the hard way.

I try to keep that in mind as Azrael leads me inside the house, but any thoughts of protecting myself are quickly swept away as a sense of unease creeps over my skin. It's just a hint of something amiss at first. But as we enter the double doors and I take in my surroundings, it settles over me like a suffocating cloud of smoke.

The first thing I notice is the light and shadows dancing across the hardwood floor in the form of the Delacroix family crest. It takes me a moment to realize it's being cast from the window above the entryway, the light of the moon illuminating the mosaic glass so that it shines directly on the floor. It would be beautiful if it didn't feel like a noose around my neck that I can't escape from.

With a shudder, I glance around the rest of the space. It's late, and it's dimly lit, but I can see a corridor ahead leading into the living room. Beyond that, I catch a glimpse of some gardens through the windows. More than anything, I want to go bathe in that moonlight, but I know that's not part of Azrael's plans for tonight.

This house is gorgeous, but there's a dark, somber energy lurking within the walls. It constricts my lungs and makes my heart race, as if it's wrapping its claws around me and pulling me into a vortex.

Instinctively, I take a step back, but Azrael captures my elbow and shakes his head.

"Come, Little Witch. No more games tonight."

I want to tell him it isn't a game, that there isn't enough sage in the world to cleanse whatever presence it is I'm feeling in this house. He doesn't give me the opportunity, though, and I doubt he would even care. He seems to carry it with him, I realize, and it's a part of him too. Perhaps he's been held hostage by it for so long that he doesn't even feel it anymore. The way it weighs him down. The way it imprisons him.

I try to get a better sense of exactly what it is I'm feeling, but I can't. Something is blocking me, and as he leads me upstairs to the far end of the corridor, I know it's going to be a full-time job keeping whatever energy that is at bay.

A shiver moves over my skin when he opens the door to what I know must be his room. It smells like him– leather and sandalwood. As rattled as I might be by this strange house, I find that scent oddly calming. I barely know him, but there's something about him that feels familiar already—something that feels much safer than the gloomy atmosphere of this place.

I swallow as he shuts the door and seals us inside.

The room is massive, with a high ceiling and arched windows reminiscent of a church. It's masculine, accented with dark wood and deep green wallpaper and bedding. Above the bed is a strange wooden carving of the Delacroix family crest. There's a crack down the middle, and I find it odd that he would keep it in such a state.

On the opposite side of the room, there's a sitting area with leather chairs and the door to what I presume is an attached bathroom.

I want to explore further, but Azrael's eyes fall on me, the black of his pupils obliterating the gold as he takes a step closer, unbuttoning his suit jacket. Instinctively, my thumb traces over the ring on my right index finger—the cat-shaped ears sharpened into points.

"Thinking of maiming me already?" Azrael arches a brow at me as his thumb skates over my jaw. "I haven't even gotten started yet, Little Witch. In fact, I believe I owe you a punishment."

I tilt my chin up, hoping he can't see my nerves. "For what?"

He offers me a lazy smile as he drags his thumb across my lips, smearing my lipstick. "Playing dumb doesn't suit you. You know what you did."

"I did nothing to warrant a punishment—" The words are cut short when he turns me in his arms abruptly, grabbing hold of the corseted mesh on the back of my dress and splitting it in two.

Heat and fear lick along my skin as his hands dip

lower, shredding the fabric of my skirt so easily it terrifies me.

I knew he was strong, but this.... this is inhuman. It takes him very little effort and all of three seconds to rip my dress in half and toss it to the floor, revealing my near-naked body. My heart feels like it's about to beat out of my chest as I stand there in nothing more than a thong and heels, listening to his breathing increase as his palm grazes the length of my spine.

I can't see his face, but I can feel his eyes burning a path down my body. His index finger dips below the string of my thong, plucking it until it snaps back against my skin and making me gasp.

I don't know what to expect, not being able to see him, and it's setting me on edge. I try to turn, but he halts me by wrapping his arm around me and splaying his palm across my belly.

The edges of his fingers trace the snake tattoo curving around my hip as he hauls me back against his body, his breath tickling my ear. "Where do you think you're going, Little Witch?"

"Nowhere." My response comes out strangled, and his dark chuckle grates at my already raw nerves. But I seem to forget them entirely as his palm sweeps up over my breast, grazing my nipple and sending sparks shooting through me.

At that moment, I have the horrifying realization of how much I like that, of how much I want more of it. When I glance down at his muscular forearm imprisoning me, the last thing I want to do is run away.

He drags his nose along the curve of my neck as he gropes my breast, and as I melt against him, I can feel the hard length of his shaft pressing into my spine.

He's huge.

I'd already suspected it, but my fear reignites as I imagine him trying to ram that inside of me.

I try to pull away, and he releases a low growl before he snatches both my arms and tugs them back, securing my wrists with one of his hands.

"Always so fucking defiant," he murmurs against me. "You're going to learn what that gets you in this house."

The sound of his tie being undone steals the breath from my lungs, and when I feel the material wrapping around my wrists, my bravery flees in a moment of sheer panic.

"Wait!" I choke out, yanking away from his grasp before he can secure a knot.

His eyes are molten hot and downright predatory as they move over my face, and I know I have to get through to him somehow. I have to find a way to humanize him again because right now, whoever's in the room with me isn't the same man who kissed me at the altar.

"Azrael." His name leaves my lips on a whisper as I take a tentative step toward him. "I'm giving myself to you freely. All I'm asking is that you don't... hurt me." Despite my best efforts, my voice falters on the last two words. Even though I didn't intend for him to see this part of me—the wounded part—I can see that he does.

His features darken as he regards me curiously. "You are a virgin."

I think it's meant to be a question, but it sounds more like a command—like he can't fathom the idea that I would ever give myself to anyone else, and if I had, there would be hell to pay.

"I am." I force the words between my teeth.

He doesn't look satisfied with my response, and I know it's because he's still questioning it. My reaction was too strong to be without a reason, and he wants to understand why. He wants to strip bare this wound, and I can't let him. I can't tell him that while I may be a virgin, I am not without damage.

Instead, I reach up on my toes to touch his face, the part of his temple that's still throbbing, pain lingering beneath the surface. I want him to know that I see his discomfort too. That I feel it. In some ways, despite our differences, we do have something in common.

We both understand pain.

He closes his eyes, shutting himself off from me, but it doesn't escape my notice that after a moment, he leans into the touch. It catches me off guard, and I'm not the only one. His eyes snap open in confusion before narrowing on my face.

"What are you trying to do to me?" His fingers clamp around my jaw as he pierces me with his gaze.

"Nothing." The word leaves my lips so quietly that I'm not sure he even hears it.

He's looking at me in that way again, like he thinks I'm doing some kind of witchcraft on him right now.

We stare at each other like that for what feels like the longest minute of my life before he surprises me again, this time by leaning down and claiming my lips with his once more. The heat of his mouth brands mine as his hand wraps around the length of my hair, holding me there as if to repeat what he's been telling me all day.

I'm his.

He's said it in every way imaginable: with his ring on my finger, his brand on my skin, and even the words he uttered to Hildebrand. But this is different than before. This claim sends my pulse skyrocketing, heats my blood, and makes my body sway as I nearly collapse into him.

I feel lightheaded from the rush of endorphins, and I wonder if this is normal. Is this how it's supposed to feel? Am I drunk off a single kiss?

Against my better judgment, my mouth parts for him again, and this time, his tongue sweeps past my lips, tasting me. He swallows my exhalation, tilting my face back like he wants to devour me. Like he needs to drink from my lips as much as he needs air to breathe.

A groan rumbles from his chest, then he releases me abruptly, glaring down at me again as he drags a hand through his hair. "What the fuck are you doing?"

I blink up at him, still breathless and half-stupefied from that kiss. "What do you mean?"

He shakes his head, muttering. "Fucking Wildbloods."

I don't know what to say, so I don't say anything.

We stare at each other, the air fraught with tension as his gaze dips down to my nipples, then lower to the small triangle of fabric of my thong.

Slowly, he starts to unbutton his shirt, never taking his eyes off me as he tosses it aside. As he does, I can't help letting my gaze roam over the broad expanse of his chest, down his muscular torso, then eventually to the ink on his skin. It covers part of his chest, wrapping around his side. The rest is presumably on his back, which is obscured from my view. It's a large piece, and it takes me a moment to process what I'm seeing.

It's an angel, his body sculpted as if it were from marble. His face is hidden beneath a hood, cast in shadow, with only his eyes peering out from beneath. The angel–much like Azrael–is a towering figure, dark and powerful, his wings spread wide. His chest, shoulders, and forearms are covered in ornate armor as if he's ready for battle. At his side, his fist clenches the hilt of the sword—a sword that's pierced a crescent moon.

I swallow, feeling strangely conflicted by the piece. While it's arresting in a way that I don't want to look away from–a beautiful piece of art–it's impossible to misinterpret. What else could that moon represent but me?

He recognizes the war in my eyes but chooses not to acknowledge it. After all, what is there to say? We are who we are: enemies at heart, now bound by marriage.

His gaze dips briefly to the tattoo on my chest, the

phases of the moon inked between my breasts, and his eyes flash with heat. For someone who has a depiction of that very moon conquered by the dark angel on his arm, he doesn't seem all that disgusted by my artwork. In fact, I think he seems to like it against his own desires.

When his hands move to his trousers, I follow them with my gaze. I've been curious about this moment, and I can't hide it.

He unzips the pants and parts the fabric, tugging them down along with his briefs before he discards those too. Just as I suspected, an enormous, throbbing cock springs free, and terror washes over me.

"Nope." The word squeaks out as I shake my head, backing away with what is undoubtedly horror written across my face.

Azrael quirks a brow at me. "Is there a problem?"

"Yes, there's a problem." I glare at the offending member. "You're going to rip me in half. Oh God, please don't let me die this way."

I don't know if I'm praying to him or a deity I'm not even sure exists. I just know I want to run, and the second the thought pops into my head, Azrael laughs. He actually fucking laughs, like this is funny. Jesus, I didn't even know the man was capable of humor, but this is the furthest thing from funny.

"Azrael—" I start to plead with him, hoping he'll come to see reason. It's basic math. That monstrosity is not fitting inside of me.

"Come here," he orders.

I shake my head again.

He sighs. "Is everything going to be a battle with you?"

I nod.

He comes to me instead, swallowing up the space between us in one stride before he turns me in his arms again and pins my back to the front of his body. Only now, it's different because I can feel his skin against mine. His cologne lingers in the air, intoxicating in a way I don't understand, just as the feeling of his kiss remains on my lips. Worst of all, I can hear that voice in my head telling me to give in.

I try to ignore it, but it's forgotten entirely when Azrael's fingers slip down beneath the fabric of my thong, stroking between my thighs. A strangled noise gets caught in my throat, and his body stiffens behind me like he's surprised.

"So wet for me already, Little Witch?"

I don't have a response for him, but it's clear he doesn't want one. His other hand settles against my throat, his fingertips pressing against the delicate flesh just enough to alter my breathing but not to take it away entirely. It feels like a warning, and I'm reminded of my own personal nightmare.

"Relax." The word caresses my ear as he strokes me between my thighs again.

I'm at war inside my head. Half of me is ready to flee at the memory of being trapped without breath; the other half is giving in to the sensations he's coaxing from my body as he touches me.

"Azrael." His name slips from my lips, and I'm not entirely sure what I'm pleading for, but he knows.

He gives it to me. He strokes me to the edge of an abyss, tension coiling every muscle in my body as I chase a high like I've never felt. But just as I'm about to fall off that edge, he pulls me back, stopping abruptly.

"Remember how I told you I owe you a punishment?" He brushes his lips against my ear.

A noise of protest exhales from my lips, and I can feel him smiling against me as he inhales me. What an asshole.

I try to yank away again, but he tightens his grip on my throat, chiding me.

"You're my wife now, Willow," he growls. "There's nowhere to run."

He drags his wet fingers from my thong and grabs a handful of my ass, kneading the flesh before he smacks it... hard.

"What the hell," I yelp.

Another smack, followed by another. He spanks me so many times I lose count until I can feel nothing but his flaming handprints covering my back side. I don't have to look to know it's red, and it's probably going to remind me of him every time I sit down for the next few days.

Just when I'm about to beg him for mercy, he stops, giving me a much-needed reprieve as his fingers find their way between my legs again. He strokes me gently, a complete contrast to the way he just obliterated my ass cheeks, and I'm having trouble keeping up with him. I don't know what to expect from one minute to the next. I just know when he stops me from coming again, I want to scream.

He shows no sympathy toward my plight. He continues to torture me, groping my body, teasing my nipples, dragging his teeth along my neck. His fingers tangle in the mass of my hair, wrenching my head back, and he renews his torment between my thighs, driving me to the point of insanity.

I'm on the verge of begging for it—something I swore I'd never do—when he scoops me up and hauls me to the bed. He splays me out across the comforter, pausing to stare down at me like he's fighting a war inside his own mind.

He wants me. Of that, there can be no doubt.

But I think he's disgusted with himself for it too. Maybe that will save me.

It's a fleeting thought, one that disappears a moment later when he leans his body over mine, spreading my thighs apart.

"Wait," I protest. "I don't think this is going to work. Seriously, you're going to kill me."

Another dark chuckle rumbles from his chest as he caresses my cheek with his thumb. "So fucking innocent, and yet so fucking evil."

His words sting, but I know they're nothing in comparison to what's going to happen next. I'm thinking of all those books I read and how they never mentioned a scenario quite like this. And I'm pretty sure my life is flashing before my eyes as he drags the head of his cock against my slickness.

I don't want it to feel good because that seems deceptive. Something that can annihilate me shouldn't feel good. But there isn't time to entertain such notions because he leans his massive frame over me and starts to push inside.

Slowly. So fucking slowly.

I suck in a breath, meeting his gaze without meaning to. At this moment, neither one of us can seem to look away. I don't know how it happened or when, but I realize I'm clutching his biceps like a lifeline, like he can save me from himself somehow.

"How does it feel?" he chokes out, like it's taking every ounce of restraint he has to be gentle with me right now.

Like I have a giant fucking cock wedging its way inside of me. It feels like he's stretching me apart. There's a sting, but it's not as apocalyptic as I imagined it would be. I can't tell him as much, though, so I just nod at him to continue.

Breathing deeply, I watch him as he closes his eyes and sinks in as far as my body can take him. It's tender and foreign, and I'm really not entirely sure how to feel about it until he starts to pivot his hips slightly, rolling them back and forth. It's a small movement, maybe just an inch or two, but it's enough to feel all of him. My nerves are on fire, my skin is flushed, and my nipples are stabbing the air as he starts to fuck me for real.

I lose myself to the sensations, the power of his

body drugging me, pulling me under a spell I didn't cast and one I don't know how to protect myself from. But I'm not the only one. It's written in his eyes when he opens them to meet mine. There's a fire in him he can't extinguish, one he's actively trying to resist, even as he stokes it with every thrust.

He's staring down at me like I'm the devil incarnate, but his body says otherwise. I can feel it in every twitch of his muscles. The tension coursing through his spine. The clench of his jaw. I watch in fascination as he gives into it, thrusting harder, deeper, claiming me in a way nobody else ever will.

My body arches up into him, tension pulling at my belly, butterflies erupting as my fingers dig into his arms. I'm so freaking close, and I think he's going to let me have it this time.

But he sees it, and he grips my throat again, a warning echoing from his lips like a thunderbolt. "No."

My body doesn't get the memo. Before the word even fully leaves his lips, the orgasm tears through me violently, stealing all of my senses. Seconds pass as starbursts alight behind my eyelids, static fills my ears, and I can do nothing but convulse around him.

It isn't until I hear the muttered curse that I realize what I've done.

"Goddammit," he groans, thrusting deeply as his own body unleashes.

I blink open my eyes, still half-disoriented, to see his head tilted back, lips parted, as he purges himself inside of me. He's a beautiful terror, this man. It's undeniable at the moment. I hate him, but even I can admit this is a sight to behold. The notion that I could have such power over a man—a Delacroix at that—is almost surreal.

But just as I suspected, it doesn't last.

After a minute, he returns to his senses, opening his eyes to glare down at me. "That makes two," he says.

"Two what?"

"Two times you've disobeyed me already."

I shrug half-heartedly, not even remotely sorry for it.

He pulls out, his gaze moving over the small amount of virgin blood on his cock with a twisted sense of satisfaction before he drags his attention back to my face.

"Don't think I'm not keeping score, Little Witch."

11

AZRAEL

Strands of deep red hair curl over my pillow, and I take in the sight of her. Her expression is soft, sleepy, sated. She stretches like a cat, and I find my gaze moving over the length of her properly, slowly, wanting to have her again.

She arches her back, twisting away as she yawns.

I chuckle.

Her eyelids fly open.

"Sleepy?" I ask, smiling as I capture her wrists to keep her arms above her head. She's on guard in an instant, and I loosen my grip. "I'm not going to hurt you."

The look on her face says she doesn't believe me, and I recall her words of earlier.

"I'm giving myself to you freely. All I'm asking is that you don't... hurt me."

I wonder what she was expecting, exactly. I can't blame her for anticipating the worst.

"Relax, Willow," I say and allow my gaze to drift from her face. She's lovely, my bride, her body made as if to fit mine.

And she's inked. I'm not sure why it surprises me, but I like it. I brush my knuckles over the valley between her breasts and her nipples tighten in response to my perusal.

Yes. Made for me, my bride.

I trace the phases of the moon inked into her pale skin, listening to her intake of breath as I do. When I slide my fingertips over her taut belly, down to the neat little triangle of darker red hair between her legs, she twists but doesn't quite pull away. She gasps when I tug on those hairs. I move my fingers to the snake curving up her hip, trace the outline of its body. With a glance into her bright blue eyes, I return my attention to that mound of hair and open her legs to see the smear of semen and blood on her thighs, on my sheets.

A groan sounds from inside my chest. A sense of satisfaction to see my mark on her washes over me. To know she's only ever been and will only ever be mine.

Releasing her arms, I bow my head over her belly.

"What are you doing?" she asks, half sitting up, her voice panicked. Her fingers grip handfuls of my hair as my tongue draws a line between her belly button and her sex, licking the length of her pussy, wanting to taste her. "Azrael!"

I do it again, taking my time and pushing her thighs apart to see her fully. She's beautiful. Perfect.

And her taste, her virgin blood, her come mixed with my own, fuck, it does things to me.

"Oh God!" Her hands turn to fists in my hair.

I look up to find her up on her elbows, her closed eyes, her hair wild over her shoulders. "Not God, but close," I tell her, climbing up to my knees. I roll her slightly on her hip and smack her ass once more before getting out of the bed.

"Hey! Ow." She turns to watch me, rubbing her ass cheek. My handprint is a prominent pink. Good. "You can't start something and not finish it." She sits up, gathers the blankets around herself.

"You already came without my permission. Besides, I wasn't starting something. I simply wanted to know how you taste." I turn my back, pull Isaiah's ring off my finger, and open the nightstand drawer.

Willow gasps loudly.

I pause, glad she can't see my face as my mouth draws into a line and my eyes narrow. I drop the ring into the drawer. It clatters, a solid, heavy weight, and when I shove the drawer closed, I hear it roll to the back.

"What the hell are those?"

I turn to her, knowing what she's referring to: the marks on my shoulder blades. Abacus had them too, identical scar-like birthmarks on our backs. Emmanuel's are fainter. "Birthmark," I say flatly.

I don't want to talk about them. Any time I'm reminded of their existence, I remember what Abacus had done to try to get rid of them. They'd driven him mad.

No. I stop myself. It wasn't those that had driven him mad. The presence of the birthmark was just a prop. Other things had driven him past the point of no return.

Willow studies me, and I think I have to get better at hiding what I'm thinking. The look on her face makes me suspect she can read my mind.

At that thought, the migraine which I was too preoccupied to focus on seems to return with a vengeance. She watches me cross the room to where I left my jacket and swallow two more pills dry.

"Come," I say. "I will wash you."

"I can wash myself just fine. We call it a shower these days, by the way."

"You have a smart mouth." I gesture to the archway that leads to the bathroom.

"You take a lot of pills," she retorts as she passes me into the bathroom.

I step on the edge of the blanket she's draped around her and when it catches, she spins to face me, arms holding the blanket up.

"Off."

She raises her eyebrows defiantly.

"I've already seen it all," I taunt.

We have a brief standoff, but she lets the blanket drop. My heart hammers against my chest. I can't help but look her over, that echo like the rattle of a snake sounding from inside my chest again. When I meet her gaze, she cocks her head and gives me a one-sided grin.

"Men are so easy." She turns her back to walk into the bathroom.

I watch her ass, proving her right. "You're very cocky for a girl who's wearing my handprint all over her ass," I say, catching up with her in one stride. I squeeze her ass cheek before stepping toward the large, round tub that the housekeeper has filled on my earlier instruction.

The bathroom itself is large, the walls the same deep emerald as the bedroom. Three arched iron-clad windows span almost the length of one wall. They overlook the forest behind the house, the glass tinted slightly for privacy. The tub was custom made for this space, the room of The Penitent—Abacus's before mine. And before him, all those other Delacroix men, The Penitents who took the marked Wildblood woman and made a Sacrifice of her to Shemhazai.

In a way, it's a sort of baptismal pool. I'm certain the original Delacroix who had it installed had just that in mind. I want to say that our thinking is more modern now, but I catch our reflection in the large antique, ornately framed window over the stone sink.

Willow Wildblood stands naked before me, taking in the oversized tub, her expression strange and her eyes too wide. I loom like an overgrown beast behind her. If that isn't evidence that we haven't come far at all, I don't know what is.

"Come, Willow." I hold my hand out to her.

She looks at the water, then at me. "What is it, holy water?"

I chuckle. "Why? Would it burn you if it were?"

"I didn't combust when I stepped into the church, but I don't want to take any chances."

"You'll be fine. Come." She hesitates, which is strange. "It's just a bathtub. You won't combust. Or drown."

She tries for a casual snort but the look in her eyes is a little like it was in that photograph with her sister, Raven, and I don't think she realizes she's wrapped her arms around herself protectively.

"What are you afraid of? I'm going to wash you, then we're going to bed."

She nods, tries for a smile and walks into the tub, bypassing my offered hand and moving to the opposite side. She cautiously lowers herself to a seat. She's uncomfortable, to say the least. I follow her in, curious, because this is not the same girl as just a few moments ago, as the cocky one who challenged Hildebrand, or the one who glared at every witness during the marking ceremony.

Instinct tells me to move slowly, and I take the soap and loofah and lather it up. She watches. I wonder if she is aware how stiffly she's sitting, how she's clutching her hands, her arms locked.

"Turn around. I'll do your back."

She blinks. "What?" She starts twisting the ring which is, I suppose, meant to be some sort of weapon with its twin spiked points like a cat's ears. On closer inspection, they're pretty sharp. I think she can do some harm with the thing.

I hold up the loofah and soap. "I'll start with your back."

"Oh." She stands up so abruptly that water splashes over the edges. She hurries toward the edge and climbs out. "I'm good, actually. Thanks." She grabs a towel off the rack and wraps it around herself. Her hands aren't quite steady. "Where are my things? My cat?"

"Sorry, your what?"

I climb out too, taking another towel and wrapping it around my hips.

"My cat." She seems almost like herself again—almost, but not quite, and in a hurry to get away from me because she's struggling to hold my gaze and her face is flushed.

That could be the heat of the water, I suppose, but I don't think so. Her behavior is strange. Out of place. "You brought a cat?"

"Of course."

"Hm. I have a dog. He's quite large. Your cat—"

"She won't hurt him. Don't worry. Unless he's wicked to her of course." Does she see the confusion on my face? Does she hear how backwards what she said is? "Where is she?"

"Well, I'll expect you to sleep in my bed, but your things are here so I suppose..." I open the door that connects my room to a smaller one. It may have been used as a sitting room once upon a time, but it's been converted for the Wildblood sacrifice. For Willow.

However long she's here.

Willow doesn't even look around, but when she hears the meow of the cat someone got past Grandmother, she rushes around me. Her relief is a palpable thing as she takes the black cat out of its carrier and hugs the creature to herself.

I watch her as she cradles it, kissing it like she hasn't seen it in a hundred years. I clear my throat and she turns to me.

"Thanks. Good night. You can close the door behind you," Willow says with a dismissive wave of one hand.

"Oh, I don't think so. Leave the... creature. Come."

"No, *I* don't think so. I'll sleep here." She looks around the room where her suitcases have been set against a corner. There's no bed, just a couch, some chairs, a vanity table, and books on a shelf. A smaller bathroom is attached to this room.

"You'll sleep in my bed. If you want to keep the thing, you'll do as I say and come to bed. Now. If not, I'll be tempted to throw it out."

The cat hisses at me as if it can understand.

"Her. She's a she. Not an it. And she goes where I go. I'm not leaving her alone in this haunted house."

"It's not haunted," I say, but it's a lie. It is. It is a dark place, and as I think it, I look at her and all the vibrance and color she is. Something twists inside me for what I will do to this woman—barely a woman—and what I will take from her. "Fine. Bring it. *Her*. For tonight." I stand aside and gesture for her to enter my bedroom again.

She considers. I expect her to argue, and I feel so fucking tired and my head hurts so fucking much that I don't think I can take an argument. But then she surprises me. She nods once and carries the furball past me. The thing looks over her shoulder at me and I swear it sneers as Willow climbs into my side of the bed—my side—and tucks the damn cat in beside her.

I open my mouth to say something but take a deep breath in and close it again. I climb into bed instead and switch off the light. When I wrap an arm around my wife, who is facing away from me, that cat hisses and scratches her claws down the back of my hand. I draw it away, cursing, but I'm too tired for anything more tonight. I turn away from my wife and stare out into the darkness of the night, praying for oblivion to take me, to give me this reprieve. Just a few hours of peaceful sleep.

12

WILLOW

When I open my eyes again, I'm surprised to find a hint of daylight streaming through the crack in the curtains. Not only did I sleep through the night, but I must have slept hard. It's an unsettling realization, considering I typically wake multiple times throughout the night, haunted by vivid dreams and nightmares alike.

I chalk it up to exhaustion as Fiona yawns and stretches beside me as if to say she had a peaceful night too. I scratch her ears and glance behind me, something like disappointment settling over me when I realize Azrael is no longer in bed. I was hoping to wake before him so I could examine those strange scars on his back, but it appears he's already slipped out to do whatever dark overlords do during the day.

I'm not sure what time it is, but I decide I should probably get ready for the day myself. I'm certain my family is worried about me, and I need to dig through my belongings to find my phone.

That's the plan, but something else occurs to me as soon as my feet hit the floor. I'm alone in Azrael's room. So, naturally, I do what any woman would do in my circumstances. I snoop.

Starting in his closet, I rifle through his clothes, amused that the amount of darkness rivals my collection. While my wardrobe consists of black and red, his is mostly black. Many of the pieces seem to be vintage, but they are well-made, and there's very little in the way of casual clothing. Out of curiosity, I reach for a long black trench coat, noting that it seems to be a favorite of his, judging by the worn leather and cologne still lingering on the material. Something about this piece feels special, and I'm not sure why. It's just a feeling I get. I don't know what possesses me to try it on and glance in the dressing mirror, but when I do, I can't help being amused at how it dwarfs my frame.

The man is a fucking giant.

I keep it on while rifling through the rest of the belongings in his closet, turning up nothing of significance. Typically, a closet doubles as a hiding space for other things. Safes. Lockboxes. Dirty secrets. But if Azrael has any of those, they aren't in here.

I return his coat to a hanger and move on to the rest of the room. I pick up every object to examine it, getting a feel for the space. Everything he owns serves a purpose. The furnishings and decorations all seem to be antiques or possibly family heirlooms.

I peek under the bed, not finding a single speck of dust. But inside the nightstand drawer, I notice the heavy gold ring he wore yesterday.

When I pick it up to look more closely at it, a wave of nausea overcomes me, and I have the strangest urge to hurl it out the window. Far... far away from me. I rotate the piece in my fingers, wondering what it is that's making my gut churn. It isn't until I notice the tiny lip and open it to reveal a hidden compartment that I begin to understand.

A lock of hair, the same shade of auburn as mine, rests inside. A cold chill creeps up the nape of my neck as a vision of Elizabeth swinging from a tree infiltrates my thoughts. It's a vision I've had many times, but never as vivid as this. I can feel her agony coursing through me, the bite of wind against her skin as she takes her final breaths... the dark, piercing gaze of Isaiah Delacroix as he watches the life slip from her.

The ring falls from my fingers, tumbling back into the drawer as another wave of sickness seizes me. I clutch my stomach, holding back the urge to retch, and meet Fiona's gaze. She's watching me with worried eyes, her hair standing on end as if she feels it too, the hatred that lives in this house, even now. It's something dark and sinister, something I don't know how to protect myself against.

"Come on." I grab Fiona and haul her into the

adjoining room, shutting the door behind us. I need to gather my thoughts. I need space.

An hour and one entirely too hot shower later, I still don't feel clean. Last night, I was so wrapped up in the moment I wasn't thinking about how twisted it is. But now I can't wash it away. Knowing that I not only allowed a Delacroix inside my body but that I enjoyed it makes me feel nothing but shame.

He's fucking demented. That's the only explanation there is. The fact that he not only keeps a lock of my ancestor's hair—the ancestor his family murdered—but that he wears it disgusts me.

How could I let him touch me? How could I allow myself to enjoy it, knowing who he is? Knowing what he thinks of my family?

The evidence of my betrayal is still imprinted on my skin. The feeling of his fingerprints still lingers where he smacked me. The ache between my thighs reminds me that I welcomed him into my body.

Worst of all is the tattoo etched into my skin, his permanent mark on me. It's a claim of ownership, a reminder that there is no escape. Even in death, his mark will remain.

Tears prick my eyes as I stare at my reflection in the mirror. I always swore I'd never let him make me cry. But how can I not after what I just saw? It feels like my heart has been wrenched from my chest, and I can't help but wonder if he'll keep a lock of my hair like some twisted trophy when I'm dead.

A faint knock sounds at the door, startling me from

my thoughts, and I wipe my eyes quickly before it creaks open. I'm sure it will be Azrael, so I'm surprised when I see a young girl peeking through the crack. She offers me a shy smile, her gaunt face and shadowed eyes catching me off guard.

"May I come in?" she asks.

"Yes," I answer hesitantly, unsure what to make of her.

She enters quietly, remaining near the door even after it's shut, her hands clutched in front of her. She's petite, and I can't tell her age, but I sense something is off. She looks frail, her body swallowed by a large knitted sweater. The long white-blonde hair that hangs loose around her face is beautiful and unique, but I can't help but wonder if she's malnourished.

It looks like something has been sucking the life out of her, and I wonder if it's this house. That same dark energy I felt lurking last night and today.

"Hello," the girl greets me softly. "I'm Rébecca, Azrael's sister. And I suppose yours now too."

There's a hopeful note in her voice as she says that last part, and something inside me softens. I honestly didn't know what to expect from Azrael's family. In my mind, I had assumed they may all be evil. But I don't think this girl has anything but innocence and goodness within her.

"Hello, Rébecca." I offer her a smile, hoping she doesn't notice the moisture at the edges of my eyes. "I'm Willow."

"You can call me Bec," she says as she shrugs a

dainty shoulder. "If you want."

"Okay," I agree. "Bec it is."

At that moment, Fiona takes it upon herself to introduce herself, walking over to greet Rébecca by rubbing against her legs.

"Oh, my God." Bec's eyes widen as she bends to greet Fi. "You have a cat?"

"I do." I smile. "I think she likes you. A rare honor with that one."

Bec looks pleased with the idea as she scratches Fi's ears. "What's her name?"

"Fiona."

"She's so pretty," Bec coos. "I love her."

It's such a small thing, but it makes me happy to hear that. "You can come visit her anytime you want."

"I would love that."

She spends the next few minutes petting Fi, much to the cat's delight, before returning her attention to me.

"I wanted to ask if you might like to have breakfast together," she says. "And then I could give you a tour."

My stomach rumbles on cue, reminding me how long it's been since I last ate, and I offer Bec a grateful smile.

"Thank you. I'd love to join you."

Over a breakfast spread that could rival a luxury buffet, Bec and I get to know each other. She chats quietly, telling me about her hobbies and asking questions about me. I learn she's fifteen, though she doesn't look anywhere near it.

She glosses over that fact and doesn't mention if she's ill, though I suspect she is. While I eat what feels like half of the food on the table, she barely touches hers. It concerns me, but I don't know her well enough to ask about it. However, I make a mental note to ask Azrael later if I'm forced to endure more of his company.

After breakfast, Bec begins a tour of the estate as promised. The house is, admittedly, beautiful. It's a mixture of rich wood, stone, and dark, polished floors. Every detail is ornate, right down to the light switches. Large, arched windows dominate the house, lending light to the gothic vibe. A stunning deep green seems to permeate every space, whether in the form of furnishings or plants, and I find it fitting. It's the same aura of color I see when I look at Azrael.

I suspect they spent a lot of time and money renovating the place over the years, but it still feels hollow inside, like a body with no soul. A family lives within these walls, but it doesn't feel like a home.

It's so different from the way I grew up. My family is close, and we spend as much time together as possible. I suspect that isn't the case here. Bec and I have spent at least two hours together and still haven't seen anyone other than the staff roaming these halls.

Bec explains a bit of the family history as she leads me through the lower level of the house. Her parents are long-deceased, as is her brother Abacus, which she tells me is more recent. A note of sadness lingers in her voice after she mentions his name, and it makes me curious how he passed, but I don't press for details.

The Delacroixes have always believed it's the Wildbloods and the curse between our families responsible for the tragedies that seem to befall them repeatedly. I'm not about to bring that up with Bec when she may be my only true ally in this house.

As she shows me through the library, the living room, and out onto the lower terrace, I get the sense that she deeply admires her two remaining brothers, Emmanuel and Azrael. But at the mention of her grandmother, Salomé, something shifts in her. It's a subtle darkening of her eyes, a rigidness to her spine that didn't exist before. But it's gone in the blink of an eye as she moves on to explain how the house is divided.

"There are two wings," she tells me. "My family maintains the west wing, but the east is closed off. You can't go in the dark wing for your safety since it's in disrepair."

I nod, though I have no such intentions of making any promises. There must be a reason it's closed off, and I want to know what it is.

A woman calls out Rébecca's name from inside the house, and the tension returns to her face as she glances at me. "Come on, I'll show you the grounds."

"Don't you need to see what—"

Bec tosses me a pleading glance, and I halt mid-sentence. I suspect that must be her grandmother calling out for her, and it's clear Bec doesn't want to be found right now. So I follow her out onto the grounds of the property, taking in the views with an appreciation I didn't expect.

The property is vast, shaded with ancient trees and beautiful foliage that lend a sense of privacy no matter where we stand. Well-maintained gardens dot the land and the dense woods surrounding us seem to go on for miles. I have an itch to explore them but have the sense that Bec wouldn't be able to make such a journey, so I allow her to show me her favorite areas instead.

When we reach the glass-encased pool house, an equal sense of longing and foreboding lingers as I glance at the pool. I've always loved water. Growing up, I think my sisters and I spent so much time swimming I'm surprised we didn't turn into prunes. But now, I can't forget how dangerous it feels too.

"Willow?" Bec's voice infiltrates my thoughts.

"Yes?" I blink at her, still slightly off balance.

"I asked if you liked it."

"Oh, yes." I force a smile. "Very much."

"Maybe we can swim together sometime."

I'm about to tell her I'd love that when a sharp voice from behind cuts me off.

"You will do no such thing, Rébecca. What did I tell you about befriending the witch?"

Bec's face falls as she dips her head and slowly turns to meet the woman's gaze. The woman, I presume, must be her grandmother, Salomé.

Before either of us can respond, Salomé directs her withering gaze over me, then to her granddaughter. "Get in the house, Rébecca. Now."

Bec offers me an apologetic glance, her shoulders slumping before she takes her leave. Tension coils in my spine, and I have to bite my tongue as I watch her go. I don't know the family dynamics yet, but I recognize that same dark energy I've felt within the house inside of Salomé.

"So you're the Wildblood." She says the name as if she means to say *trash*.

I offer her a sweet, condescending smile. "I am."

"Marked by the devil, I can see." Her attention drifts to the crescent moon peeking out of the décolletage of my black dress, and her face twists into a sneer as she takes in my visible tattoos and jewelry.

"If you say so," I reply, refusing to let her see she's getting to me.

"I suppose you'll do," she says after a beat. "After all, I doubt you'll be around too long."

Her words don't sound like a prophecy but a threat.

"I suppose we'll see," I answer in challenge.

Her eyes narrow, and it's clear she's not used to anyone talking back to her. "Stay away from my granddaughter," she issues the decree with unwavering authority. "Or you'll see the devil come out of me."

I roll my eyes and turn my back on her, choosing to walk away. But it doesn't stop me from hearing her final words as I go.

"The only good Wildblood is a dead Wildblood."

13

WILLOW

I spend the rest of the morning unpacking my things, intentionally decorating the room in a way I know will grate on Azrael. I prominently display my apothecary bottles, tarot cards, crystals, and whatever witchy belongings I suspect will raise his hair.

When I glance at the clock again, I'm dismayed when I realize it only took me an hour to settle in. Time seems to pass so slowly in this house, and I haven't even been here a full day. I can't imagine what a year will feel like.

I shudder at the thought, trying to figure out how to spend the rest of my time today. My phone is charging, and I know I need to check in with my family, but I'm not sure I'm ready to answer all of their questions just yet.

I could read. Or take a nap with Fiona. But I feel too restless for that.

I find it strange that I haven't seen Azrael this morning. Bec and I walked through most of the house and the grounds and never crossed his path. Part of me hopes I never have to see him again after the discovery I made in his nightstand drawer, but I know I won't be that lucky.

I'm sitting on the floor of my room, trying to ground myself, when I hear the door shut in Azrael's bedroom. Tension bleeds into my muscles as I listen to him move around, his footsteps creaking around the hardwood floor.

I'm holding my breath when the adjoining door between our rooms opens. I wonder if he'll go away if I just pretend he isn't there. But of course he doesn't.

"What are you doing?" His voice reverberates over my skin as if he were right beside me, even though I know he isn't.

"Trying to manifest a different husband," I answer in a serious tone as I peek one eye open. "Unfortunately, it doesn't seem to be working."

His eyes flash, and I can't tell if he's annoyed or amused. But it's obvious that whatever the case may be, he's exhausted. His face is drawn, shadows lurking in the hollows, and I wonder if he slept at all last night with me in his bed.

I suspect he imprisoned me there on the advice of the old adage to keep your enemies close. He'd probably rather hear my every breath, my every move, than await me sneaking into his room at night to stab him in the back.

"I didn't hear you complaining about me last night when I impaled you with my cock," he answers dryly. "And despite your naivety, you didn't even die."

Irritation lances through me as I tear my eyes away, hoping he can't see the flush creeping over my skin. I know how stupid it sounds now, but what did he expect when he married a virgin and unveiled that weapon of mass destruction in his pants? He doesn't need to throw my inexperience in my face, particularly when his archaic family demanded my virtue.

"Did you need something?" I grit out. "Or have you just come here to ruin my day?"

His brows pinch together slightly, and I know he's questioning my sudden hostility toward him. But I'm not going to tell him. He can stew on it and analyze his faults until the end of time for all I care. He has plenty of them, even if they aren't outwardly visible. I should know because I've been tallying a list in my head all morning.

"I came to see that you were settling in," he says, his eyes moving around the room in disdain as he examines my belongings. When he notices my altar with a charcoal portrait of Elizabeth Wildblood on display, something I can't identify flickers through his gaze.

"Yes, I've made the room more to my taste," I agree. "All I need now is my own bed."

"That won't be happening."

"Why?" I tilt my face up to meet his gaze. "I fulfilled my obligations to you last night. You took my virgin blood. Now we just get to be miserable together until one of us inevitably dies."

At this, storm clouds roll through his eyes, and he stalks toward me like a slow-moving predator—so calm and sure of himself as he descends upon me. Before I can even utter a protest, he tugs me up from the floor, caging me in one steel arm as the other fists my hair and forces my head back.

"Tell me," he growls. "Was it an obligation when you came on my cock?"

I shiver, searching my brain for a smart-ass retort, but my sharp tongue seems to have dried up under that withering gaze.

"Was it your obligation that made you so fucking wet for me?" The heat of his words licks along my skin before he grazes my ear with his teeth. "Should I see how obligated my wife is feeling today?"

I let out a quiet gasp as he nips at my ear and drags his teeth even lower, down my throat, to the wildly beating pulse that can't hide the truth.

"I'm still sore," I choke out, my only defense as my traitorous body melts against him.

"You seem to think that's a problem." He inhales me like he can't help himself, his grip tightening on my hair. "Do I need to remind you that you have two other holes I've yet to fuck?"

I open my mouth to respond, but all that comes out is a strangled sound at the imagery his words provide.

"I imagine your ass won't fare any better after I've buried my cock inside of it," he murmurs, his voice dipping an octave. "I doubt you'd be able to sit for a week."

My knees nearly buckle when I feel one of his hands sliding up between my thighs. I don't even know when he released his hold on me or how he got beneath my dress without me noticing. But I'm starting to think this man has a little sorcery in him too.

"Are you wet for me now, little liar?" His fingers brush over my thong, and he groans in satisfaction when he feels that I am.

Clearly, there's something wrong with me. Something really fucking wrong with me. There has to be for me to respond this way to him.

His fingers tease my clit through the thin material, and I close my eyes, fighting the pleasure I want so desperately to deny. How is it possible to feel this way with someone I hate? Someone I most certainly despise.

I have to hold onto that feeling. It's the only way I'll survive him. But then that voice is in my head, reminding me I won't survive him. Suddenly, I'm at war with myself, wondering why I shouldn't enjoy it if it's the only chance I'll get to experience it.

Before I can come to any conclusions, Azrael stops, leaving me cold and unsatisfied as I blink open my eyes to meet his.

"Only good little witches get to come," he tells me smugly as he releases my hair and kisses me on the lips. "Think about that before you challenge me again."

I have about five different insults on the tip of my tongue ready to hurl his way, but he doesn't give me the chance. Before I even realize what's happening, he's hauling me into his room, manhandling me into one of his sitting chairs.

"Stay there," he commands.

I glare at his back as he retreats into the bathroom, only to reappear a few moments later with a wet cloth and some lotion. I realize what he's doing just before he turns my head, dipping it forward so he can access the tattoo on the back of my neck.

I'm expecting more of his roughness, but his touch is gentle as he cleans me, almost reverent. But I know that can't be right. There's nothing but hatred between us. That's the only thing that makes sense.

Even as I tell myself that, goosebumps erupt along my arms as he cleans me with an attentiveness that feels at odds with everything I know about him. I don't want to think about why it matters to him if the tattoo heals properly, so I chalk it up to him not wanting his brand on me to be ruined.

He allows it to dry and applies some lotion afterward, his thumb grazing the ink before his fingers wrap around my chin and tilt my head back to meet his gaze.

"You belong to me now, Willow," he says. "Get used to it. I want you ready for dinner with me at six o'clock. And if it wasn't already clear, you will be in my bed tonight."

"Oh my Goddess." Raven groans in relief when she answers my video call. "I've texted you like a million times, and you haven't answered any of them. I was getting really freaking worried. Nanna had to stop Mom from sending the calvary."

"Willow?" My mom crowds the screen as she snatches Raven's phone, my sisters all trying to get a peek from behind her. "Are you okay?"

"I'm okay, Mom. I'm sorry it took me so long to get back to you. I was unpacking and—"

"You're okay?" she asks again.

I can't help noticing the dark circles beneath her eyes, and I feel terrible that I can't do more to settle her nerves. The only thing I have to offer is my reassurances, though I'm not sure she'll believe them. "I'm okay, I promise."

"He hasn't hurt you?" she whispers.

"No," I tell her. "Everything is fine. I swear."

"Clara, she's okay," Nanna interrupts. "I told you she would be. She's strong."

"Hi, Nan." I wave at her as she winks from behind Mom, her subtle way of letting me know she's keeping a close eye on my mother.

Before I can get another word in, I'm bombarded with questions from all of my sisters and even my father. I scarcely have a chance to answer them before they start talking over each other and arguing over whose questions are the most important.

They ask me about Azrael's estate, his family, and the wedding. I give them vague details about most of it, which is all I can manage with their eagerness to touch on every subject. It's only after thirty minutes that they all seem to be satisfied that I am, in fact, alive and well and the world isn't imploding. At least not today.

"Say goodbye, everybody," Raven tells them as she snatches the phone back. "It's my turn to talk to her."

"Wait!" Cordelia screeches. "I have to show her the shirt I made for her."

Raven snorts, adjusting the phone so I have a clear view of my youngest sister and her wild red curls. She holds up a black tank top that's been embellished with rhinestones to say, 'Hi, this is my resting witch face.'

I can't help but laugh as she beams proudly. "I love it, Cordelia."

"I knew you would," she says. "I'll give it to you next time I see you so you can wear it."

"I'm sure Azrael will love it too," I reply dryly.

Cordelia offers me a coy smile as if to say that's exactly why she made it.

"Okay, we're off now," Raven says, turning the phone back to her as she marches upstairs to her room.

I know what's coming, but I play dumb as I rifle through my crystals, trying to get a feel for the right one.

"Tell me everything," Raven hisses the moment she enters her room and shuts the door.

"I already told you everything," I mutter, choosing an amethyst and setting it beside my jewelry kit.

Raven rolls her eyes. "I mean the stuff you didn't tell Mom and Dad."

"Like what?" I shrug.

"Are you really going to make me say it?" she asks.

I cut some wire to wrap the crystal, avoiding Raven's gaze. "I don't know what you're talking about."

"Seriously?" she grumbles. "You're going to do me dirty like that after everything we've been through?"

Now it's my turn to roll my eyes. "Dramatic much?"

"Just tell me," she presses.

"Tell you what?"

"Oh, for crap's sake. Mother Goddess, grant me strength to deal with this nightmare of a sister."

"I thought I was your favorite sister," I muse.

"Did you survive his monster cock or not?" she screeches so loud my eyes widen in horror.

"What the hell, Raven," I hiss. "Could you ask any louder? I don't think the whole city heard you."

"I'm sorry, okay." She blows out a breath. "But it's a serious question. I was worried about you."

"I told you, I'm fine."

"I know that's what you told me," she says. "But I want to know the truth. Come on, Willow. It's me. We tell each other everything."

I sigh, setting the crystal aside as I meet her gaze. "I survived. It wasn't... terrible."

She leans closer, far more interested in this conversation than I ever expected her to be. But then again,

Raven is a virgin. I'm the only reliable source she has for this information, apart from her friends, I suppose.

"By not terrible, you mean..." She leaves the words hanging.

I shift, trying to figure out how to reply. "Well, I didn't die."

She snorts. "Obviously. But it was good, though?"

"It was... unexpected." I feel my cheeks heating as I admit it. "I don't know how else to describe it."

"So you'll do it again?" she asks curiously.

"God, Raven, I don't know. Probably. I mean, he's my husband now."

"More like captor," she mutters under her breath.

When I don't respond, she changes the subject, much to my relief.

"What are you making?"

"A necklace."

"For me?" She bats her eyelashes.

"Not everything is about you," I say. "This is for Azrael's little sister."

Raven's features pinch in concern. "Don't tell me you're replacing me already."

"As if I could." I return my focus to the necklace, trying to find a chain to accompany the crystal. "Bec is young and really sweet. I'm worried about her."

Raven lets that settle over her for a moment before she asks. "Why?"

"I don't know. Something's off. I haven't figured it out yet. But I want to make sure she's protected."

A beat passes, and I worry that Raven still feels like

I might be replacing her. But when I look at her, I can see she's not jealous. The concern has returned to her eyes because she knows Bec isn't the only one who might need protection in this house.

"Use the silver chain," she says quietly. "And don't forget to bless it."

14

AZRAEL

I leave Willow to entertain herself. I'm tired, fucking exhausted. I had woken early this morning with my head pounding, feeling like I was suffocating. The same damned nightmare played again, but this time it felt like there was a hundred-pound weight on my chest—like that weight was stealing any breath I managed to take.

There was one difference in the dream, though. Elizabeth Wildblood was absent.

It was Willow who came riding up in that cart wearing ragged clothes, a lock of her hair having been ripped from her head. Willow whose eyes I met on Proctor's Ledge as she was taken to the hanging tree, the noose dropped over her head, tightened around her neck. Willow not with the hate Elizabeth had in her eyes but something else, something different. Willow with that hollow darkness I glimpsed in the photograph at her home, her sister laughing and her trying to but looking haunted instead.

When I gasped awake, I was shocked to find myself staring into a pair of green eyes. It took me a minute to realize what the weight on my chest was and why it felt like my breath was being stolen.

That goddamned cat sat on my chest, staring at me like the Queen of fucking Sheba, and she didn't budge when I opened my eyes. Instead, she just kept on looking at me as if I were the fucking intruder.

"Goddamned cats," I mutter again at the memory of the morning. Well, the middle of the night.

I'd gone to grab her, intending to toss her across the room, but she hopped off me just in time and nestled into the curve of Willow's arms. Just like earlier that night, she set her furry little face on Willow's shoulder and sneered.

"You watch yourself," I'd said to a cat. A fucking cat.

I'd drawn the blanket over Willow's shoulder and gotten up because that was the end of sleep for me. Given the time of year, though, could I expect differently? I changed into running clothes and went out to run, and when I reached the lake at the far end of the property, I sat looking at the tree where I found my brother almost a full year ago.

After too long at the lake and as the sun rose, I returned to the house, showered in a guest room so as not to wake Willow and headed to the library. Well, through the library and to the stacks where a secret door leads to the dark wing. To my hideaway. It's where I find myself now, breathing in the closed-up smell that clings to this place. Trying to make sense of cobwebs swaying in a draft I've never been able to identify the origin of. I've lived here most of my life and this wing is still a mystery to me.

Abacus and I were born in France, as was Emmanuel. My grandparents had lived in the Paris house all of their married life, and I don't think my father was expected to leave it. Mom worked in a Parisian café when she met dad. She'd been working to pay her way backpacking through Europe. Neither was older than seventeen. She'd graduated high school early and was taking a gap year before attending university. She never did get there because the way they told it, they fell in love at first sight.

I smile to think of it.

If Grandmother had been more welcoming or even simply accepting of Mom, I wonder if they'd have left France to take up residence in the New Orleans home that had been empty since my great uncle, Tobias, had passed away a decade earlier. Although, as Grandmother tells it, a Tithing was overdue, and with the Wildbloods settled in New Orleans, it was inevitable the next Penitent would come here. Given the tragedies that had been multiplying, and knowing my grandmother, I can see how her twisted mind would add two and two together and come up with eight.

The birth of Abacus and myself—well, the birth of Abacus—was a sign to her that my parents' union was not blessed. Abacus was born average. Not deformed, not lacking in any way, but simply average. I was the stronger of the two of us, bigger and quicker to hit all those milestones doctors measure. But I was born second.

When Emmanuel came, my parents had a reprieve because Grandmother found no fault with him. However, after his birth, there were several miscarriages. My parents always wanted a big family, and that was one area where they and Grandmother agreed. But each miscarriage, always around the twenty-week mark, was another sign to Salomé Delacroix that her son's marriage should not have been, that the next Penitent was not to be born to this woman.

Back then, my brothers and I didn't know about the curse. Our parents kept us well sheltered as far as that went. But in time, as Grandmother became more and more adamant that our father leave our mother and marry an appropriate woman—a Society woman—they left Paris and took up residence in the New Orleans house. It was Dad's anyway as the oldest living male of the family. Once they left Paris, they'd cut off all ties with Grandmother.

Rébecca was born shortly after our arrival in New Orleans. I still remember how small she was, how happy Mom especially was with her girl. She'd always wanted a daughter even though she loved my brothers and I wholly.

Before the time of Rébecca's birth, they began renovations on the house that my great-uncle had let go to ruin. They were set to begin with the dark wing upon their return from the yacht trip they never came home from.

With a heavy sigh, I turn into the room that houses my mother's beloved piano. Electricity is spotty in the dark wing and non-existent in this room, so I begin the task of lighting the candles and take in the boxes upon boxes stacked all around the room. My parents' things, which Grandmother had ordered packed and put away first thing upon her arrival. I guess it could have been worse. She could have burnt them or made us move back to France.

But by then, there was no doubt that the time of The Tithing was drawing near as far as she was concerned. The Wildbloods had four daughters and one of them was rumored to be marked with the crescent moon. It was, to her, a sign from Shemhazai himself come to her in a dream.

The thought of Shemhazai makes my head pound harder, and so I shove it aside. I sit on the piano bench, lift the piano lid, and begin to play. The tattoo on my arm is visible, and I try not to see it, remembering the way Willow looked at it. At me. How she seemed to be physically repelled by it as if sensing its dark energy. It was as if she knew what Shemhazai would take from her.

I wear him on my body and I, too, feel that repulsion. It's not for what he'll demand of me. I know that well enough, and I'm prepared to pay the price if it will save my sister and keep my remaining brother safe.

It's what I am expected to do to her that has me

battling myself. It's Grandmother's stories of the past, of the curse. It's what I've read in The Book of Tithes that chronicles the tragedies my family has suffered over centuries. How those tragedies somehow, as if by divine intervention, abate once The Tithe is paid and the Wildblood witch sacrificed.

It's insane, I know. Yet here I am. Here we all are.

Just to clarify one thing about that divine intervention. It's not any God in heaven I am talking about. Grandmother believes in one God: Shemhazai. The leader of the fallen angels, or Watchers, who were sent to look after humans and who instead took the women for themselves and created a species of man and beast. Well, beast or God, depending on who you ask.

Nephilim.

The children of fallen angels and human women.

Until, that is, the great flood was sent to wipe out the race—genocide, according to Grandmother. The leaders of the Watchers, Shemhazai among them, and my own namesake, Azrael, were punished for eternity. Well, eternity by our human standards, I suppose.

According to my grandmother, the Delacroix family is descended from this race. To her, it explains our great height, our strength, and our abundance of blessings. Only since Isaiah Delacroix had the misfortune of meeting and falling in love with Elizabeth Wildblood did things go so wrong for our family.

Well, falling in love is how she explains it. His lecherous advances being rejected is probably more likely the case if he's anything like the dream version.

However you say it, though, generation after generation, both Wildblood and Delacroix have paid a heavy price.

But I digress.

I close my eyes and focus on the music, an ancient requiem that banishes the migraine and envelops me in its darkness. In a darkness that is somehow a comfort because it brings with it oblivion, at least for as long as it lasts.

My mother, Amélie, taught me how to play. She had an incredible talent for the piano, and I inherited about an ounce of it. Actually, she could pick up any musical instrument and play beautifully, but the piano was her beloved. I still remember the look in my father's eyes when he would watch her as she created the loveliest music. I am so grateful to have this piece of her left for me, a single thing Grandmother can't take away.

I lose myself in the notes, pounding on the very same keys my mother pounded on. I play until the tips of my fingers are numb, until the light filtering in through the dark, heavy drapes covering every window turns a deep orange marking the setting of the sun. I have passed a full day here, which is not an unusual thing. Time seems to move more quickly when I play.

And I am very aware of time. Of days. Nearly three-hundred-sixty-five of them. Just a few more days until the anniversary that I will need to mark. A full year since Abacus's death.

Rest in peace, brother.

Between his death and The Tithing, it's no wonder my head feels like it's going to explode.

I stop abruptly, hitting the final note that becomes a haunted echo in this haunted house. Willow was right about that. I sit here for a long time, my hands resting on the smooth wood of the piano lid. I look at the ring on my left hand. My wedding band. And I know it's idiotic, but in some way, I feel a quickening inside myself. Something new.

Maybe it's simply that, the fact that it's new. She's new. Maybe it's that she's so full of color and life, so much so that energy has no choice but to manifest as that vibrant red hair, those clear blue eyes that sometimes look like shards of glass—at least when they're looking at me. But that thing, that quickening, it is hope. Hope even in the face of everything.

Or hell, maybe it's a thing as simple as attraction. The woman makes me want. I take my fill of women as I need to, never denying myself, but it is just that: sating a need.

With her, it's something else entirely. Lust. A hunger like I've never felt before. A yearning to touch. To possess. A thing I fear will never be sated, not with her.

The chime of the clock echoes from the main hall of the house. I check the time on my father's antique watch. Six o'clock.

I get to my feet and, after glancing at the last photograph taken of my family days before our parents' final trip, I blow out every candle and make my way back from the dark wing to the library. If I wasn't sure before whether my grandmother knew where I spent the days I vanished from the house, I am now. Because there she is, seated in my armchair studying the stained-glass window, a tumbler of whiskey on the table between the two chairs. Without turning to me, she pushes the glass toward the empty chair. Grandmother doesn't drink. It's a vice.

"Grandmother." I cross to that chair because there's no sense in doing anything but that, and I take a seat, picking up the tumbler and sipping from it.

"Azrael," she says with a smile that turns the blood in my veins to ice. "I understand the witch will be joining the family for dinner."

"The witch is my wife. And yes, she will eat with us."

"Why?"

"Because she needs to eat."

"She can eat with the servants. You've already given her a room of her own in our home, which I am against."

"Yes, I'm aware."

"You've allowed her to roam freely."

"Do you expect me to keep her under lock and key for a full year?"

"It does not need to be a full year, as you know," she says.

The muscles in my face tense as I try not to show any emotion. Once The Tithe is collected, it falls to The Penitent to make The Sacrifice within a calendar year. Each Sacrifice is marked in The Book of Tithes, a logbook of sorts, and historically, The Sacrifice is made anywhere from a few weeks after the marriage to a full year.

"The sooner the better, if you ask me."

"Lucky for her, it's not up to you."

She narrows her watery gaze on me. "You've taken her to your bed." She grins a knowing grin.

"And?"

"Don't let the whore turn your head. You can have any woman you want. You've fulfilled your obligation with this one."

"What do you want, Grandmother?" I ask, checking the time.

"I want what needs to be done to keep our family safe and prosperous."

"And you want me to hurry up about it."

She nods.

I get to my feet. She rises to hers and we face one another.

"You understand what is required of me, do you not?" I ask.

"Of course. Your sacrifice, too, will be great, and we will honor you for it."

"Not that part. The other. The fact that it will be my hands that spill her blood."

She simply raises her chin, stubborn as ever. She is obsessed with this curse, with making The Sacrifice. Over the last decade, it has consumed her and stolen the little bit of humanity she had left. "Your family needs you, Azrael."

"It will happen on my terms and in my time. If you'll excuse me, I'll collect my wife for dinner." I set my empty glass down and head toward the door.

"Rébecca may not have a year," she calls out from behind me.

I stop, because this always makes me stop.

"If we were to lose her," she says from closer than I expect. "You'd never forgive yourself. I know you."

I rub my forehead, not sure I'll make it through dinner with this migraine.

The door opens and I hear Rébecca. "He's usually in here when you can't find him," she's saying. She giggles and starts to say something else, too, but as soon as she sees us and realizes I'm not alone, she stops dead in her tracks. I swear she shrinks a few inches in front of the old woman.

"What did I tell you about associating with the witch?" Grandmother says, stalking toward my sister, who takes a step backward. At the same moment I grab hold of my grandmother's arm, Willow, whose hand Rébecca was holding, pushes my sister behind her.

"She didn't seek me out. I heard some music and got lost searching for the source," Willow says, although I can see her guilt.

Was she snooping? And how did she hear the music?

Grandmother is seething. She turns to me, rage making her face go beet red. She tugs her arm out of my grasp, so angry she spits the words she speaks. "You let her wander around this house, who knows what she'll do! What more curses will you allow this witch to bring down on our heads for your own selfish desires, Azrael Delacroix?"

Willow snort-laughs.

"How dare you, witch?" Grandmother practically hisses.

"She's not..." starts my little sister, but she stops when she sees Grandmother's face.

"You realize calling me a witch is not an insult, don't you?" Willow taunts.

Grandmother sets her sights squarely on Willow but speaks to me. "Azrael," she starts in that calm, quiet way she has. It is the very same tone that she used just before she administered her punishments when we were younger. "You should teach your wife some manners. Keep in mind you would not be the first Penitent to take a second Wildblood when the chosen one refuses to heel."

Ah. There it is. She knows Willow's Achilles' heel, just as she knows mine.

Willow's hands fist but before she can speak, there's another sound. "I don't feel well," comes a small voice from behind Willow.

We all turn to find Rébecca has gone pale as a ghost. I rush to her and crouch down to hug her just as Emmanuel enters.

"There you all are. I'm starv... Bec?" He rushes toward us as Grandmother, her head held high, walks out of the library with her long black skirt whipping around her.

"I'm sorry," Rébecca says, burying her face in my shoulder. "I found Willow outside and she was lost."

"Was she?" I ask, glancing up at my wife.

"It's not your fault, sweetheart," Willow says, quickly averting her gaze from mine and setting a hand on Rébecca's shoulder.

I glare at her and what she sees in my eyes has her pulling her hand away. "Emmanuel, take Bec to get dinner. We'll join you shortly." I straighten up and wrap a hand around the back of my wife's neck. "Once I've had a word with my wife."

Emmanuel glances between us, and one corner of his mouth curves upward as he leads our sister out of the library and closes the door behind them.

15

WILLOW

The door to the library closes with a sound of finality, sealing me inside the space with my new husband—a husband who's currently glaring at me as if he can't decide whether to throttle me or fuck me.

He steps closer, wrapping his fingers around the tender flesh of my neck as he forces my head back to bear the full brunt of his smoldering gaze.

"What do you think you're playing at with Rébecca?" His voice is calm, but there's an undercurrent of rage that slightly terrifies me.

I know that beneath the veil of his anger is fierce protectiveness of his sister, and right now, he sees me as a threat. I can only imagine how he'll feel once he realizes I've given her a necklace for protection. He'll probably believe I cursed the thing.

"I'm not playing at anything," I bite back. "She

enjoys spending time in my company, and I enjoy spending time in hers."

His fingertips press deeper into my throat, and my heartbeat quickens as I consider how easily he could end me right now. "She isn't part of your game," Azrael growls. "I won't fucking tolerate you toying with her."

His words light a fire beneath my skin, and while it might not be wise, I can't help the vitriol that spews from my own lips. "But you'll tolerate her living in fear of Salomé?"

His eyes flash, his grip tightening even further. "You know nothing of our family."

"I know what's right in front of me," I hiss. "How blind must you be not to have noticed that girl lives in abject terror of the woman?"

Azrael's breathing accelerates, a storm raging in his eyes as he uses his grip on my throat to slam me back against the bookcases, rattling the contents behind me. "You know nothing," he echoes, his voice betraying an edge of rawness.

I've hit a nerve, and now he's manhandling me to prove his point. But I won't back down, regardless of how much it pains him to hear the truth.

"You'll stay away from her," he orders.

At this, I can't help the caustic laugh that bursts free. "What are you so afraid of, Azrael? That she might be influenced by the filthy witch? As if I could be any worse than your bloodthirsty lineage. How do you think she'd feel if she knew the truth about the violence that lives inside of you?"

He flinches unexpectedly at the insult, and his grip on me falls away, allowing me an unobstructed breath. When he notices the indentations on my skin from his fingers, it only seems to add salt to the wound.

I learn something about him at that moment: he doesn't want to be a monster, but he was born one all the same, merely for being a Delacroix. As much as I want to believe in the power of our free will, I don't know that the beast inside him can be slayed. I've only seen a glimpse of it, but that darkness haunts him. It may be dormant right now, but it won't be long before it makes another reappearance.

"Shut your mouth."

His voice is a warning... one I don't heed.

"Or what?" I challenge. "You'll do it for me?"

His nostrils flare, darkness pooling in his eyes as he grabs a fistful of my hair and wrenches my head back. I gasp at the sound of fabric tearing, and it's only when I feel the cool air against my skin that I realize he's torn the strap of my dress.

He robs me of the rest of it a moment later when he yanks it off, and I barely have time to process it before he's spun me around, his large body caging me in against the bookcase.

"You know what I think, Little Witch?" He drags his nose along the curve of my neck, inhaling me as his words thrum against my skin. "I think you like me angry. I think you want to feel the full brunt of my cock as I split you in half."

A choked sound of protest falls from my lips as he bites my neck, teeth sinking into the delicate flesh.

"If you wanted to be punished so badly, all you had to do was ask."

His breath blows across my spine before I feel the crack of his palm reverberating off my ass cheek. Instinctively, my body bows forward at the impact, but there's nowhere to go. I'm trapped between the hardness of his body and the bookcase.

"Azrael." I squeak out his name as he kicks my legs apart, tearing the thong from my body and leaving me completely naked before him.

"Try again," he growls. "Perhaps now you will recognize me for what I am: your Lord and your God."

The hostility in that remark makes it evident he didn't forget my snub at the marking ceremony. I refused to utter those words then, and now he's determined to prove just how true they are.

A shiver rolls over me as he palms my breast with one rough hand while his other snakes between my thighs, cupping me there.

"Still sore for me?" he mocks.

I bite back a response as warring pleasure and annoyance surge inside of me. I shouldn't like this, but God help me, I do. Maybe it's easier to give in when I feel his hatred. Maybe it's easier to hold onto my own that way.

"Do your worst," I tell him.

A low rumble of irritation resounds from his chest

as he pinches my nipple and makes me suck in a sharp breath. "You'll regret those words."

The sound of his zipper coming undone elicits goosebumps on my skin, but when I feel the heat of his rigid cock pressing against my spine, my knees nearly buckle. It was easy to be brave when I had a temporary lapse in memory. Now I can feel the pulsing, throbbing beast, though, and I know I wasn't overexaggerating the size of him last night.

I consider waving the white flag then and there, but my pride won't let me. I don't know if I'm ready for his roughness, not really. But he's about to give it to me regardless, which I realize when he fists my hair and presses my face into the solid frame of the bookcase. With his other hand, he yanks my hips back, putting me on display for him. A toy to use. A doll to toss around.

"You haven't figured it out yet, Willow," he murmurs, his cock sliding against my butt as he releases my hair, only to grab my throat again. "But you will come to understand that every breath you take is granted by me."

I gasp as he impales me without warning, thrusting so deeply I swear my life flashes before my eyes. Before I can draw another breath, his fingers tighten around my neck like a vice, squeezing.

"When I'm finished with you, you will feel me everywhere," he grits out.

Blackness creeps along the edges of my vision as he starts to fuck me, thrusting deeply as he holds me in an unyielding grip, controlling the very thing that gives me life.

My head spins, my heart races as instinct takes over, and I begin to fight. I buck against him, nails clawing at his forearm. It doesn't faze him. His only reaction is to fuck me harder, fingers pressing into my skin, the length of his cock obliterating me as his body slaps against mine.

My vision dims, and I part my lips, desperate for air, still clinging to life as tension coils in my body, stringing me taut like a bow. Just when I'm about to accept my fate, that this might be the end, he releases me, and I choke on the air that enters my lungs. A rush of adrenaline surges in my veins, and before I even realize it's happening, a violent orgasm tears through my body and nearly brings me to my knees. If it weren't for Azrael's strength holding me up, I would be on the floor.

A tear leaks down my cheek, followed by another as I come back to my senses, trying to process what just happened. My ears are ringing, pulse thrashing, eyes burning as Azrael's growl of pleasure behind me rolls over my back. His rough hands are all over me now, pawing and groping as he fucks me like a man possessed. When I dare a glance at him over my shoulder, his eyes capture mine, and they don't let me go.

It feels intimate to see him this way. So off balance, drunk on me in a way I never could have imagined. He feels it too, and he wants to punish me for it. He makes that clear when he moves for my throat again.

"Azrael," I choke out his name like a safe word, and everything halts as he stares down at me with ragged breaths.

His eyes are conflicted, torn between punishing me or giving me what I'm silently begging for. Ultimately, whatever he sees in the depth of my gaze sways him, and he pulls out of me reluctantly, only to lift me into his arms and wrap my legs around him.

We're face to face when he thrusts back into me, his strength unwavering as he holds me up as if it's nothing. He doesn't take his eyes off me as he rolls his hips, taking up a different rhythm that's less frenzied and more intense. I don't know what possesses me to do it, but I reach up to stroke his hair and press my lips against his. It seems to catch him off guard.

He freezes for a moment before he kisses me in return, a kiss that deepens with every thrust, every hitch of our breaths. His tongue sweeps over my lips before plunging into my mouth, tasting me like he can't help himself.

He's so hard for me, I can feel him creeping toward his oblivion as tension bleeds into his muscles. It won't be long, and the realization that time is running out makes us both frantic. I paw at him, my fingers tugging at his hair while he shoves me back against the bookcase, the impact shaking the wall and forcing the breath from my lungs. He swallows that breath and every other that I give him.

The shelves behind me groan beneath the weight

of our bodies, books toppling to the floor as a guttural sound crawls up his throat and spills between my lips.

He comes even more violently than I did, his cock pulsing, warmth filling me—yet still, he doesn't stop. A shudder moves through him as I roll my hips, nibbling at his mouth, drinking him in like I've been put under a spell.

I can't explain this strange energy thrumming between us. The only thing I know is that it's not of this world. It doesn't listen to reason or logic. It doesn't care about our mutual hatred or the barriers I swore I wouldn't allow to crumble in his presence.

Something is happening here, something I can't control, and I know I'm not the only one who feels it.

Azrael proves it when he jerks inside me one last time, a final powerful shudder. "What the fuck are you doing?" he growls against my lips.

It's the same thing he asked me last night, and I don't have an answer for him. As much as I'd like to take the blame, to pretend that I wield such power, I know this isn't me.

As his eyes settle on mine, I wonder if this is part of the curse. If every other Wildblood that's been sacrificed came to feel such conflict about their captors.

It doesn't make sense. None of it does. It's something only Elizabeth knew since there are no remaining survivors to ask.

Azrael looks just as uncertain as I feel when he finally relinquishes my body, setting me upon my feet. Briefly, his gaze drifts to the come leaking down my thighs, the evidence of his claim on me. Something flickers in his eyes, and I wonder if he's thinking about the rules we are to abide by. There can be no child between us. It's why his family dictated that the sacrificed Wildblood should already be on birth control, a rule I readily agreed to when I got the shot in preparation for the Tithing.

My first thought is that he'll grab something to wipe it away. But instead, he tucks himself back into his pants and reaches for my torn dress.

"What are you doing?" I ask as he slips the material over my head, tying the two pieces at the back.

"It's time for dinner," he says.

"I need to go change," I protest, glancing down at the very noticeable strap hanging loose from the bodice. "I need to clean up–"

"No." His word echoes like a gunshot through the room, silencing me as I glance up at him in question. "You'll go to dinner just as you are."

I stare at him, questioning his sanity for the hundredth time since I met him. "You want me to go to dinner like this?"

"Yes." His fingers skate over my jaw, a gentleness to his touch that's a complete contrast to his commanding voice.

"With your come still leaking down my thighs?" I ask in disbelief.

His eyes flare, betraying just how much he likes the idea. "Yes," he answers gruffly. "Exactly like that."

Before I can protest further, there's a knock at the door, effectively ending the conversation.

"Yes?" Azrael calls out.

I recognize the voice of the housekeeper as she replies. "Your grandmother asked that I remind you dinner is ready, sir."

IF I THOUGHT THERE WAS A SNOWBALL'S CHANCE IN HELL I could get out of this dinner, I would have taken it. But Azrael hauls me to the dining room, his palm guiding me along until it's too late to run.

As we make our grand entrance, silence falls over the table, and all of his family's shocked gazes fall upon me. If I didn't already know how obvious it is, their expressions are confirmation enough that it's no secret Azrael just had his way with me.

Heat flushes my cheeks as I try to smooth out my tangled hair, but it makes no difference. I can feel the dried mascara that bled from my eyes when he choked me. My lips are still swollen from his kiss.

When Salomé narrows her gaze on my ripped dress, I find myself wishing a crater in the earth would just swallow me whole.

Emmanuel shoots his brother a questioning glance as he helps me into my seat, and Rébecca stares at me ,wide-eyed and innocent.

"Are you okay, Willow?" Her voice severs the quiet

tension in the room. "You look..." She doesn't finish that thought, but she doesn't need to.

I look wrecked. That's what she meant to say. But something in her expression tells me she doesn't have the slightest idea what happened. I think she's been far too sheltered to understand the depravities of men.

But who am I kidding? Because clearly, I'm just as depraved.

"Azrael." Salomé's indignant tone pierces my ears. "I'd like a word. Now."

"It will have to wait." He takes a seat at the head of the table, nodding at the food. "Dinner is ready."

She clenches her jaw, casting a withering glare my way, as if I'm responsible for his refusal.

I shoot her a sweet smile in response, only because I know it will piss her off.

Dinner is a stilted affair. While the food is lovely and elegant, Salomé's company most certainly is not. She continues to mean-mug me through all four courses while Emmanuel and Bec carry most of the conversation. Emmanuel is well-spoken, charming, and intimidatingly large, just like his brother. He's handsome like Azrael too, but there are subtle differences between them—most notably their distinct eyes.

While he asks me casual questions about my family, I feel the heat of Azrael's gaze on my face. It seems to caress my skin like a physical touch, and I wonder if he notices me squirming in my chair as his come sticks to my thighs.

I try to focus on the food, devouring almost everything the chef sets on the table. I plow through the butternut squash ravioli and baby kale salad, embarrassingly famished after Azrael's ravishing.

The only thing I don't touch is the lamb. The smell nearly makes me gag when it's presented. I'm hoping nobody noticed, but I don't get so lucky.

"Is there something wrong with the food?" Salomé asks right in front of the chef. "Is it not to your tastes?"

"There's nothing wrong with the food." I offer the chef an apologetic glance. "It's just... I'm a vegetarian. That's all. But everything else is so delicious, and I don't think I can possibly eat another bite anyway–"

"Vegetarian," Salomé scoffs. "How puritanical of you."

I wonder if she recognizes the irony of her words, considering the Puritans were the same lot who used to hang witches for not complying with their ideals.

I snort, barely able to hide my amusement when Emmanuel takes it upon himself to interject. "More for us, right Azrael?"

Azrael scowls at his brother, and I wonder what's set his mood ablaze.

Emmanuel takes it in stride, smirking as if it's a private joke between them before he returns his attention to me. "Tell us more about you, Willow," he says.

"As if we haven't heard enough this evening?" Salomé scoffs.

Emmanuel shrugs. "I find her fascinating. It's not every day you get to have dinner with a Wildblood."

"It's Delacroix now," Azrael corrects him.

"No, actually, it's not." I shoot him a glare. "I haven't legally updated my name, and I have no intentions of doing so."

Azrael tosses me a reproving glance that feels like a spanking. "A conversation for another time."

"Let her keep her name," Salomé muses. "All the better not to taint ours."

"A conversation for later," Azrael repeats, his patience wearing thin.

"Back to your family," Emmanuel suggests, redirecting the topic.

I reach for my wine glass, drinking the last of it in one unladylike gulp as I try to manifest an end to this dinner.

"I think you've monopolized enough of my wife's attention this evening." Azrael narrows his eyes at his brother. "Don't you?"

Emmanuel smiles, eats a few bites, and silence settles over the table. But it's not even a minute later that he's observing me again. "So what about your sisters?"

My brows pinch together in concern. "What do you mean, my sisters?"

"Tell us about them."

"For God's sake, Emmanuel," Salomé snaps. "I can't take one more minute of this. We don't care to hear it."

Emmanuel chuckles to himself before adjusting his features to appear properly chastised, but the damage is done.

Salomé tosses her napkin onto her plate and rises from her seat. "Rébecca, let's go upstairs."

I glance at Bec, noting the way her shoulders slump in defeat. Despite the fact that she ate very little tonight, she seemed to be enjoying herself.

When I look at Azrael, he can see the challenge in my eyes. The question.

Are you going to do something about this?

There's a moment's hesitation on his part, and I'm convinced he won't. This seems to be the status quo of their fucked up family dynamics, and I have a hunch they've been coasting on autopilot this way for many, many years.

"Bec can stay," he says, his eyes falling on his sister. "If she wishes."

Salomé's face mottles with red, and it looks like she's about to blow a gasket. The petty part of me hopes she might. I barely know the woman, but everything about her feels malevolent.

"Azrael—" His grandmother starts to argue, but he cuts her off.

"It's her choice."

Bec glances between them, terror streaking through her eyes. It pains me to see, and I wish Azrael could understand the position he's just unknowingly put her in. Perhaps he thinks he's helping, but by putting the choice back onto Rébecca, he's also making it her who's willfully defying Salomé's wishes.

I don't know what consequences her defiance

would garner, but whatever they may be, they are clearly motivation enough for Bec.

She shakes her head reluctantly, dipping her gaze to avoid eye contact as she rises from her seat. "It's okay. I'll just go."

I want to protest, but I know it will only add fuel to the fire. Salomé won't back down if it comes from me. It needs to come from Azrael, and right now, in front of everyone, isn't the time to address it. I'll have to do it later.

"Goodnight, Bec," I tell her softly.

She offers me a shy smile. "Goodnight, Willow."

16

AZRAEL

I eat my meal like a man famished. I want to say it's because of having spent a full day in the dark wing without having eaten, but as I watch my wife devour her meal with gusto, I think it may have to do with the events in the library. Or maybe it's seeing her across the table, hair tangled, makeup smeared, lips swollen, and dress torn that has me feeling so fucking starved.

I can still taste her mouth on mine, feel her teeth scrape across my lip. Her breath lives inside me now.

And my come is inside her.

Fuck.

I swallow a large mouthful of wine to drown the rumble inside my chest.

My come is inside her, running down her thighs. My seed is a part of her.

My gaze dips to the soft curves of her breasts, the crescent moon birthmark she does not hide, the very tip of the tattoo that runs down the center of her chest. I imagine those breasts swollen, her belly blossoming with my offspring. I reach rudely across my brother for the bottle of wine to refill my glass and drink it like it's water.

Willow watches me. I glare at her because, not for the first time, I feel the strange current running between us. It's like a live wire connecting us even now, even as my family is gathered, my brother peppering my wife with questions, staff coming and going, refilling glasses and removing dessert plates. Throughout it all, it's as if it's just her and me and this thing between us.

This thing.

This curse.

That's what it is: the curse. Has every other Delacroix felt the way I do about their Sacrifice? Have they lusted the way this woman makes me lust? Hell, I could have bent her over and taken her a second time in that library. A third. And it wouldn't be enough.

I shift in my seat, my cock readying itself. This strange new hunger will not be sated. How long will I be able to stand it?

My gaze shifts to her neck, to the bruise forming in the shape of my fingers. Her struggle only intensified the building tension between us, but when I'd loosened my grip on her neck and she gasped for air, *fuck*. What happened then shook me as thoroughly as it did her. She came with a violence that almost had me spilling my seed, but when she called out my name as I reached for her again, when she turned her head and looked at me with those eyes like molten ice, that charge simmered, lava tempering, and I wanted more. I wanted her closer still, and fuck, when she kissed me, I lost my mind.

"Finished?" I ask, pushing my chair back loudly and abruptly standing.

In my periphery, I see my brother's eyebrows rise, but I'm addressing my wife. I can't sit here another minute and see her looking like that and not touch her. Take her. Try somehow to sate this hunger because there is too much at stake to feel lust for this woman.

Willow stands, too, and I wonder what she was thinking as she slowly wipes the corners of her mouth with her napkin before dropping it on top of her dish. "Finished."

The blue of her eyes has gone darker. My wife wants me as much as I want her. That is some comfort.

I gesture toward the French doors that will lead outside.

"Don't mind me," Emmanuel says from the table.

"We won't," I say without a backward glance. I set my hand at my wife's back and open the door. She steps outside and shudders, wrapping her arms around herself. I slip off my jacket and set it over her shoulders.

Willow is clearly not expecting such a gesture and I'm reminded of what she said before the marking ceremony.

"Don't think I'm trying to be a hero," I make clear.

"Don't worry, I won't."

Her comment makes me smile and, in spite of herself, she slips her arms into the jacket, which is about eight sizes too big for her.

Benedict barks from where he's tethered by a short chain outside the kitchen door.

"Christ. I'll be right back." I go to get him. I'm sure he's locked out here on Grandmother's orders. "Hey boy," I crouch down to release him, and he nuzzles his nose in my hair and neck, tail wagging, happy to see me. "Let's walk." I stand and watch him run right to Willow.

I remember her asshole cat last night and decide to let him go. I won't let him hurt her, but he's huge and has no idea of his own size. Having him come charging at you if you don't know him can be frightening.

"Oh, aren't you a sweetheart!" Willow drops down to her knees as he nears her and Benedict, the traitor, greets her in the way he does Rébecca, nuzzling her, sniffing and licking her, almost careful around her.

"It's because he smells me on you," I tell her with a smirk, drawing the dog away and sending him off into the woods.

She straightens. "Or maybe he just has good taste."

"He likes me too, Little Witch. What does that say?"

"Even the best of us have lapses in judgment. Besides, Fi doesn't like you."

"Fi?"

"Fiona. My cat." She points to my hand where the asshole had scratched me.

"She's wild like her master." Willow shifts her gaze higher to the scratch marks she herself left in the library. I bend closer, slide my hand up her back, under the mass of hair and wrap it around the nape of her neck. "I'll tame her master, though. Teach her how to take it rough and like it. Oh, wait," I straighten, grin. "You already like it."

She flips me off, and I laugh out loud, some of the tension easing.

"Where are we going?" she asks as we take the steps off the patio, past the pool house and toward my mother's greenhouse. There is a more direct route, but that would take us past the cemetery. I find I want to hide her from Shemhazai's sight, at least for now. I don't know why or where the thought comes from, but there's no question about it.

"Nowhere particular. We're just walking."

"Why?"

"I need some fresh air. You don't?" I look down at her, and she glances up at me.

"I'd rather walk alone."

"No, you wouldn't, little liar." I caress the nape of her neck with my thumb and hear her breath catch. We walk in silence, and I know she likes this—being outside in nature, under a clear, starry sky.

"What's wrong with Bec?" she asks after a while.

"You noticed."

"It's hard not to. She told me her birthday is in a few weeks, that she'll be sixteen."

A weight settles over my shoulders, a sadness, a sense of powerlessness, spreading through my insides.

"She looks twelve, Azrael. And she's not well. She hardly eats. I don't know. But something's wrong."

"Do you think I don't know that?"

"What is it?"

"We don't know. Doctors can't figure it out. She was born small, always has been small, but over the last few years she's just almost stopped growing."

"Does she have her period?"

"What does that have to do with anything?"

"At nearly sixteen, most girls have their periods. It's natural. A milestone."

I look straight ahead. "I don't know. Grandmother would know. She looks after her."

Willow shakes her head, stops and steps in my path, setting her hands on her hips. "Really? Are you blind?"

"What?"

"Rébecca is terrified of your grandmother. And that woman, there's something not right about her."

"She's not terrified—"

"And you giving Bec the choice tonight to stay or go, do you have any idea what position you put her in?"

"What the hell are you talking about? I told her she could stay if she wanted to. She chose to leave."

"Christ, you really are blind." She turns to walk on but the path splits here, and she takes the one leading toward the cemetery.

"This way." I pull her back.

"I'm serious, Azrael. Maybe take her to a different doctor."

I look straight ahead, forehead furrowed. We have taken her to many doctors. She just doesn't get better. My grandmother's words play in my head. What I need to do to save Rébecca.

"I know someone. I can take her," she offers.

I look down at her. "We have specialists. I don't want to talk about this anymore."

"She's been our family doctor for years. She delivered all of us and—"

"I said we have specialists. Drop it."

"If you promise to think about it, I'll drop it. For now." I look down at her eager face. "You accused me of playing some game with her, but I'm not. I wouldn't want to see her hurt. Just think about it, okay? I'll drop it for now if you promise to think about it."

"Fine. I'll think about it."

She nods and we fall into silence. It's not uncomfortable though. In fact, I feel more at ease than I have in a while, and my headache's staying away.

Benedict begins to bark which is unusual. I stop to listen. He's close but off the trail. "Stay here," I tell Willow.

"Where are you going?"

"He doesn't usually bark. Stay on the trail. I'll be right back."

"I'll come with you."

"Stay." I head into the woods, calling for him. He doesn't stop barking, though and when I get to him, he's standing at the single gate near the back of the property that's unused. The huge solid door was here when the property was purchased centuries ago. I don't think I've ever seen it opened.

"What is it, boy?"

He whines, sits. I follow his gaze to the door, then look at the overgrown grass around it, the ivy creeping along it and up the twelve-foot wall. I test the chain. It's locked tight, the ancient wooden door with iron fixtures undisturbed.

"There's nothing here. Come on," I say, petting him to reassure him, but he just whines. "Come, Benedict." He lifts his nose in the air and bounds back toward the trail, disappearing from sight. I follow the path to where Willow should be waiting, but she's gone.

I look up and down the path but don't see any sign of her.

"Willow?" I call out but get nothing. Before I can decide which way to go, I hear a loud splash. Fuck. The lake? No. She wouldn't have found it, would she? "Willow?" I call again, hurrying toward the back of the property where I hear Benedict. I can imagine him running along the bank in and out of the lake, making as big of a splash as he can.

I run faster, stopping only when I come to the clearing where the forest opens up and find them.

It is beautiful here, the most beautiful spot on the grounds, with a riot of colorful flowers blooming almost year-round and the water clear and crisp. Mom loved bringing us swimming here when we were younger.

When Grandmother came, she forbade it, of course, but Abacus, Emmanuel, and I would sneak out here anyway and swim on hot summer nights.

Benedict is paddling around in the small lake. Grandmother can apparently smell a wet dog a mile away so it's rare that we bring him here, but it's not him I'm worried about. It's Willow. She's standing at the foot of the tallest tree on the property set at the far end.

The tree.

I slow my steps as that familiar sadness, that immense sense of loss, overwhelms me.

Once I reach her, Willow glances up at me, her face paler than usual, one hand resting on the tree. She feels it too. I see it.

"What happened here?"

My head begins its pounding, and my throat closes up as I try to tamp down all the fucking emotions. One year. It's been one year, but it feels like yesterday I came across his body. Yesterday when I stopped right here, in this spot, and cut down my brother's dead body.

"What the hell happened here?" she demands.

"Nothing," I say, not sounding remotely like myself.

"Not nothing." She touches the tree. "Someone died here."

"Let's go back to the house. This was a bad idea."

Willow shakes her head. "Did you hang a Wild-blood witch from this tree?" Her question catches me off guard. It's not what I'm expecting, not remotely. Her eyes are ablaze, shards of glass that would slice me through if they could. She spins to face me fully when I don't respond. "Did you, you fucking psycho?"

"It's not what you think."

"No? Then what is it?"

I glance up at the branch he'd used, and I can almost see the image of him hanging there.

"You're a family of murderers." She slaps both hands against my chest.

I look down at her, half-hearing what she's saying, half-reliving that moment, the morning I found him.

"You motherfucker! You barbarian!" She pounds her fists against my chest, pulls at my hair and nearly scratches her nails down my face until I catch her wrists.

"Why did you come here? You don't belong here," I tell her.

"Did she? Did my ancestor belong here? Hanging from your fucking tree?" She rages, struggling against me.

I grip her arms and give her a good shake. "You don't have a fucking clue what you're talking about."

"No? Tell me then. Explain it to me. Because from what I know, once The Tithing takes place, every one of the Wildblood Sacrifices is dead within a year. That's just history. They all die! Explain that, Azrael! Is that what you're going to do to me? Hang me from a tree? This tree?" she asks more quietly, her voice breaking, her skin pink and stained with tears. She quits fighting, and I release her.

"Shut up, Willow. You don't understand," I say, more quietly too.

"I understand just fine. I understand that you're a goddamn sadist and a murderer." She shoves me, but when I don't budge, she takes a step away to put distance between us. "May you rot in hell, all of you, for what you've done to us. Although you know what? You're already living it, aren't you? That's what I feel in that house. Hell. Maybe that's what's killing Rébecca!"

We're both struck silent, Willow wincing at her own words, and looking as shocked to have said them as I am to have heard them from her lips.

But I get over my shock faster. Every muscle in my body coils, and heat surges through my veins. I back her toward the tree, the very tree Abacus died on.

She puts her hands on my chest. "Azrael. I didn't mean..." She shakes her head. "I care about Rébecca. I'm sorry, I wouldn't—"

"You are right. Someone did die here, but it was no Wildblood witch." I spit the words.

At that revelation, her eyes grow wide. She searches my face, the fury gone, replaced by something else. Morbid curiosity? No. Concern? No, surely not that.

It takes her a minute to put it together. We've kept Abacus's suicide a secret, but she's not stupid. I'm sure the Wildblood family has done at least some research.

"Bec said..." She looks up at the tree. "Oh, Azrael. You had a twin."

"Shut up, Willow." My throat closes up again, and my head throbs. "Just this once, do as you're told and shut the fuck up."

Her hands move to curve around my shoulders, then creep up my neck to cup my face. Her fingers come to rest on my temples, then she does something unexpected: she rises up on tiptoe and, eyes open, kisses me.

I'm taken aback, and when she does it, the throbbing in my head softens, then stops altogether.

She draws away but keeps her hands where they are, and I find myself searching her face.

"What are you doing to me?" I ask quietly, no anger, no fight in my tone. Just sadness. That sense of loss.

"Shh." She bites her lip, then kisses me again.

This time, I wrap my arms around her, taking a handful of hair in one hand and tugging her head backward to kiss her hard on the mouth.

She doesn't resist, wrapping her arms around my neck as I take her mouth, wanting—no, needing—to devour her whole. I push my jacket off her, then rip what's left of her dress away until she's naked and we're kneeling on the ground. She draws back to pull my shirt over my head and reaches for my belt.

"What are you doing to me?" I ask her again between frantic kisses, laying my body over hers until she's lying back on her elbows. I push her legs open to look at her. "I don't know what the fuck you're doing to me," I mutter before bending my head to devour her wet pussy. Greedy, as if starved, I don't take my time to tease or taunt. I scrape my teeth over her clit and hear her moan, her fingers weaving into my hair to pull me closer, thighs on either side of my head. Her breaths are my name as I lick the length of her, tasting all of her, tasting myself on her.

"Azrael!" she cries out. Her hands turn to fists in my hair, thighs squeezing as she arches up, throws her head back, every muscle tensing as orgasm tears through her.

When her body dips and her legs fall open, limp, and her hands drop away, I settle on my knees and watch her. Her eyes are closed, one cheek to the grass, sated, my little bride. My Little Witch.

When I grab my shirt and draw it back on over my head, she turns lazily back to me, reaching for me as she licks her lips. The sight of that little pink tongue has me wanting to bend my head to kiss her again, to capture it between my teeth as I drive into her again, but I can't. After last night and this evening, she's got to be sore.

We look at each other for a long, long moment until Willow shivers.

I reach for her destroyed dress but toss it aside and wrap her in my jacket. "Let's get back. It's getting cool."

She nods, and I help her up. Benedict comes bounding out of the water, almost soaking us as he shakes himself off.

"What was he barking at?" she asks as we get back to the house.

"Nothing. There's a sealed off entrance to the property there but it's undisturbed."

"What?" she asks, stopping on the step to look up at me, her expression suddenly panicked.

"It was nothing." Before I can say more, the French doors open. My grandmother stands looming over us. She takes in what Willow is wearing and I'm very aware of my hand around the back of Willow's neck.

"Well, I hope you two won't be too tired for church tomorrow morning."

"Church?" Willow asks, glancing up at me.

"Yes, church. We are not heathens, and you'll be attending. Azrael, a word." She stands back, making space at the door.

"Grandmother, now—"

"It cannot wait."

Christ. "I'll be right there." I turn to Willow.

"It's fine. I'm tired anyway."

Grandmother snorts at that. "I can guess why."

Willow rolls her eyes and walks past the woman without another word. I enter the house and close the door behind me. Grandmother waits until she hears my bedroom door open and close before turning to me.

"Are you sure she's on birth control? This could be a trick. Getting herself pregnant to save her neck. She wouldn't be the first Wildblood to try it."

"Grandmother—"

"The way you two are carrying on, well, I just want to warn you, Azrael. It's not as though that harlot could harbor anything but ill feelings toward you. You'll do what needs to be done, child or not, if it comes to that."

"Jesus Christ." I push my hand through my hair and walk away.

"Azrael! Do you hear me?"

"I'm going to bed, Grandmother. Goodnight."

17

AZRAEL

I lie awake, staring up at the crack in the wood carving over my head as Fi, or *the asshole* as I decide to call her, sits on my chest watching me. She was perched there when I opened my eyes, but I didn't have the same nightmare as usual. No pressure, no choking weight. We have a moment, the asshole and I.

"Scram," I tell her.

She doesn't. Instead, she decides to clean herself in a show of defiance she probably learned from her master. Once she's finished, she resumes her staring.

"You don't scare me, cat," I tell her.

With a sigh, I turn my head to look at Willow. She has her hands tucked beneath her cheek. Her eyes are closed, her lips slightly parted. Her face is completely relaxed, and her hair is everywhere. I extend an arm to cup a lock of it, and the cat digs her sharp little claws into my chest in warning.

"Relax," I tell the asshole. She does only once she sees I'm not hurting Willow.

What happened at the tree last night was... Well, I'm not sure what it was, but her blurted words betrayed her fear even if she won't admit it. She knows some tragedy will befall her. Does she know that it will be at my hands? That it *must* be at my hands?

The thought of it, though, of what she said about hanging her from that tree makes my hands clench, makes me feel both sick and furious at once.

I am not those things she accused me of being. Not yet. But my ancestors were, weren't they, if I'm being honest? It's all written in The Book of Tithes locked in my desk drawer in case I ever doubt it. Every Wildblood witch whose life was stolen by a Delacroix logged, like you'd log inventory at a warehouse.

Christ. We're a sick bunch.

I draw my hand away, take a deep breath in, and move to get out of bed. The cat jumps off me—good riddance. Once I'm off the bed completely, she makes herself at home on my pillow. I roll my eyes and walk into the bathroom to have a shower and get ready for this day, which I am sure will be a long one.

When I return to the bedroom, I find Willow awake and sitting up against the headboard cuddling the cat.

"Morning," I say, not missing how her gaze moves over my chest to the towel I have wrapped low around my hips.

"Morning."

I pick up my father's watch from the nightstand

and wrap it around my wrist, checking the time. "You'd better get up. We leave in half an hour."

"Church? You're really going to make me go to church?"

I shrug. "It's easier to just go. I don't care if you believe or not."

"Do you believe?"

I study her, but rather than answering, I turn and walk into the closet to get dressed. I know she's been looking through my things, but haven't said anything. I smelled her subtle perfume on my coat. The idea that she put it on is unexpected, and I like it.

I'll go through her room soon myself.

Once I'm dressed, I return only to find she hasn't moved.

"You really do need to get up and ready." I walk into the bathroom to comb my hair and grab the things I need to clean her tattoo.

"Do you believe in God, Azrael?" she asks again. "I mean, you are supposedly descended from angels, aren't you? Fallen ones, at least. That makes you Nephilim, I believe?" she says, her tone mocking.

"Come here," I tell her as I sit on the leather chair. "I need to clean the tattoo."

She gets up and walks over to me. I notice she's wearing one of my T-shirts and I raise my eyebrows.

"I was too tired to search for my own," she tells me with a shrug as she pulls it off and tosses it onto the bed. My gaze sweeps over her naked breasts, her flat belly, the pink thong through which I glimpse that tiny triangle of dark red hair at the apex of her thighs. When I look up and meet her eyes, she's grinning.

I clear my throat. "Kneel." I point to the space between my knees, annoyed at how unselfconscious she is and how like a fucking teenager I am whenever I see her naked. Hell, she's not even fully naked.

"Kneel," she mimics and settles on the floor between my legs, her back to me. "Why don't you answer my question?" she asks as she gathers her hair and draws it aside.

I notice she hasn't removed the wedding ring. The deep garnet nestled in a bed of diamonds suits her so perfectly. I chose it instinctively, thinking I didn't much care. Grandmother was beyond irritated when she came to give me the brass band she'd planned to have me present to my bride.

I take my time to look at Willow like this, liking my mark on her, liking it very much.

"I believe there are things I cannot explain," I say as I begin the task of cleaning the area.

"So, you believe you're descended from fallen angels?"

"I don't think about it."

"Wasn't the great flood sent to wipe you all out?"

I wait for the area to dry as I squeeze lotion out of the tube and meet her taunting gaze when she turns her head.

"Sad we survived?" I ask, pushing her head down to make her look away. "I like you like this, by the way."

"What? On my knees? You would."

I smear lotion into the mark, tracing the lines of the Delacroix insignia, and I don't miss how her back arches in response to my touch. When I'm finished, I weave my fingers into her hair and tug to shift her position so she's facing me.

"Ow," she mutters, although I'm not hurting her.

I draw her face closer to the erection currently pressing against my slacks. "I actually prefer you positioned facing this way if you're asking."

"Like I said, you would." She clutches my thighs as I draw her higher on her knees. I take in her tits, brushing my knuckles over one nipple and watching it tighten. "I need to get ready, Azrael."

I let go of her, and she stands, thinking this is over. But once she's up, I take hold of her hips and draw her toward me. I'm eye-level with her pussy, and I bend my head to inhale deeply.

"Azrael!"

"I like you better with my smell on you," I say and tug the thong down to lick her sex. Her breath hitches, and I chuckle as her fingers weave into my hair. I stand, snapping the elastic back into place. "But I don't have time to fuck you properly, so it'll have to wait. You think you can wait, Little Witch?"

Her face is flushed, and she's clearly disappointed. She rallies, smiling broadly as she closes her hand around the crotch of my pants. She squeezes. "You think you can?"

I lay my hand over hers and slide up and down once, twice. My chest rumbles, and I lean down to kiss her before scraping my teeth over her lower lip. "I think I'm going to take that mouth of yours tonight. Make better use of it." I draw back, spin her around and slap her ass. "Get dressed."

"Asshole," she mutters as I walk to the door.

I open it and stop to look back in. "Wear something appropriate."

"Appropriate," Willow says, all innocent smiles that show off those pretty white teeth. "Yes, sir." She mock salutes.

"Appropriate," I emphasize, and step into the hallway. I close the door just as Emmanuel steps out of his room. He looks like he just got home, never mind if he slept.

"Morning, brother. Long night?" I ask, patting his back.

"I fucking hate Sunday mornings," he grumbles, pushing his hand through his unruly wet hair. He glances at my closed bedroom door. "Where is your bride? Can she walk this morning?"

"She'll rally."

The bell chimes, announcing five minutes before we need to leave. Grandmother likes us to be prompt. Emmanuel and I head down to find Grandmother and Rébecca coming out of the kitchen.

"Hi!" Bec says, brightening when she sees us. My mind wanders to what Willow said about her being terrified of Grandmother. Is that true?

"Not so loud, Bec," Emmanuel says to her.

Grandmother clucks her tongue. "You look like you've been out all night."

"Hey, I showered, so at least I don't smell like it," Emmanuel says. "I need to grab toast."

"There's no time!" Salomé yells to his back as I bend to kiss my sister's cheek.

I notice the necklace Bec is wearing. It's new, or at least, I haven't seen it before. I almost comment but she notices me looking at it and tucks it into the collar of her dress with a quick glance up at Grandmother. I'm reminded again that she's almost sixteen but looks like a much younger child. I wink to tell her I'll keep her secret because she's clearly hiding it.

"Where is your witch?" Salomé asks as I straighten.

"My wife, you mean?"

She makes a dismissive motion.

Before I have to answer, we hear a bedroom door open and close and heels clicking down the hall. Emmanuel comes around the corner just as we all turn to see my wife stop at the top of the stairs. She's practically beaming, and I see why when she slowly, ever so slowly, descends the stairs, giving us all time to take her in.

"What in the name... Azrael! You cannot allow this... this..." Grandmother is practically spitting.

Emmanuel chuckles. "This morning just got more interesting."

"Oh, Willow!" Bec says when Willow stands on the bottom step. "You look so beautiful!"

"What she looks like is a harlot. We will be a laughingstock!"

She does look fucking amazing in a black dress, red cloak, and over-the-knee boots that I may have her leave on when I punish her for this transgression. The flame red lipstick is the cherry on top.

"Change! Now!" Salomé orders.

Another chime sounds. We have to leave.

"No time," Willow says sweetly, shrugging her shoulders. "We don't want to be late for my first ever Mass!"

"I will not allow you to shame us this way!"

"She's fine, Grandmother. We'll be late. Let's go." I wrap my hand around the back of my wife's neck and lead her out, not missing her victorious grin—which I am sure Salomé will make her pay for later. "What happened to appropriate?" I ask as I open the passenger side door to the Series 1 Jaguar E Type. It was my father's, and I'd had it modified to fit my taller frame. This car put a smile on his face like nothing else could. Willow looks at it, raises her eyebrows, and gives me an approving nod before climbing in. I close the door and get into the driver's side. The rest of the family will follow in the Rolls Royce.

"Whatever do you mean?" she asks innocently.

"I'm going to enjoy punishing you, wife."

She sets her hand on my thigh. "Oh, I'm sure you will, husband, but it is already worth it. Nice car, by the way. Wouldn't expect it of you."

"It was my father's," I tell her, then shut my mouth because I have no idea why I'm telling her this.

"Really?" she asks, and I see her studying me in my periphery. "The jacket too?" She touches the ornate gold threading on the lapel.

I nod once, surprised she has noticed.

"You must miss him," she says softly.

My jaw tightens, as do my hands on the steering wheel. She rubs my arm and drops it. I'm sure she noticed my white knuckles.

Mass at St. Trinity Cathedral is a long, drawn-out affair. Emmanuel nods off. Bec kneels and stands and kneels again on the hard wooden kneeler from which Grandmother has removed the cushions for both herself and my sister. My wife is, as expected, gawked at by the men and women alike, with the former wearing a very different expression than the latter.

The men at least wither at my glance, and I keep my hand around the back of my wife's neck for the entire Mass, not liking anyone's eyes on her.

Once the service is over, we walk out of the church along with the rest of the congregation. I make it a point to hurry to my car, which I tipped the valet earlier to have ready, not wanting to talk to anyone in particular.

"How do you sit through that weekly? Please tell me I won't have to," Willow mutters to me.

"It's not over yet," I tell her as I pull out onto the street.

"What do you mean it's not over?"

I draw a deep breath in, exhale. Mass I can tolerate. The next part, though, takes all I have to get through it.

"You'll see," I say tightly, because there is no describing it. I wish there was some way to not have her see the next part, not to have her be present for it. But it's just a matter of time. As The Sacrifice, she is already a part of the ritual.

When we arrive back at the property, I hand the keys off and walk Willow through the house and out the back.

"Where are we going?" she asks, hurrying along in her heels. "Can you not go so fast?" she asks more than once. I have her hand and need to remember to match her stride. Her legs are not as long as mine.

"Better?" I ask, slowing my step.

She nods. "Where are we going, Azrael?"

"The gifting," I say.

Something in my tone must transfer to her because she doesn't ask any more questions. My family joins us a little farther back on the path, and we weave our way to the churchyard. I feel Willow draw back as we near it and tighten my hold on her hand.

"What gifting?" she finally asks, as the shadow cast by the angel's great wings falls upon us.

"Shemhazai," I say, turning into the churchyard to face the ten-foot-tall statue.

"What the..." Willow starts but stops, shuddering as I tug her closer. She closes her free hand around my forearm and doesn't pull away from me.

Grandmother comes up behind us, her own victory

apparent as she sees Willow clinging to me before the hulking form of Grandmother's true God. She faces us, and I'm glad to see Emmanuel holding Rébecca's hand and coming to stand on the other side of Willow.

It's strange, this, us gathered as we are, with the great angel looming over us and casting his dark shadow over us here, now just as he casts his shadow over our lives. The altar is cleaned and ready for the offering, an altar large enough to carry a Wildblood witch.

Grandmother stands as if she were Shemhazai's priestess and the four of us, well, what are the four of us? One a Sacrifice, one a Penitent—truly, that makes two Sacrifices, does it not? And Emmanuel and Rébecca? What are they?

"The gifting, Rébecca," Grandmother snaps.

Bec steps forward, looking too small, too fragile before the beast. She bends to pick up the bundles of flowers in their baskets waiting to be placed before the angel. The task takes time, with each bloom laid carefully, and Grandmother stands unblinking as she presides over the proceeding.

Willow is trembling now. Does she feel the malevolence of the angel? Or is it that she feels what is buried beneath the altar?

Grandmother doesn't miss Willow's discomfort. She relishes it, in fact.

Once Rébecca is done, she looks up at Grandmother, who nods. My sister hurries back to take Emmanuel's hand. There was a time many, many years ago when we'd be made to kneel here before the statue. That time ended when Abacus and I came of age, and Grandmother no longer ruled.

"Let's go," Emmanuel says grimly and without waiting, he takes Bec and heads back to the house.

Before I can walk away, though, Grandmother steps toward us. She looks down at Willow, whom she towers over, then up at me. "The Sacrifice should be presented to Shemhazai. The Penitent must make an offering showing good faith that The Tithe will be paid."

I see Willow's face in my periphery.

"You know what must be done, Azrael."

"Now is not the time, Grandmother."

Her face hardens, that satisfied smirk diminishing. But she recovers. "I look forward to bearing witness at a time of your choosing then," she says in that cruel, mocking way of hers.

With that she walks away. Willow watches her go, her mouth hanging open.

"What was church all about if she worships this thing?" she asks, still watching my grandmother's disappearing back.

"Appearances," I say flatly, knowing how sick it all is... and realizing how complacent I've become.

18

WILLOW

"Do you even realize how fucking creepy that is?" I glare at the statue, that same dark energy I felt at first glance making me take a step back.

"Says the woman who dabbles in magic," Azrael responds dryly.

"The magic we practice doesn't hurt anyone," I tell him. "Meanwhile, how many wars have been started over religion? How many people have died at the hands of someone swearing it was God's will? I'll tell you this... if there is a God or gods, they aren't nearly as vengeful as their flock are. In fact, I'd imagine they're quite sick of the evils performed in their name."

Azrael's eyes seem to almost glow in the sunlight as he gazes upon me, and for a moment, I find myself wondering if it could be true. If he could be descended from angels. After all, they said the devil was the most beautiful of his kind.

"And what about me, Willow?" His fingers brush over my cheek, sending a cascade of sparks through my nerve endings. "Am I a vengeful disciple?"

At that word, a visible shudder moves over me, and his eyes narrow in question as his thumb comes to rest on my chin, tipping it up.

"Well?" he demands.

"I suppose you'll reveal the answer to me in due time." I swallow, recalling Salomé's words, which had felt like a threat. "Will you pave your own way or follow the path that's been dictated for you?"

His eyes flash, and I barely have time to react before he kisses me roughly, tugging at my bottom lip with his teeth and smearing my lipstick. I imagine he's been thinking about doing this all day, judging by the ferocity of it. Just as I'm relaxing into him, parting my lips and offering myself for devourment, he stops cold.

"I'll tell you what." His fingers move to the knot of my cloak, untying it and slipping it from my shoulders, the red material pooling on the ground behind me. "I'll be a good sport. We can roll the dice. I'm always up for a challenge."

I don't know what he means, but the rough edge in his voice makes my thighs clench together in anticipation.

"And the best part is you get to decide." He dips his head, the warmth of his breath fluttering over my ear.

"How?" I croak.

"I'll give you a head start. If I capture you, then you

get to worship me like a god. If I don't, then I'll be the monster forever chasing after you."

My chest heaves, my pulse skyrocketing as he grabs a fistful of hair and wrenches my head back, his lips brushing against my ear.

"Run, Little Witch, while you still can."

His words may have well been the sound of a starting pistol because that was what they sounded like in my head. The moment he frees me from his grasp, instinct takes over, and I dart toward the woods.

I don't know where I'm going, but I weave my way through the trees, taking myself off the beaten path. Branches and leaves crunch beneath my boots so loudly that they sound like echoes all around me. I know without a doubt he will catch me, and part of me anticipates it. But the other part of me, the Wildblood in my DNA, anticipates an escape from my shackles just as much.

The two halves of me are at war as my blood thrums inside my veins, my skin flushes, and the wind bites against my face. Though the trees are vast, I suspect Azrael has tracking capabilities that far exceed my hiding skills. But that's the point, isn't it? It isn't a question of my inevitable capture.

It's the thrill of the chase for him.

I run until my lungs burn and my legs feel like they will give out beneath me, and when I stop to catch my breath, I listen. I don't hear him. I don't hear a sound around me except for those of the forest: the birds, the breeze, and the quiet stillness that exists here.

My eyes dart around, seeking shelter, when I spot the perimeter fence in the distance. It's a stone wall, and though it will be a challenge to climb, a thrill courses through me at the idea of crossing that barrier.

I head in that direction, pausing occasionally to hide behind a tree and listen for my hunter. And after a while, I begin to wonder if he's even giving chase. It's too peaceful. Too quiet. I don't trust the silence, but it doesn't alter my course.

When I finally reach the twelve-foot stone wall, I swallow at the enormity of it. Either I'm going to break something, or I'm going to pull off a miracle. Never one to let fear stop me, I decide to go for it. The first stone I set my foot upon feels sturdy enough, and it gives me the confidence to keep going. I don't look down, and I settle into a rhythm of finding solid ledges to balance on my ascent.

The breeze caresses my skin as I work my way up, followed by an unexpected chill. It's a warm afternoon, so I know it can only mean one thing.

There's a predator in my midst.

Before I even have time to glance back, I feel his fingers wrapping around my ankle, tugging.

I fall back into his arms with a shriek, my heart slamming against my chest as I meet his hungry gaze.

"Caught you." He says the words so smugly it makes me want to scream. Because I wanted to win. At least... for a little while.

"I suppose that makes me your God." He sets me upon my feet, his heated gaze carving a path of fire along my skin. "And you, my little sinner, need a lesson in worship."

My breath catches in my lungs as he forces me to my knees, his fingers reaching for his belt. I watch as he unbuckles it, revealing the length of his throbbing erection beneath his briefs.

"You did this." His words are gruff and accusatory. "And now you're going to repent for it."

My nipples tighten as he grabs a fistful of my hair and rubs my face against the bulge in his briefs. I know what he wants, and any bitterness I held at being captured flees as I kiss him there.

He groans, fist tightening, voice gravelly as he issues his command. "Again."

I kiss him again, working my way along the material until I reach the band. When my tongue darts out, licking along that seam to taste his skin, I feel a tremor in his arm.

He may have won the game, but the god is only as powerful as the woman on her knees before him, making him shudder.

It gives me courage, and I move of my own accord, tugging down his briefs to unleash his cock. It bobs in front of my face, angry and so hard it looks painful.

I want to ease that ache for him. It's an unsettling thought, just how badly I want that.

Azrael sees the hunger in my eyes, and it pleases him very much. "Good girl," he murmurs, stroking my hair as I lick the entire length of his shaft. "Show me again."

I lick him again, this time all the way down to his balls, and he releases another groan of satisfaction. It makes my insides clench, and heat blazes deep in my core, stoking a fire of need in me.

I continue to taste him, throwing myself into the act and savoring every lash of my tongue. Every sigh. Every clench of his fist in my hair.

"Enough," he growls. "Open your mouth for me."

I hesitate, blinking up at him, unable to hide my nerves. "It's not going to fit."

Dark amusement flickers in his gaze. "It will fit. Now open."

A battle of wills takes place in my mind, instinct telling me he'll choke me to death with that monster and the more deranged part of me insisting maybe it wouldn't be a bad way to go.

In the end, I do as he bids, trusting him for some reason I can't identify.

"Such an obedient little wife." His fingers wrap around my throat as he pushes his cock between my lips. "I'm going to own every part of you."

The velvet of his skin brushes over my tongue until my jaw is stretched as wide as it will go, and he can't fit anymore. I don't know that I even have half of him in my mouth, but it makes no difference to him.

His fingers tighten as he closes his eyes and pulls back, only to rock forward again, fucking my mouth just like he'd promised. "Christ," he rumbles as I wrap my lips around him and relax into it. "Do you know how much I wanted to do this to you today in that church?"

Goosebumps break out along my skin at his confession, and I look up at him in silent acknowledgment, but he doesn't see it. His eyes are still closed. The pressure from his fingers on my throat tightens as he starts to fuck my mouth for real.

"All I could think about was that goddamned lipstick," Azrael grits out. "How tempting you were to every pair of male eyes in those pews. And here I am, the only one who will ever touch you. The only one who will ever own you this way."

His other hand cups the back of my head, fingers raking over my skull as he thrusts deeper, making me gag. Tears leak from my eyes, and my hands come up to his thighs, gripping him there as his cock slides in and out of my mouth.

Tension cords the muscles in his arms, holding me like a vise as he uses me for his pleasure. I should be offended, I think, but all I feel is enraptured by the sight of him getting off on me. When he opens his eyes again to meet mine, electricity sparks between us.

"God, you're fucking beautiful like this," he chokes out.

I whimper, the sound vibrating against him, and it sends him over the edge. His entire body goes rigid as his cock spasms in my mouth, his come spilling over my tongue and leaking down my throat. I swallow instinctively, and he makes a feral sound of approval as he watches like the dark God he's playing at.

It's insanely hot, if I'm being honest. I don't want to admit it, but he is. He's fucking beautiful.

A beautiful terror.

"Good girl," he praises me again, slowly withdrawing his cock from between my lips. As he does, some of his come leaks down my chin, and he catches it with his fingers before bringing them back to my lips.

"All of it," he commands, our gazes locked on each other.

My lips part, and he pushes his fingers inside my mouth.

His eyes flare when I suck them clean. "Tell me, Little Witch," he murmurs. "Are you aching for it?"

I nod, no shame to be found as I watch him, silently begging for a release. He offers me a lazy, hungry stare as he pulls his wet fingers from my lips and captures my chin.

"How bad?"

I groan in frustration, not wanting to admit it. But he doesn't move. He doesn't do anything except watch me, and I know he's going to make me beg.

"So bad," I whisper.

His lips curve wider, tormenting me before he reaches down for my hand and pulls me to my feet, nodding at the perimeter wall.

I turn to face it wordlessly, my breath accelerating when he kicks my legs apart and presses my hands against the stone, arching my hips back. Cool air hits my skin when he tugs my dress up, his fingers sliding along the length of my thong until he feels the sticky arousal between my thighs.

"So wet for your monster?" he questions. "Or is it your God?"

That landmine feels like a trap, so I don't answer, and he rewards me by slapping my ass. I squeak out a strangled noise, and he chuckles as he soothes the sting with his palm. I'm afraid he's going to demand an answer, so I'm relieved when his fingers move to where I need them the most.

I'm in agony, and just the slightest brush of his thumb over my clit nearly makes my knees buckle. He hums his approval and grabs my hip to steady me as he slips two of his fingers inside of me. I gasp at the feeling, then bite back a moan as he retreats, only to thrust them back in.

At the same time, his body presses close to mine, the heat of his chest warming my back as his lips settle over the beating pulse in my throat. He kisses me gently and fucks me roughly with his fingers, the contrast mixing me up and sending me into a tailspin.

"God or monster?" he asks again.

The only sounds coming from my lips are garbled responses that increase with the intensity of his thrusts. I feel like I'm deliriously high, riding a tidal wave that's about to crash, and I want it. I want it more than anything. So when he asks me again, just as I'm cresting the tipping point, I can't be held responsible for the word that leaves my lips on a cry.

"God."

Starbursts explode behind my eyes as the orgasm tears through my body with a violence that feels unnatural. It robs me of my faculties, and before I can stop it, I'm collapsing. Azrael catches me in his arms, dragging me back as the aftershocks continue to ravage my body, sparks slowly fizzing out as my senses come back to me.

I'm breathing hard, still half-drunk on him when his lips brush against my ear. "That's what I thought."

His victory annoys me, but I refuse to let it show. I can't be held responsible for what I say in the throes of... whatever that just was.

My body slumps in exhaustion as he pulls my dress back down and zips up his trousers. We still have to get back to the house, and I genuinely don't know if I can make the journey. Perhaps he'll just leave me here to live amongst the trees like a nymph.

Azrael seems to sense what I'm thinking, and without another word, he picks me up like it's nothing, wrapping my legs around his waist and securing my arms around his neck.

"Come on, Little Witch. Let's get you back home."

Home.

The word rattles around my brain like a record stuck on repeat the entire way back. Azrael smirks as his gaze flickers to mine occasionally throughout the walk, and I can just imagine what I must look like right now. I'm pretty sure my hair is wrecked again, and I can feel the lipstick smeared around my mouth, along with the dried mascara that bled down my face. He's left his mark on me the way he likes to do.

It should come as no surprise when we finally reach the terrace that I'm subjected to another spectator for the occasion. Of course it has to be Salomé sitting there, her face twisted in disdain as she eyes me like I just emerged from a brothel. Other than the tension in Azrael's back, he barely seems to acknowledge her as we move past.

But I can feel her eyes on us as we go, and before the door shuts behind us, I hear her muttered disapproval. "Wildblood whore."

19

WILLOW

Tick. Tock. Tick. Tock. Tick. Tock.

The pendulum swings beneath a familiar clock face, marking the ebbing of time with every breath I draw. Restlessness settles into my bones as I turn, only to find hourglasses tumbling through the landscape of my mind like weeds. Granules of sand drift away as if to signify the seconds of my life.

Careful, child.

A shiver runs through me as Elizabeth's voice reverberates off the walls around me, a constant echo.

Careful.

"Why?" I ask. "What are you trying to tell me?"

There's a long, agonizing pause where I wonder if she's gone, if her spirit vanished before she could finish her warning, as it sometimes does. But then I hear her faint voice as if it's carrying on the breeze.

Protect yourself. They will come for you. You must... keep close... the chosen one.

The urgency in her request sends a ripple of terror through me, and again I ask why, but I know it's already too late.

She's gone, disappeared into a void, a place I can't follow her.

It doesn't stop me from calling out for her as fear wraps its ugly claws around me. I don't know what she means. I need more. I need something else to grasp onto, but there's nothing. I'm alone in this room full of clocks, sand slipping away through hourglasses, and soon the light dissipates like an ominous warning, leaving me in total darkness.

"Elizabeth!" I scream for her, clawing my way through the black, only to hit wall after wall. "Come back, please!"

"Willow."

A different voice splinters my consciousness, distorting everything around me. I spin around, searching for the source, but I can't see him.

"Willow," he says again.

There's an edge of concern in that voice, and the familiarity blankets me like a warm caress. It gives me a sense of safety I shouldn't feel.

"Azrael." I open my eyes, stirring from a tormented sleep.

"You were having a nightmare." His thumb brushes over my jaw, his eyes as haunted as I feel.

"Oh," I croak.

"What was it about?" he asks.

"I don't know," I lie. "It's all jumbled."

He frowns, and I know he isn't buying it. But I can't tell him that I've had these dreams every night for as long as I could remember. Strangely, they've been absent since I started sleeping in his bed. I had wondered why, but I guess it doesn't matter since they've returned with a vengeance.

Elizabeth's warning still lingers in my mind as I try to untangle my thoughts. What was she trying to tell me?

"Better now?" Azrael tucks me against his body, his arm sheltering me.

I don't want to admit just how much better it is. His warmth. His strength. The enemy at my back who's starting to feel more like a comfort with each day that passes. I know I shouldn't give in, but exhaustion weighs heavy on me as I nod anyway.

I drift back to sleep in his arms, and when I wake again, I'm groggy and disoriented. A glance behind me confirms Azrael is already gone, and I wonder where he goes or how much sleep he actually gets.

I've been searching the house, but I haven't found the entrance to the dark wing Bec mentioned. The only one I've discovered is sealed off, but I suspect there must be another one somewhere. I intend to find it, and perhaps when I do, I will uncover some of Azrael's secrets and what he hides behind those walls.

I check my phone, shocked when I see that it's already afternoon. I must have fallen into a deep sleep after my nightmare. I rarely ever sleep this long.

The sound of the bedroom door opening startles

me, and when I turn to meet Azrael's gaze, he seems on edge.

"You're awake," he observes.

"Yes," I murmur. "I didn't realize the time."

A moment passes, and I wonder if he's going to mention the nightmare.

Instead, he delivers some unexpected news. "You have visitors."

His tone betrays his discomfort over the notion, and immediately, I perk up.

"My family is here?"

"Your sisters." He nods. "They're waiting for you in the sitting room."

I can't hide my relief. It hasn't been long since I last saw them, but I've missed them so much.

Azrael watches me scoop Fiona up and dart to the connecting door to my room.

"Willow." His voice halts me.

I turn to look at him, and he seems conflicted. I'm not sure if it's because he's aware that he now has five Wildblood witches under his roof or if it's something else. But whatever the case may be, he seems to decide against sharing his thoughts.

"Don't be too long," he mutters, turning his back on me as he takes his leave.

I smile to myself, secretly amused by his discomfort, and go about my preparations for the day as quickly as I can manage. It takes me fifteen minutes to make myself presentable, and while I'd been trying to be respectful of the differences between our families before, all bets are off after Salomé made us attend church.

I dress in a black leather mini skirt, a cropped velvet bustier top, and the same over-the-knee boots that I'm certain almost gave her a coronary. For the pièce de résistance, I pin Elizabeth's onyx brooch in the center of the bodice. It's an heirloom that's been passed down to every chosen Wildblood woman, and I wear it proudly as a sign of our resilience. Our defiance. My message to Salomé is as clear as I can make it.

You will not change who I am.

Since our outing to The Society's church, I've decided if she wants to shove her religion down my throat, she can have a taste of mine. I've been leaving things around the house for her to find. Crystals, bundles of dried herbs and flowers, vials of elixirs, and the most entertaining: a stuffed piece of felt that I fashioned to look like a voodoo doll.

I'm anxiously waiting for the moment that she finds them.

Feeling that same energy, I grab the Ouija board before I leave my room and head downstairs to join my sisters. I'm eager to see them, and I want them to know I'm okay.

I'm half-expecting a somber greeting when I reach the sitting room, but there's nothing that could have prepared me for what I actually find.

Cordelia, Winter, and Aurora are all sitting together on one sofa, trying to stifle their laughter as Raven sages the room around them. Most notably, she's focusing on the area around Emmanuel, who happens to be sitting on the largest chair, watching her with disdain.

"Raven," I squeak out. "What are you doing?"

"What?" She blinks at me innocently. "This room was full of bad energy. I'm trying to dispel it, but it doesn't seem to be working."

I can't help the laugh that bursts from my lips, which only seems to further sour Emmanuel's mood. But truthfully, Raven has a point. What is he even doing in here?

"I'll take that as my cue to leave," Emmanuel says gruffly, rising to his feet.

But he doesn't go, not right away. It's impossible not to notice the way his eyes move over Raven, darkness flickering in their depths. It sends a chill through me because I recognize that look all too well. It was the same expression Azrael wore when he first set eyes upon me and realized I was his chosen Sacrifice.

"Raven," I bite out.

She doesn't seem to hear me because her eyes are locked on his, a strained expression on her face.

"Raven," I say again.

This time, my voice seems to sever the connection, bringing them both back to the room around them. Emmanuel's jaw ticks, and he dips his head in lieu of a goodbye as he takes his leave.

"Willow!" Cordelia flings herself at me before I can process what had just happened, wrapping her arms around me and squeezing so tight I can scarcely breathe. "I missed you!"

"I missed you too." Tears prick my eyes as an unexpected wave of emotion takes me captive.

It isn't long before they are all taking turns hugging me, even though they know I'm not a hugger. When it's Raven's turn, I give her a sharp look before whisper-hissing in her ear.

"What the hell was that?"

"I don't know," she grumbles. "You'll have to ask him. The man is obviously certifiable."

"Why was he even in here?"

"I have no idea." She shrugs as I release her, her eyes looking everywhere but at me.

Something about this whole situation seems off, and I don't like it.

"Stay away from him," I warn her. "He's dangerous."

Even as I say it, I don't know if that's actually true. But still, he's a Delacroix, which is reason enough to be wary.

"It's fine, Willow. I want nothing to do with him." Her eyes flicker to the Ouija board beneath my arm. "What are you doing with that old thing, anyway?"

I smirk, amusement coloring my voice as I reply, "What do you think I'm doing with it?"

"Fucking with them?" She laughs.

I nod, not even trying to deny it. My sisters and I only ever played with the Ouija board once, just to see if anything happened. It's not something we actually use as a divination tool, but I brought it here because I suspected I might have a use for it.

"I figured I'll just leave it here for them." I set it on the coffee table. "They can wonder what we were up to in here."

"Oh wait, even better." Winter digs around inside her hobo bag, retrieving a piece of paper and a pen before she starts to scribble on it.

We all wait to see what it is she's doing before she sets the paper on top of the board, bold black runic symbols scratched into the surface. They are perfectly harmless, but the Delacroixes don't need to know that.

Cordelia is the first to burst out laughing, and soon, we're all in stitches. I can just imagine Azrael's face when he sees it. But even better will be Salomé's mouth twisting like she just sucked on a lemon.

"You're going to get me in trouble," I tell them.

"Really?" Aurora asks, her voice tinged with concern.

A somber mood settles over the room as I shake my head, trying my best to appease them.

"No, not really. I was just kidding."

"So, you're okay then?" Winter presses. "They haven't been... terrible?"

"No," I admit. "They haven't."

I'm not going to tell them about Salomé. I don't want them to worry. So instead, I launch into a conversation about Bec and mention that I'd like to get her in to see our family doctor, although I'm not quite sure how I'll manage such a feat under Salomé's watchful gaze. Bec doesn't leave the house other than to go to church, I suspect.

My sisters tell me they'll help me figure something out, and the conversation seems to flow easily from one topic to the next. Cordelia gives me the shirt she made me, and Winter gives me a new crystal necklace she wrapped. Before I realize it, hours have passed, and it's almost time for dinner.

I don't want them to go, but they seem to be aware that staying isn't an option. I can only imagine the hell that would break loose if Salomé had to sit down to dinner with all of us.

"Will you come to visit Mom and Dad soon?" Aurora asks. "They want to see you."

I suspect our parents aren't aware of their visit here today. If they knew, they'd be sick with worry.

"As soon as I can," I assure them.

They all give me more hugs, preparing themselves for a goodbye none of us want. But when they linger, faces drawn, I know there's something else they came to tell me. It isn't until Raven removes a handful of letters from her bag reluctantly that I realize what it is.

"They're increasing," she tells me quietly, handing them over. "These are all just from the last few days. They've been watching the house. They know you're gone but don't know where."

"They're threatening us," Aurora adds. "All of us."

I glance up at her in horror, helplessness settling over me.

"Don't worry." Raven tosses Aurora a chastising look. "We'll be okay. We're being careful."

Guilt sinks into the pit of my stomach, making me feel sick. "This is all my fault."

"It's not," Raven argues. "You know they would have come for us regardless. They're demented."

"No," I whisper. "If I hadn't been so naive—"

"This isn't your fault," Winter reiterates Raven's sentiment. "We're a sisterhood, remember? They fuck with one of us, they fuck with all of us."

I know they're trying to make me feel better, but it doesn't. The Disciples might have come for us either way merely for the fact that we were rumored to be witches, but it was me who put a target on our backs. The group is just a reborn version of the same bloodthirsty Puritans who committed murder under the guise of religion. I didn't know they were watching us. I'd had no idea that the boy who'd seemed so interested in me at sixteen was one of them. I'd ignored my intuition, and I allowed myself to be swayed by his charms, only to discover he was the devil in disguise.

Now, that man is pacing his prison cell like an animal, waiting for the day he can take his revenge. The horrific truth is, I don't know how to stop him.

"Don't go anywhere alone," I plead with my sisters. "And take protection with you. Even if it's just in the yard."

"We will," they promise me. "Same goes for you."

20

AZRAEL

While the Wildblood sisters visit in the sitting room, Emmanuel and I meet in the library.

"Five witches in the house. Is Gran twitchy?" Emmanuel asks.

I grin and close my laptop. "See the papers this morning?" I ask and watch the casual look on his face darken. He nods once. Two women have been found murdered over the last week in the New Orleans area. "Both are from families who have been known to dabble in witchcraft."

"Or pretend to," Emmanuel says. "It makes for good business in New Orleans. Didn't one have some sort of shop in the French Quarter reading cards or some nonsense?"

"You already looked into it then?"

He shrugs a shoulder and slides into one of the armchairs. "I was bored."

"Is that so?"

"What else would it be?"

My brother doesn't get bored, and he doesn't do anything that doesn't somehow serve him—unless it comes to Bec. For his sister, he'll do anything. I drop the question for now.

"You're right about the shop," I start. "Girl was young. The second woman was over sixty and lived alone in a small, decrepit house outside of the city. Doesn't sound like the police are linking the murders."

"Are you worried for your witch?" he asks.

"She's safe here. But her family may not be, if it's what we're thinking."

Emmanuel's jaw tenses. I'm not sure he's aware of the movement. "The Disciples have been off the radar for years. You think they're back?" The Disciples are basically witch hunters who gave themselves that title centuries ago, as if they act in the name of some god. They'd been around since before the time of Elizabeth Wildblood, having originated in Europe and spread, like a disease, to North America and beyond.

"There's no mention of the mark they leave on their victim but that could be on purpose. Don't want to scare the general population into thinking there's a serial killer on the loose, and it protects against a false confession. Talk to your detective friend yet?"

"I have a visit planned tomorrow afternoon, in fact," Emmanuel says.

"Good. The family, are they safe?"

"I'll walk by the house after my meeting."

"Will you?" I ask, standing, wanting to wrap up this meeting because there's something I want to do while Willow is occupied. "Wouldn't have anything to do with Raven Wildblood, would it?"

He stands too. "What would it have to do with Raven Wildblood?"

"You think I didn't feel your eyes boring into my back when I looked her over during The Tithing ceremony?"

"Hm. Well, this is just me doing a good deed, brother." He puts an arm over my shoulders as we walk to the door.

"Mhm. You know the rules, right?" He can't touch another Wildblood. None of us can as long as The Sacrifice is given to us.

"I know the rules," he says.

I stop to face him squarely and take him by the shoulders. "She's not for you, brother. Leave her alone."

He studies me, takes a long minute to answer. "Just walking by the house to make sure they're safe. That's all, Azrael. Scout's honor."

"You were never a Boy Scout."

He just shrugs, and we walk out of the library. Emmanuel heads to the front door, both of us pausing when we hear the combined laughter of all five Wildblood sisters. It's so rare to hear laughter like that in this house.

No, not rare. It just doesn't happen.

With a sigh, I walk up the stairs, to my bedroom

and through it to Willow's connecting room. I close the door behind me, feeling a little twinge of guilt as I take it in.

She's unpacked most of her things, the suitcases now out of sight. I see the asshole's large bed and play area in one corner and wonder why the damn thing chooses to sleep in my bed rather than here. Well, maybe not sleep. It's more like staring me down as she sits comfortably on my chest, probably trying to steal my breath or whatever it is cats do.

The drapes are open, letting in the light. It smells like her in here, sweet and woodsy, citrusy even. I've never smelled the perfume on anyone before and wonder if she makes it herself. I wouldn't be surprised, judging from all the vials.

I cross to the vanity and the first bottle I pick up and sniff confirms what I think. It's her scent. Palo Santo something or other. I put the lid back on and set it down, looking at the various tubes and bottles and finding her lipstick. I remember how it ringed my cock when I fucked her mouth. Her black eyeliner is here, too, and several containers of powders and little pots of pigment in every possible shade. Bec would have a field day in here. She doesn't so much as own a tinted lip balm. Salomé's doing. I'm going to change that, I think, as I look at Willow's collection.

Over the back of her chair, she's draped her red cloak. I pick it up then set it back down. I don't throw my clothes over the backs of chairs. I am meticulous with my things. It's how I'd noticed she'd been in my closet. The hangers were askew. She's not as neat. Throughout her room are scattered various silk scarves and knick knacks that remind me of the room where the Tithing took place. I look into a plethora of bottles, sniffing contents, unsure what they are. I pick up crystals and set them back down, wondering what she does with them. I go into her bathroom. Although she mostly uses mine, and I suspect she's been using my shampoo and soap, she has her own here and I pick up the first bottle and look at the label. It's from a local shop in the French Quarter that I've seen in passing. Zen Apothecary. I open it, sniff the contents. It's exactly how her hair smells when it doesn't smell like me. I reach for the bar of soap but stop myself. What the hell am I doing? Looking through her room is one thing, but sniffing her shampoo? That's a little creepy.

I walk back into the sitting room and flip through the stack of magazines, leaving the notebooks she's written in alone. I'm not going to snoop into a diary if she keeps one. When I'm finished and on my way out, my gaze falls on the tall glass jar with its burning candle within. I go to blow it out, although it's not going to do any harm, but when I do, I see among the dried flowers and crystals a small frame containing an image. It's a sketched portrait. I'd noticed it briefly the first time I'd come in here. It's black and white—well, apart from the tell-tale red hair that is the Wildblood inheritance. The hair on my arms stands on end as I pick up the frame and look closer at the picture.

I know who it is. Of course, I do. I see her almost

nightly in my dreams, although that's changed since Willow has been sleeping in my bed.

This is Elizabeth Wildblood exactly as I see her, exactly as my imagination conjures her up. It's uncanny.

Except here, it's not hate in those eyes that look so much like Willow's. Her expression is earnest, serious, but kind. Not as though she is looking at the face of her enemy but at her kin.

I wonder at the age of the portrait. Wonder if it's been passed down through the centuries.

The candle in its glass flickers although there is no draft. I meet Elizabeth Wildblood's eyes again. I'm not welcome here.

I set my jaw, put the frame back where I found it, and walk out of the room. I walk down the stairs, feeling irritable when I hear the murmur of voices coming from the sitting room. I observe the Wildblood sisters in a huddle almost, their faces serious, none of the laughter of earlier now. I wonder what they're up to. I clear my throat to make my presence known.

They practically jump, and I don't miss the panic in Willow's eyes as she quickly tucks envelopes into a shirt she's holding.

When she meets my eyes again, she's flushed.

"Dinner is ready," I say.

"Okay," she nods.

My gaze rakes over her, lingering on the skin left exposed by her top.

"I just need to finish saying goodbye to my sisters," she tells me. "I'll be there in a minute."

My cue to leave. I glance at the sisters, pausing for a moment on Raven. Have she and my brother met before tonight? Have they had any contact at all?

Willow clears her throat and I realize I'm hovering.

"Right. Don't be too long." I turn and walk away, hearing her usher her sisters out and saying a hasty goodbye before hurrying up the stairs.

When she returns, her hands are empty. I lead her into the dining room for dinner.

21

WILLOW

I wake with a jolt, breath heaving and skin flushed as my eyes dart around, taking in my surroundings. I'm in Azrael's bed, but he's not here. A glance at my phone confirms it's three o'clock in the morning—the witching hour.

A cold chill moves over me as I try to shake off the nightmare that pulled me from sleep, but Elizabeth's voice curls around my ear like a whisper of dread.

Careful, child.

Her warnings have increased lately, but it makes little difference if I can't understand what she's trying to protect me from. It could be any number of things. Salomé. This house. The fate that's been written for me from the moment I was born a marked woman.

I've felt off balance, and no amount of energetic work has helped. There's been a sinking feeling in the pit of my stomach from the moment I saw the news articles Raven sent me. Two local witches had been tortured and mutilated, their bodies found dumped in the street like trash.

While it's always possible it could have been a random act of violence, I can't help thinking it has something to do with Caleb Church's associations and the group that calls themselves The Disciples. Before they set their eyes upon our family, rumors had abounded for years that they were hunting women around New Orleans... women who were known to dabble in witchcraft.

When I met Caleb Church, I didn't know about his affiliation with the group or their reputation for performing violent exorcisms and baptisms alike—if you could call nearly drowning those they wish to convert a baptism, that is.

A shudder moves over me as I recall that feeling of suffocation. The choking, burning, clawing as blackness dimmed my vision.

I was young and naive when Caleb snuck me into his place of worship. Foolishly, I had believed it was because he wanted a quiet moment together. A stolen kiss, maybe. He'd only ever been sweet. But instead, he stripped away the charming persona he had carried and showed me who he really was.

He told me he wanted to 'get the Devil out of me,' and in his mind, rape and murder were the only ways to absolve a sinner like me. If I hadn't been wearing my ring that night, he would have succeeded.

That was the first time I truly felt the power of Elizabeth Wildblood in my veins. I'd channeled her strength somehow, and I survived. But I've never been the same since. The experience changed me, and not for the better.

I learned after that night that my parents' warnings about the evils of this world weren't just talk. Now I feel those evils everywhere. The men and women who burned and hanged witches aren't extinct. They just hide in the shadows, feeding their murderous appetites in the dark among their own kind.

For well over a decade, bodies have been turning up on the streets. Women who were mothers, sisters, daughters. Women who were members of the magic community.

It was undeniable that someone was targeting them. The police kept insisting they would find whoever was responsible. But then, one day, not long after Caleb had been sentenced to prison, the murders just... stopped.

Time passed, and people moved on. They forgot about those other women. But I haven't. I still think about them every day, connected to them in a way I can't explain. Maybe because I was almost one of them.

After what happened with Caleb, I couldn't help but believe they were responsible. His group of Disciples was insane, and they didn't hide the fact that they were targeting witches. But I knew it couldn't have just been Caleb involved in their murders. He was only nineteen when I met him, which means someone else had been carrying the torch long before he came of age.

When things died down, I suspected it was only a matter of time before it started again. They were under a microscope during Caleb's trial. They had to lay low. But now, I fear they have chosen to make a return. Sure enough, when I roll over to check my phone, there's a new message from Raven.

Did you see?

I eye the news article she attached, my stomach somersaulting when I read the headline.

Local voodoo priestess murdered, business torched.

My hand trembles as I click on the link, scanning the details through blurry eyes. I only make it halfway through the article before my phone rings and Raven's name flashes across the screen.

"Couldn't sleep either?" she asks when I answer.

"No," I murmur.

There's a long, heavy pause before she speaks again. "I don't like this, Willow. This has The Disciples written all over it."

"I know."

"I think we should do another binding spell," she suggests. "This week. Do you think you can get here?"

I consider it, deciding it doesn't really matter what Azrael says. This is important. "I'll see what I can do."

More silence fills the line before I ask the question I've been dreading. "Have there been more letters?"

Raven's hesitation confirms it. "Yes, and that's not all."

"What is it?" I ask.

"There was a message spray painted on the front

door." She swallows audibly. "It said 'come out, witch. You can't hide forever.'"

I squeeze my eyes shut, clutching my stomach as I shake my head, feeling like I'm going to be sick. "Raven."

It's all I can manage, but that one word conveys everything my sister needs to know. She understands me. We're all connected this way.

"We have protection," she assures me. "Mom and Dad have issued a lockdown on the house. We're not even going outside unless it's during the day, and we're together."

"I still don't like it," I tell her. "We don't know what they might do."

"They want you," she reminds me softly. "We'll be okay here. And you will too. As strange as I think it is to say, it's probably good that you're where you are right now."

"I'm not worried about me," I argue. "And we don't know what they will do. You can't get complacent. You have to stay vigilant."

"I know," she assures me. "We will. I promise."

"I'll talk to Azrael," I tell her. "I'll let you know what day I can be there this week."

"Okay," she agrees. "Try to get some rest."

I tell her I will before disconnecting the call, but that's a lie. The last thing I want to do right now is rest.

I set my phone aside, glancing over at Fiona. She blinks back at me with sleepy eyes, shamelessly keeping Azrael's spot warm for his return.

"Traitor." I give her a quick pet, shaking my head in disbelief. "You're supposed to be team Willow."

She yawns, boops my hand, then goes back to sleep before I slip out of bed and into my room to grab my black silk robe. There's a draft in the house tonight.

I finish tying the knot at my waist, sneaking a glance at my altar, when I notice Elizabeth's portrait has been knocked down. As I pick it up to examine the cracked glass, something twists in my gut. This was no accident. It was intentional.

A glance around the room confirms my suspicions when I notice the metal garbage bin full of burned remnants. On closer inspection, I can just make out the faint outline of a letter on the Ouija board I left downstairs. And beneath that are some of my crystals, charred herbs, and the vials of elixirs I planted throughout the house.

It doesn't take a genius to figure out this was Salomé's doing. Azrael didn't seem to care, or if he did, he hasn't said anything to me about it yet. But I can't see him being this petty. This has the old hag written all over it.

I toss the ash back into the bin and wipe my hands. I guess that's a point for her.

Setting the bin aside, I sneak into the hall, the floorboards creaking beneath my feet. I can still see the light in Salomé's bedroom at the opposite end of the hall. It's no surprise the woman doesn't sleep. Evil rarely does.

I set out in search of my husband, the house's

silence an eerie feeling around me. I tiptoe down the stairs, cautious that one noise might summon Salomé, and move around the house like an apparition. Every room I pass through is empty, but as I near the library and step into the darkness, I can hear that faint melodious sound again.

I pause to listen, realizing it must be a piano. But for reasons I can't explain, this seems to be the only room in the house I can hear it. I know it's because it must be in the dark wing, as Bec called it. But I haven't yet figured out how to get to that part of the house.

Given the age of the house, I consider that there might be a secret door, but as I run my fingers along the shelves, I don't notice any discrepancies. In the movies, it's always a book that has to be removed or something equally as dramatic, so I take note of the Delacroix collection. There seems to be a vast array of books, many of which appear to be leather-bound first editions of the classics, along with French titles I've never seen. A large selection of old tomes rests on one shelf, their spines battered from years of carrying their hefty weights.

I drag my fingers over them, pulling out a couple to inspect them. They are bound with leather straps and untitled, so I don't know what they contain, but I'm curious. Just as I'm about to untether one to see for myself, a faint voice behind me nearly scares me half to death.

"What are you doing?"

I shove the tome back into place, whipping around

with a sheepish expression to meet Bec's gaze. I half-expect to find a look of reprimand in her eyes, even though she's been nothing but sweet to me. I can only imagine how strange it is for her to have someone snooping through her house.

But a strange expression flickers across her face when her eyes dart to the tome I replaced, which only makes me more curious.

"I heard music," I confess. "I can hear it in the library but no other part of the house."

"It's Azrael," she tells me. "He plays the piano at night."

"Oh."

There's so much I want to ask about that, but I don't want to look too eager, and Bec seems uncomfortable with the notion of explaining. I imagine it's because the piano is in the dark wing, and she knows it's a place we aren't supposed to venture.

"I couldn't sleep," she says. "I came down to get a glass of water and saw the light on in here."

"Are you feeling alright?" I ask cautiously.

She nods reluctantly, shifting her weight while she works up the courage to ask me something. "Could you..." She hesitates, her hands twisting in front of her nervously. "Could you fix my necklace for me?"

"Did it break?" I ask, concern bleeding through my voice.

It's never a good sign if a protection necklace breaks.

"Something like that." She dips her gaze, leading me to believe it had some help being broken.

"I can fix it," I assure her. "Where is it?"

"I'll go get it." Her eyes light up with relief. "Can I meet you in your room?"

I nod at her, and she slips out of the library, barely making any noise as she goes. It makes me wonder how much practice she's had sneaking around these halls, trying to stay hidden.

With one glance at the tome, I make a mental note to return later to examine it before I switch off the light and go back upstairs. Thankfully, when I reach the top floor, Salomé's light is off. I don't know if she's asleep or lying in wait, but I'm hoping it's the first.

In my room, I do a quick job of hiding the burned remnants Salomé left for me. I have about a minute to pick up a few stray pieces of clothing before the knob twists quietly, and Bec peeks her head in.

"Can I come in?"

I offer her a reassuring smile, sad that she feels she needs permission for every moment of her existence.

She closes the door and bows her head as she clenches the necklace in her fist. Her body language is guarded, like she's afraid I might get angry. And when she reaches me, it falls upon me to offer her more encouragement.

"Let's see the damage. I'm sure whatever it is, we can find a fix for it."

Reluctantly, she opens her hand, revealing the bent wires and shattered amethyst that's now in three pieces. Definitely not an accident. Wherever the chain is, I'm sure that's in pieces too.

I consider it for a moment before returning my gaze to meet Bec's. "Why don't we make something interchangeable instead? You can wear it as an anklet or bracelet, depending on the clothes you choose that day."

I don't have to say it's so she can hide it because Bec seems to understand, and her smile is my answer.

"I would love that."

"Okay, first, we need a new stone or crystal. Come here. I'll let you pick."

She watches me curiously as I move to my altar, pulling my jewelry box from beneath it. When I open it, I choose a few pieces that will all work equally well for protection, laying them out for her to choose from.

"How do I decide?" she asks.

"Try feeling them," I suggest. "Whichever one speaks to you. You'll know when you feel it."

Her eyes brighten as she takes her time, examining each offering before returning to a piece of black tourmaline several times. I can tell that's the one, but I give her time to reach that conclusion on her own.

It takes her several minutes to work up the courage, a sure sign that she's not used to making decisions of her own accord.

"I think I like this one."

"Perfect," I tell her. "Do you want to see how it's made?"

She nods, sitting beside me on the floor as I get to

work, cutting wire and carefully wrapping the stone. This time, I use a length of rope to secure it, pausing to measure her wrist and ankle, which are equally tiny. It concerns me, and I know Bec can see it when she hastily covers them back up. There's so much I want to ask her about her condition, but I know I need to build a relationship with her first. Trust has to be established before she'll tell me the truth about what's going on here, which I suspect is far more than she's divulged.

"I think this will do." I extend the bracelet when I finish. "Do you want to try it on?"

She slips it onto her wrist, her face lighting up as if it's one of her most cherished possessions, and for some reason, that only breaks my heart more.

"Thank you," she whispers. "I love it."

"Of course." I smile. "If you have any more trouble with it, don't hesitate to come back. There's always a way to fix these things."

She nods, her eyes moving over the other jewelry in my case with interest. She doesn't ask, so I push the box in front of her in offer.

"Do you want to look through it? I have a lot of pieces in there."

"They're so pretty," she remarks, her dainty fingers picking up a few pendants and rings to examine them. "What do you do with all of them?"

"I sell them," I tell her. "Mostly. I also make some for friends and family."

"Where do you sell them?"

"There's an apothecary shop in New Orleans.

Solana, the owner, has a space for my jewelry and some of my candles and the elixirs I make."

"That's so cool," Bec says. "I wish I could do something like that."

"You can help me anytime you want to."

"I would love that." Her words are genuine, but I can't help noting the sadness in her voice. I'm not sure if it's because she doesn't think Salomé will ever allow it or if there's another reason.

"Hey, I have an idea," I tell her.

"What?" She blinks up at me.

"Are you tired?"

She shakes her head.

"Good." I get up and walk to my closet, searching the hangers for something I think will fit her. "My sisters used to do this when we couldn't sleep. We'd get all dressed up with nowhere to go. It passes the time."

Bec seems to like the idea, and when I notice her eyeing one of my black Wednesday Addams-style dresses, I pluck that one from the hanger.

"Here, try that one." I rummage around for accessories, choosing a red headband and heart-shaped glasses to accompany my robe.

While Bec puts on the dress, I grab some makeup, too, picking out a few items that will work well with her skin tone. She laughs when I turn around, and she notices the glasses on my face. It's such an innocent thing, but it makes me happy because I think it's the first time I've heard her laugh.

"How does it look?" she asks, peering down at herself.

"Perfect," I tell her. "I think it suits you. Have a look in the mirror."

She does, and I can see the moment she falls in love with the dress. I wonder if she's ever been able to choose any of her own clothes and make another mental note to ask Azrael about it later. I doubt he'd let me take her shopping, but it's worth a shot to ask.

"I look like an actual teenager," she says.

"You're beautiful," I tell her, wiggling the makeup at her. "Now comes the fun part."

She sits on the velvet ottoman at my instruction, and I apply light makeup to her face, mostly focusing on the eyes, swiping them with some glittery shadow. She peeks at my makeup case when I reach for the nude lipstick.

"Can we do the pink one?" she asks.

"Bold choice," I tell her. "I love that."

I apply the pink lipstick for her and then work on her hair, splitting it down the center and braiding the fine strands. As I work, she examines some of the items from my altar, asking about each of them. I take my time explaining, observing that she's asking out of genuine curiosity and not fear. But when she picks up Elizabeth's brooch to examine it, I can sense that she feels the significance of it. She doesn't ask, but I explain anyway.

"It belonged to Elizabeth Wildblood," I say. "It's

been passed down to every chosen Wildblood woman since her death."

"It's beautiful," she murmurs, her voice carrying a note of sadness. "Maybe it's like a protection stone too."

"In a way, it is," I confess, but I can't hide my sadness. Because the truth is, there's no protection from my fate.

Bec feels the weight of it in her hand, seeming to sense the shifting of my energy. "Who knows? Maybe it's even powerful enough to break the curse."

I don't know how much she knows about the curse, but it seems like an innocent observation. The observation of someone who still has hope.

"All done," I tell her. "Want to see?"

She nods, rising to look at herself in the mirror. Emotion steals her voice when she does, but I can tell she's happy.

"Thank you," she says softly. "I didn't even know I could look this pretty."

"You're pretty no matter what you wear."

She pauses while she takes herself in, lost in her thoughts before she answers. "You'll be a good mother."

A sharp pain twists my gut. It's something I've known my whole life I'll never have—a family of my own. It's a loss I've felt deeply every time I considered it. Every time I had to stop myself from even dreaming about it.

Bec doesn't know. I don't think she has any idea

that Azrael and I are both fated to die tragically, and I don't know if that's better or worse.

A wave of grief washes over me as I consider how great that loss will be for her. To lose another brother. And here I am, allowing her to get attached to me, only to have that ripped away too.

Tears prick my eyes, and I suck in a shaky breath, determined not to let them fall. I can't let her see that pain. But as I'm thinking about it, a new fear alights in my mind. The sudden realization that once Azrael and I are both gone from this world, there will be nobody but Emmanuel left to protect Bec from Salomé.

I open my lips, the question on the tip of my tongue. I want to ask about her illness again, but the door swings open before I can, startling both of us.

"Bec?" Azrael glances at her in concern before his eyes narrow on me. "Why is she dressed like that?"

"You mean like a teenager?" I reply dryly.

Bec's shoulders slump, and I shoot Azrael a glare, hoping he'll pick up on what he's doing. I think it shocks both of us when he actually does.

"You look... beautiful," he tells Bec, softening his tone. "Just don't let Salomé see you like that. She'll have a fit."

I roll my eyes. He was so close. So close to nailing it, then he had to go and ruin it with that last part.

"I'll return your dress tomorrow if that's okay." Bec gathers up her pajamas, barely able to meet our gazes now.

"Keep it," I tell her. "I want you to have it."

She looks equally grateful and terrified because I'm sure she realizes she'll never be able to wear it in front of Salomé. At least not until Azrael puts her in her place.

"Thank you." She hesitates, almost turning to go, unsure how to say goodbye exactly.

Even though I'm not a hugger, I hug her, and it seems to relax her. If only it had the same effect on Azrael, who's glaring at me like I'm trying to convert his sister into a witch.

"Goodnight, Az," Bec tells him, quickly scurrying past before she closes the door behind her.

"What are you doing?" Azrael growls.

I smile at him sweetly, removing the headband and glasses and tossing them into a drawer. "What's the matter? Worried I'll rub off on her?"

He grits his jaw and shakes his head. Any amusement I may have felt dissipates when I recognize the worry in his eyes. It isn't that I'm rubbing off on her. It's the same fear I felt earlier staring back at me.

He's worried about what will happen to her if she gets close to me, only to have it snatched away.

"Come," he murmurs tiredly. "Let's get back to bed."

22

AZRAEL

The whole of the following day, Willow seems off. I don't know if she's seen the news of the murders or if it has to do with the bundle of letters her sisters gave her that she was quick to hide. As I'm walking her down to dinner, I decide now is the time to ask exactly what they were. "What did your sisters give you yesterday?"

"Huh?" she asks, eyebrows rising.

"You had a bundle you took to your room."

"Oh. That. Just some clothes and things. Nothing really."

"Hm. I got the impression you didn't want me to see them."

"Did you?"

I study her, see how she doesn't quite meet my eyes. She's a bad liar.

"There was a stench in the house today, Azrael,"

Grandmother says, ending our conversation as Willow and I enter for dinner.

Willow rolls her eyes.

"I've opened all the windows in the sitting room to air it. I hope we can get it out."

"Is that the best you can come up with?" Willow asks her. "Really?"

Grandmother holds her dish out to be served a slice of roast, her lips tilted upward in one corner. "Your sisters won't be welcome here going forward. You belong to us now, girl," she says to Willow directly.

"I *belong* to you?" Willow raises her eyebrows. "I certainly do not—"

I put my hand on hers, a gesture Grandmother doesn't miss.

"Bec, how did your appointment go?" I ask my sister, ignoring my grandmother altogether. Bec had an appointment with her doctor.

My sister opens her mouth to answer but Grandmother is quicker. "No change. They've increased her dosage."

"I don't want more of the medicine. It makes my stomach hurt," Bec says, eyes pleading.

"What is the medicine?" I ask.

"Are you a doctor now?" Grandmother asks me. Admittedly, I've always let Grandmother take the lead when it comes to Rébecca. I was young when she started to have strange bouts of illness, but they went as mysteriously as they came. Although over the last year she has only seemed to grow sicker.

"If her stomach hurts when she takes it, then they need to find her an alternative."

"Medicine isn't candy but it is necessary."

"Bec, what is the diagnosis exactly?" Willow asks.

"I don't think the witch needs to be involved in a private family matter, do you, Azrael?"

"They don't know," Bec tells Willow, ignoring Grandmother. She seems different tonight. More confident or something. I wonder if it was her dress-up session with Willow. "They can't figure it out."

"Where is your brother?" Grandmother asks, changing the subject as she stabs a bloody piece of meat.

I notice Willow helping herself from a casserole dish set beside her and don't comment although I am sure Grandmother has noticed. I requested something appropriate for vegetarians, and Willow seems to be enjoying it, so I'm glad.

"Yeah, actually, where is Emmanuel?" Willow asks.

"He had an appointment," I say, realizing how late it has run and fairly certain where he is.

"Your sisters seem nice," Bec says.

"You should meet them," Willow answers. "You'd love them, and I know they'd love you."

Grandmother snorts, cutting into her meat angrily.

We finally get through dinner, and I'm glad to see Bec eat about half of her dessert, which is more than she usually does. I make a mental note to ask the chef to make it again. Just as coffee is being served, I hear the front door and a minute later, Emmanuel enters the dining room, eyes bright and looking energized.

"Where have you been? You missed dinner," Grandmother says, her disapproving gaze moving over him.

"I'll grab a sandwich later," he tells her dismissively. He glances at Willow, then at me. "Talk later? Bec and I are binge watching the last season of The Vampire Diaries. Ready?" he asks her.

"Haven't you two watched the series like three times now?" I ask.

"Yep." Bec smiles wide and pushes her chair out. "I hope you're not going to get all emotional like you did last time," she mutters to Emmanuel with a roll of her eyes.

I raise my eyebrows.

He holds up his hands. "I'm a romantic at heart. What can I say?" He pokes Bec in the ribs. "Snitch." He picks up her spoon and shoves the last of her dessert into his mouth. "Now I may have to eat all the popcorn myself."

"You got popcorn?" she asks as they disappear down the hall.

"Salty and sweet. And M&Ms."

"Yes!" Bec touches her fists to his. It's such a normal gesture for a normal girl and to see it fills me with something akin to hope, at least momentarily.

"She'll be sick tomorrow," Salomé proclaims, then stands. "Goodnight," she says to me and heads out of the dining room but stops on the threshold and glances back at us. "Oh, I meant to ask if you've chosen the date to present The Sacrifice to Shemhazai yet?"

"You'll be the first to know."

"Good. It's about time Rébecca understood what is coming. Before she forms any attachments. The girl has been shielded from the reality of what being a Delacroix means for too long."

I don't have a chance to respond before she's gone.

"Christ," I say, standing. I turn to Willow who is staring at the empty space where Salomé just stood. "Let's go."

"What does she mean?"

"Nothing."

"Clearly, it's not nothing. She's brought it up twice now."

I hold out my hand for her and she pushes her chair out and stands.

"Azrael, I want to be prepared."

"Let's go outside. I could use some fresh air."

"It's going to storm."

"I'm not afraid of a little rain. Are you?"

"Azrael—"

"We'll talk outside." She opens her mouth, but I interrupt. "I want to go to the lake."

At that she pauses, then acquiesces, and we head out to the lake. It's been a warm day and the temperature is still high although a storm is expected.

"My grandmother may talk, but she has no say in anything that happens to you. All right?" I tell her once we're out of earshot of anyone listening from the house.

"Yes, sort of, but here's the thing. Something is going to happen to me. You and I both know that. Within a year, I'll be dead."

I keep my gaze on the path and am silent until we reach the clearing. Strangely, since the other night out here with her, it doesn't feel so bad to be here. In a way, I feel closer to Abacus.

"Let's have a quick swim," I say, pulling off my shirt.

"Why won't you answer me?"

"Willow. Drop it. It doesn't matter."

"It matters a great deal to me."

"What I mean is..." I start but stop when her gaze falls to my tattoo and I see how her expression changes, I stop talking.

"Wait a minute." She reaches out to touch it, tracing the lines of the angel curving around the right side of my body. Did I think she would somehow not know what it was after our visit to the cemetery?

She moves around me, her fingers feather light on my back, her breath warm on my shoulder. When she comes to stand before me again, she takes my hand, opens it. In astonishment, she takes in the golden cuff inked into my skin. It's the same as Shemhazai's battle-ready statue wears.

All I'm missing is a cloak and a sword to be him.

To *be* Shemhazai.

And that's the point, isn't it? That was Salomé's point.

Willow has seen the tattoo before, but she didn't know exactly what—or who—it was.

"It's him." She shudders, wrapping her arms around herself. Her shoulders curve inward, and in her eyes is something akin to disbelief or disgust. "It's the angel from the cemetery."

"He's a demon, not an angel," I say because it's true. I know it, and I think she does too. All that talk of witchcraft aside, she has a sixth sense.

Color drains from her face before my eyes. "Is that what you'll be when you do what Salomé seems to expect from you? When you *present* me to that thing? A demon?"

It's hard to look at her, but I make myself do it. She deserves that much. I brush her hair back, let my fingers move over her chest to the crescent moon on her breast, gliding lower to undo the top buttons of her dress until I expose a part of the tattoo.

It's in that moment I make the decision. Or perhaps I'd already made it on the night of The Tithing. Maybe it was having her in my house. My bed. I don't know. But I do know that I don't want to hurt her. I can't hurt her.

"Mom used to bring us here when we were little," I say, turning away from those too-keen eyes. Because if I don't do what I'm supposed to do, what Salomé expects of me, what will happen to my family?

"It used to be a happy place with so many happy memories," I hear myself say, wondering how I sound remotely normal. "I often wonder why he chose to die here."

She follows my gaze to the tree. "Your brother?"

"His name was Abacus." A light rain begins to fall, the start of the coming storm. I pull my shirt back on, wanting to hide Shemhazai from her view. Wanting to hide her from his eyes.

"Maybe Abacus felt the happy memories too. Maybe it was a comfort for him to be here at the end," she says gently.

I smile at her kind words. I think she means to comfort me with them.

"He was first-born, did you know that?" I look at her as we settle on a stone bench beneath a sheltering tree. "By a few minutes, but still."

She remains silent and I'm not sure why I'm telling her any of this. I think I need to.

"We were very close, Abacus and me. And Emmanuel too. Rébecca came much later."

"Did Salomé always live with you?"

I shake my head. "My parents died when Abacus and I were eleven. That's when she moved here to look after us. The night before we turned eighteen, Grandmother took me to get this tattoo. Well, the first part of it. It took some time to finish."

"Your grandmother took you to get that? I'd think she'd associate tattoos with Satan or something."

I chuckle. "Not this particular mark, no. It's Shemhazai. Our ancestor, according to her."

"Did you have a say in it?"

"I didn't even know where we were going, and remember, I'd had seven years of being ruled by her iron fist. I'd learned it was easier to do what she wanted than to fight her."

"But not anymore?"

"No."

"Did Abacus get one too then? A rite of passage or something?"

"No. No rite of passage. And no, she didn't think he was strong enough to wear Shemhazai, even though he was first-born."

She looks confused.

"Abacus didn't look like me or Emmanuel. He wasn't as tall or as strong. He was average. Normal. To Salomé, that meant he was not chosen by Shemhazai. In a way, she chose me to be The Penitent, I suppose. But she doesn't determine what happens anymore. That's why I'm telling you this, Willow. You don't have to be afraid of her." I touch a lock of her silky hair, brush the backs of my fingers over her arm. "We should go in. The rain is picking up."

She ignores the last part. "I'm not afraid of her. I just want to understand what is going to happen to me. What is this 'presenting The Sacrifice' nonsense?"

"You truly don't know?"

"How could I? No Wildblood Sacrifice has ever returned to tell the tale." She shrugs my touch off when she says it and rubs her arms warm.

"Historically, The Penitent presents The Sacrifice to Shemhazai at Shemhazai's altar."

She raises her eyebrows, waiting.

"It's a ritual, like The Tithing, how it's all conducted. The Delacroix family stands as witnesses, although Bec is too young no matter what Salomé says."

"What happens at the ceremony exactly?"

"It's not going to happen. You don't have to worry."

"It's never going to happen, or it's not going to happen right now?"

I stand up. "Let's go in," I say, storm clouds moving closer as the rain picks up.

"Azrael?" She's on her feet too. "Tell me. Tell me what would happen exactly."

"You'd be presented. That's all. You'd kneel before the statue—"

"I wouldn't kneel."

"Letting it be known you're there of your free will—"

"That's a real stretch, but go on."

"And I'd make an offering. Something of yours."

"Like what?" she says tightly. Does she hear the long, low rumble of thunder?

I watch the dark clouds closing in. "It's not going to happen, Willow. Don't worry about it." I push wet hair back from her face. Our clothes are getting soaked. "We need to go inside."

"You say that so casually, but you're not The Sacrifice," she continues as if she doesn't feel the rain at all, but I watch the sky light up with electricity.

"Willow—" I start but am interrupted by a loud crack of thunder.

She shrugs off my hands and takes a few steps away, folding her arms across her chest. "Tell me what kind of offering. What have your ancestors offered in the past? You keep records, don't you? I thought you kept a book or something," she snaps. "What could it be? Clothes we wear? Jewelry? A finger? An organ? Just tell me. Because I felt the same thing at that altar as I did when you wore that ring. The ring with Elizabeth's hair in it."

"Christ. When did you..." I shake my head. "I don't wear the ring."

"You *did* wear that ring, Azrael. Own it. Tell me what it is you will offer your demon god."

"He's not my demon god."

"Whatever he is," Willow says.

"Salomé believes—"

"I don't care what Salomé believes! What I care about is that you believe it too—at least some part of it or I wouldn't be here. Or The Tithing wouldn't have taken place. And I guess in some way, I believe it too, or I'd have done what my family urged me to do. Run. But historically, if we don't offer the chosen one, more Wildbloods are lost. Killed. Dead. Better one dead Wildblood witch than a whole family, right? So here I am, and here you are. So please just fucking tell me so I know. So I'm prepared. I deserve that much, don't I?"

Her eyes are ablaze, wet with emotion, so much emotion I'm struck silent. But she's right. She does deserve to know. And I need to own it, as much as I hate it.

"Hair. I'd offer him a lock of your hair. That's all."

"Hair." Tears well to overflowing, and she takes more steps backward as I try to go to her. Rain is coming down hard now.

"I'm not going to do it, Willow. I don't want to hurt you."

"But you're going to. We're both here, aren't we? You're going to. Salomé wants—"

"Salomé can want whatever the hell she wants," I try to maintain control of my tone, which is raised. "She can say what she wants. But I decide."

"Tell me why, at least. Explain to me why your ancestors and you, now, in this modern time, still come for the chosen Wildblood. Explain to me why we're still doing this centuries after Elizabeth's death."

I shake my head, then push a hand into my hair because she's right. It is outrageous that I believe in this curse, but I do. So does her family. So does she. It's why we're here. Exactly why she and I are both here.

"My parents' yacht disappeared years ago; their bodies were never found. No crew was found. It's like they were never there at all. Abacus? Abacus went insane. I found him. I found him, and do you know what he'd done before hanging himself? He'd tried to cut out the birthmarks. He'd butchered himself. That's how badly he'd wanted to escape the Wildblood curse."

"A curse you don't think you deserve for what your ancestors did to us?" She turns to walk away.

I go after her, grabbing her by the arm and turning her back to me. "My ancestors, maybe, but Abacus? My mom and dad? Do you think they deserved to be punished? Do you think Rébecca does?"

She tries to shrug free, but I don't let her go. "No, I don't, but do you really think taking me, offering that thing a lock of my hair, do you really think it will heal Rébecca? Will it bring your parents or Abacus back?"

"It won't bring anyone back from the dead." I loosen my hold and she takes two steps backward, tilting her head as she studies me like she's trying to make sense of something nonsensical.

"But you think it will heal Rébecca?" she asks, sounding astonished.

I hear what she's saying, how unbelievable it sounds. How fucking ridiculous. I shake my head.

"And what about you?" she continues, yelling now over thunder and sheets of rain, wiping away the hair that's sticking to her face. "What happens to you after some accident befalls me and I'm off your hands and all your problems are solved? Your sister is miraculously healed. Hell, maybe your parents are found and your brother rises from the dead. What about you, Azrael? Because historically, no Penitent has lasted more than a few months after the Wildblood witch is dead. You're not going to walk away from this, either."

"You think I don't know that?"

She shakes her head, a deep line between her

eyebrows. "Are you willing to throw away your life along with mine?"

"I'd happily give up my life if it would save Rébecca's," I say over the pounding rain.

"What about taking her to a different doctor then for starters? What about modern medicine instead of—"

A blinding blast of lightning makes her stop mid-sentence as it strikes the center of the lake.

Willow stares, mouth agape.

"Fuck!" Without waiting for her to say another word, I bend to lift her, haul her over my shoulder and run for the chapel because it's closer than the house.

She bounces on my back, clutching the waistband of my pants for balance.

I turn to watch the storm that seems to be chasing us. When we get to the churchyard, I weave through the path, not slowing when I have to pass Shemhazai's altar. Only when we reach the stairs to the chapel do I slow down, setting Willow on her feet beneath the overhang. Her eyes are locked on the demon-angel.

"Willow," I say, taking her small face in my hands and turning her to look at me, wiping away water, seeing something I haven't seen in her eyes yet, not really.

Fear.

"That thing is evil, Azrael."

She looks up at me, shivers. I hug her close.

"I'm not him," I tell her. "And I'm not going to let anything happen to you. I swear it."

Her forehead creased, she opens her mouth to answer. Before she can utter a sound, a bolt of lightning strikes the very altar at the angel's feet, and for a moment, the night is electric. A sound like nothing I've heard before rumbles louder than the thunder that follows, and as I push Willow through the door into the church, I look back over my shoulder at the thing. At the altar now split down the center, the malevolent angel wearing his hood, carrying his sword and watching us. As if he heard every word we just said.

23

WILLOW

Tension lingers between us as Azrael leads me back to the house, settling me into bed alone. He has no intention of staying, and I don't know if that's better or worse. We waited out the storm together in silence after I'd shrugged him off, the howling wind and thunderous booms shaking the chapel as if to prove we've angered the heavens.

A balance is yet to come due, and in the end, it will cost us both our lives.

We've been avoiding this reality, but now it hovers over us like a dark storm we can't escape. My nightmares are increasing, the clock of doom flickering in my subconscious, an ever-present reminder that my time is limited.

There's a part of me that wants to trust Azrael, to believe in what he says. When I look at him now, noting the anguish on his face, I can feel his pain. How he, too, is torn by this curse.

I have always believed in Elizabeth. I have always felt it was my duty to remember what was done to her. But for the first time in my life, I find myself questioning the bigger picture. The reason behind the curse. Even if she didn't intend it to be so, she has cursed every chosen Wildblood woman with the hastily spoken words she uttered before her death.

Centuries later, we continue to die. And for what?

It was easier to believe in the sacrifice when I hated Azrael Delacroix. But every time I see him now, that hate transforms into something else. It's been slowly ebbing away with every kiss, every stolen touch, every moment I spend in his presence, realizing he isn't at all who I thought he was. Instead of being satisfied with the knowledge that we both will die, one from each family, to balance the wound inflicted, all I feel is inexplicable sadness.

I don't want to die.

But I don't want him to die, either.

It's a bitter truth to swallow when it's all I ever thought about before I married him. I thought it would somehow put my spirit to rest in my grave, knowing that he, too, would be gone from this world.

Now, the idea makes my chest painfully tight.

"Try to get some sleep," he murmurs, showing me his back as he returns to the door.

I swallow, eyes blurring with unshed tears. I can't bring myself to speak before he takes his leave. But I feel the loss of him. I feel his absence like a cold chill in the air around me.

Feeling my discomfort, Fiona settles on me, purring as I close my eyes and try to sleep. But sleep doesn't come. Instead, it's Elizabeth's voice that arrives, louder than it's ever been.

There are two paths before you, Willow. Listen, and your heart will guide you.

I let those words rattle around my brain, unsettled by the strange sentimentality in her voice. She's only ever been cautious. Serious. But right now, she's telling me to follow my heart, and my heart is telling me that there are enough enemies around me. I don't need to make one of Azrael too.

I want to trust him, but can I?

I glance up at Fiona, and she returns my gaze with judgment in hers.

"Typical of you," I mutter.

Seeming to predict my next move, she abandons me for Azrael's side of the bed, leaving me to get up. I don't bother with a robe tonight as I head for the door in my black silk nightgown. I don't really care if Salomé sees me at this point.

Her light is on again as I walk down the hall, but I don't hear anything from her room. I wonder what it is she does in there, then I wonder if I could ever sneak in to snoop around without getting caught.

Bec's light is off tonight, and I hope she's getting some rest for her sake. I noticed she looked weaker than usual today, and I'm truly worried for her.

I take the stairs slowly, pausing when I hear the sound of a door creeping open on the second floor. It sounds like it must be Salomé's room. Light footsteps echo down the hall, and I linger in the darkness as I hear another door open. This time, I'm fairly certain it's Bec's. I wonder what purpose Salomé would have for going into her room in the middle of the night when Bec is surely asleep.

Something keeps me rooted to the spot, and I listen for anything out of place, but everything is quiet. Yet, I can't deny this strange feeling in my gut. It isn't just my dislike for Salomé. Something isn't right here, in this house... in her orbit.

She's the darkness in this place. She's the one sucking the very life from it. I don't doubt she'll happily dance on my grave once I'm gone, but I can't help wondering about her intentions. She's so eager to be rid of me, to see me dead, when she knows history has dictated it will happen in due time regardless.

What is her hurry?

With that thought in mind, I close my eyes and ask Mother Goddess to protect the good in this house from evil—to protect us from her. Then, I slowly continue my descent, winding my way through the house until I'm back in the library.

A solitary lamp lights the room, an indicator that Azrael has been here, and when I press my ear to the stacks, I can hear the music again.

I linger there momentarily, my eyes drifting to the old tomes I wanted to examine. But the emotions of the day have been too much already, and right now, all I want is to speak to Azrael. To make peace.

I work my way along the shelves, pressing against each frame to see if anything budges. They all seem solid and unmoveable, and I'm not sure it will work. At least not until I feel one give slightly. It's heavy and takes some effort, but with a solid push, it starts to turn, revealing a dark, musty corridor.

I stare into the abyss, goosebumps breaking out along my skin as I consider venturing down that path. I can't see much apart from the light spilling in from the library that illuminates the stone. Beyond that, it's dark, but there's no doubt this is where Azrael is. The music is coming from the other end, loud and melancholy.

With a deep breath, I steel myself and set out along the corridor, my bare feet slapping against the cold stone floor. The journey feels long, and the energy shifts as I venture further into this part of the house. It's different here. The memories of a family that once existed within these walls still linger. I can understand now why Azrael comes here late at night when he's restless.

When I reach the end of the corridor, the entrance to the piano room beckons me, but I find myself stopping in the doorframe, eyes moving over the sight before me.

Candles flicker throughout the space, casting a soft glow over the imposing man in the center of all of it. His large frame moves in tandem with his fingers as they float over the keys with a haunting proficiency.

The melody is one I don't know, but it's beautiful

and gut-wrenching all the same. It's strange how powerful music can be. I've always known it, but seeing him this way makes me feel something I can't explain, like we're bound together in a way that makes me feel his pain. It's something I've only ever experienced with my own family.

But this connection is stronger. It's a pulsing, electric beat in my chest. The string of fate wrapped around my wrist, tugging me in whichever direction he moves. It's a voice whispering in my ear.

Go to him.

I do.

It takes me several steps into the room before he looks up, his eyes catching mine. His shoulders stiffen at first glance, and a flicker of vulnerability moves through his gaze. He didn't expect me to see him here.

"Hi." I offer him a nervous smile.

"Hi," he echoes. "What are you doing down here?"

I move closer, my hip brushing the curve of the piano as I enter his orbit close enough to smell his cologne but far enough to guard my heart if he rejects me.

"You left me alone," I murmur, my words betraying the emotion behind them.

His eyes darken, fingers reaching out to wrap around mine. "I thought that's what you wanted."

"It isn't." I stare at him, my voice little more than a whisper. "It isn't at all."

His eyes move over my face, and with a jerk of his

hand, I'm standing before him, pinned between the piano and his muscular thighs.

"Do you have any idea what this does to me?" he asks roughly as his fingertips graze my face, down the length of my neck, before dipping to my hard nipple poking through the silk of my nightgown.

"What?" I croak.

He responds by dragging his finger along the hem to my shoulder strap, pushing it to the side before he repeats the action on the other side. The material slides down over my skin to gather around my waist, baring my breasts for him.

With a growl of satisfaction, Azrael grabs a handful of my ass, holding me in place as he dips his head forward to suck my nipple into his mouth. A whimper escapes me as he pulls me forward, mauling me with his teeth and tongue.

"Azrael," I pant, my fingers reaching up to tug his hair.

"I know," he rumbles against me. "Fucking Christ, I need to be inside you."

The piano's keys play a chaotic tune beneath my ass as he tips me back, using the instrument as leverage when he stands abruptly. He grips my waist with one hand, balancing me while the other reaches for his zipper.

His cock is a solid weight in his palm when he retrieves it, and he wastes no time before he nudges it against me. I'm already wet for him, and my body accepts him greedily when he thrusts up inside me and I wrap my legs around him so I feel his full length.

I cry out, fingers clawing into his back as he mauls me with his mouth. It's a brutal kiss, one full of need like I've never experienced. I know he feels it too. This thing between us is growing. Changing. Tethering us together. Is it the curse wrapping its claws around us, or is it something else?

He's barely touched me, and I'm on the verge of coming undone. But I can't. Not until I know the truth.

"Wait, Azrael." My lips retreat from his, and he glances down at me, eyes full of torment.

"What is it?" he asks, his body slackening against me, his cock pulsing inside me even in stillness.

"Promise me," I whisper, "that I can trust you."

His eyes flash, and he tips my chin up when I waver in the silence, forcing me to keep my eyes on his. "You have my word, Willow. As long as I live and breathe, I will protect you. I will keep you safe."

I gulp back my emotions, nodding as I press my lips against his. "Okay. Then I believe you."

He grunts as he thrusts into me again, deeper and harder than before. It isn't sweet. It's primal. A claiming. A different mark of ownership. One that I'll feel everywhere tomorrow.

The first orgasm rips through me with an intensity that travels all the way to my toes. I barely have time to catch my breath before the second is chasing after it, and I don't know how it's even possible, but he gives me another. And another. He fucks me endlessly for what feels like hours as he shifts me around, positioning my body in ways he seems to understand will give me exactly what I need. He drapes me over the top of the piano, his large palms swallowing up my hips as he fucks me from behind. When my legs are on the verge of collapse, he picks me up and settles us both onto the bench, face to face. He rocks me down against him while he kisses me, our teeth clashing, breaths mingling, hearts beating wildly against each other.

I can't look away from him, and he sees it. Does he feel it too? Does he feel this thing between us?

"Willow," he grits out my name between his teeth, tension ratcheting in his body.

I kiss him. I kiss him like I'll die if I don't. It sends us both spiraling together, his fingers digging into my skin. Our breaths are fire in our lungs as he comes inside of me, pulsing violently as a sound of agony tears from his throat.

I feel it, then, that same question he's been asking of me.

What are you doing to me?

I don't give voice to it, but I don't need to. Azrael recognizes it in my eyes as we stare at each other, coming down from the high, the only sound between us our ragged breaths.

We stay like that, tangled up in each other, neither of us willing to move. His palm rests on my back as I nestle against him, breathing him in. Exhaustion weighs heavy on me, and I know there are still discussions to be had. I want to talk to him about Bec and

Salomé going into her room at night and so many other things, but I can't seem to move. The longer I lay there, sagging against him with the strength of his body supporting me, the further those thoughts drift away until there's nothing.

Nothing but silence and bliss as I fall to sleep in his arms.

24

AZRAEL

Willow doesn't stir as I drape my jacket over her shoulders and carry her back out through the corridor, through the library, and up the stairs to my bedroom. Once I'm inside, I close the bedroom door. She left the light beside her side—well, my old side—of the bed, on. The asshole has made herself comfortable on my pillow again. She raises her head, her eyes sleepy slits until she sees me carrying Willow and sits up, suddenly alert.

"Relax, I didn't hurt her," I tell her, whispering the words, wondering why I'm explaining myself to a damn cat.

She watches as I lay a still-sleeping Willow down and tuck her in. She must be exhausted. All of this, everything that's happening, has got to be weighing on her.

Fi settles back down and nuzzles into Willow's

neck. Willow moans softly and turns toward the cat in her sleep. I watch her looking so sweet and soft and wonder how I ever thought I could go through with it. How did I think I could hurt her?

I shake my head and glance out the window, just barely seeing the red glow of the tabernacle lamp in the chapel. My chest tightens, and just before I'm about to switch out the light, my gaze catches on the wood carving over my bed. I have to peer closer to be sure but that crack that's been there for as long as I can remember has, I swear, grown, widened as if it will split the carving in two.

I'm reminded of the altar breaking into two pieces tonight. The angel's rage. Is this a product of that rage too? No. It feels different in here. It always has. The malevolence in the churchyard is absent here.

My cell phone buzzes with a message. I reach into my pocket and retrieve it.

Emmanuel: Meet me at Bloody Mary.

I check the time.

Azrael: Now?

Emmanuel: Unless you need your beauty sleep.

I send him the middle finger emoji then type out my reply.

Azrael: Give me twenty minutes.

Willow makes a sound, and I shift my gaze back to her. She opens her eyes momentarily, smiles, then closes them again. She's still asleep. I hope she's having the sweetest of dreams.

I bend to kiss her forehead as I switch out the light.

From my closet, I retrieve my coat and head out into the hallway. Salomé's light is still on. I wonder how much sleep that woman gets. I pass her room as quietly as possible and go down the stairs. The keys to the Jaguar are in the pocket of my coat and I head out of the front door, locking it behind me even though the property is gated. Feeling somehow like I need to do it.

I park a few blocks from Bloody Mary, wanting to walk. I haven't been to town in a long time. Emmanuel and I used to come often. We've always liked the French Quarter and especially Bloody Mary, the little bar with its secret entrance off Bourbon Street. Tourists don't find this place. It's not on any app and has no virtual presence. It's refreshing.

As the night winds down, people on the streets are thinning out. I wonder why Emmanuel wanted to meet in town rather than coming home.

I take the turn into the alley that houses the bar's entrance and push open the nondescript door. The familiar smell of the place washes over me. I've stayed away too long. I stop to take it in, then look around the good-sized, dimly lit room with its old furnishings and ancient oak bar. The bottles of liquor spanning the wall aren't fancy, and I'm not sure the last time Mary, the owner, dusted the place. But when I see her watching me from behind the bar, I give her a genuine smile.

"You're late," Emmanuel says from our usual table.

I pull out my chair, noticing the folder he has in front of him as Mary brings over a tumbler. The bottle of whiskey, ours and probably the most expensive thing she has in this place, is already on the table.

"Well, well, stranger. It's good to see you."

"Good to be here, Mary. How's business?"

"Can't complain. You boys need anything, just holler."

"Will do," Emmanuel says, pouring me a whiskey and topping off his glass.

"How was movie night, by the way?" I ask, remembering he and Bec were going to binge watch The Vampire Diaries before he headed out to check on the Wildbloods.

"It's a series, not a movie. And the storm cut it short. What?" he asks, probably seeing my mood darken as my mind wanders to what happened at the churchyard.

"A lightning bolt from the storm split Shemhazai's altar in two."

His eyebrows disappear into his hairline. "What?"

The hair on the back of my neck stands on end and I find myself turning to look over my shoulder. It's almost as if I expect the angel to be standing at my back.

"It split the altar?" he asks, disbelieving.

I nod. I don't tell him it happened just as I swore to Willow I wouldn't let any harm come to her. Because what I do or don't do when it comes to this Sacrifice impacts him and Bec as much as it does me.

"Gran will lose what's left of her mind. Cheers to

that." He lifts his glass, touches it to mine which is still sitting on the table between us and drinks.

"What did you find out? Why did you have me come here rather than coming home?"

Earlier tonight, he met with Larissa Heart, the detective working the murders. Larissa's grandmother used to work for our family when we were very young. She was a kind woman. I still have fond memories of her being a warm presence in our lives after our parents passed away and Grandmother moved in.

Larissa is a single mom with a two-year-old daughter, and Emmanuel has always had a special relationship with her. It's the only relationship he has with a woman outside of the family that is not sexual as far as I can tell. He told me once as casually as he could that he'd promised Mrs. Heart a few days before she passed away that he'd look after Larissa and he's kept that promise, even interacting with her young daughter on regular intervals. I know he doesn't like to appear remotely kind-hearted. Grandmother's upbringing led us to believe it was a weakness, but I'm glad to see Mom and Dad's influence persisting in my brother. I hope I will be as strong as he is when push comes to shove with Salomé.

The fact that Larissa is the detective on these murders is a stroke of luck for us.

"I don't have good news," he says. He drinks another swallow of whiskey. I still haven't touched mine.

"Tell me."

He glances over my shoulder, but we're alone, and no one will eavesdrop on us here. At home, it's always a possibility. Grandmother's superhuman hearing. At least that's what she tells us. I wouldn't be surprised to find out she'd bugged all the rooms.

"Both victims had the cross carved into their foreheads." He slips the folder toward me. I place my hand over it but take a moment to digest his words. To ready myself for what I'll find because I know what it contains. It's no less brutal when I open the folder, though, and look at the photographs. There are two, zoomed in close. At least I don't have to see the rest of the butchering they did. It's only their foreheads bloody and mutilated, bearing The Disciples' signature. The sign of the cross.

"Christ."

"Police are withholding that detail."

I lean back in my chair. "The Disciples are back."

"There's more."

"What more?" I pick up my glass and bring it to my lips.

"They're targeting the Wildbloods."

His words stop me. "What did you say?"

He takes out his phone, scrolls to something and turns it around to show me. It's a photo of the front door of the Wildblood house. Barrett Cromwell is sanding it down, a can of paint ready at his side, but I can read most of what he's trying to clean up. Someone spray painted a message on their front door. Their fucking front door.

...witch you can't hide forever

Emmanuel looks as concerned as I feel. It's absolutely not like him, and it tells me he has more of a stake in this than I realized.

"Someone was on their property. At their door, Azrael. Someone got that close to them."

"I'm guessing there's no security system in place."

"Not apart from their spells." He rolls his eyes. "Which aren't going to keep them safe."

"How do you know that?"

He takes a moment to answer. "I talked to Raven."

I knew it. "What's your deal with her?"

"That's not the question you should be asking."

"Well, I am asking it. You know the rules. You—"

"The message was for Willow, Azrael," he says, turning the subject around absolutely.

The blood in my veins runs cold, and I have a sudden image of Willow, her eyes closed forever, her face desecrated and bloody. That cross carved into her forehead.

"Willow is safe at the house. No one can touch her there. I won't allow it." I don't sound remotely like myself when I say it. I swallow the contents of my glass and reach for the bottle to refill it.

"You're probably right that she's safest at the house, for now."

For now. He doesn't need to elaborate. She's safe until I fulfill my obligation as The Penitent. "Her sisters, though, are not."

"Does Willow know any of this?"

He nods. I feel my forehead crease. She hasn't said a word. But then I remember how jumpy she and her sisters were when I went into the sitting room. How quick Willow was to hide those letters from me.

"And the Wildbloods don't know who is targeting them exactly?"

"They know about The Disciples, but that's as far as I got. There's more, though. I can tell." He stands. "I'm going back over there."

I study my brother. No, this is not like him at all. "Is that what she wants? Raven?" I add in case it wasn't clear.

"I didn't ask."

Ah. There he is, the Emmanuel I know.

I stand too and nod. "Arrange for security. Don't tell them. I'm sure the Wildbloods won't agree to a Delacroix's protection."

He snorts. "No, they definitely won't agree to that."

"How was Bec, by the way? How did she seem to you?" I ask as I take some cash out of my wallet and leave it on the table.

"Good, actually. Better than she's been in a while. She showed me her new dress," he says as we head to the exit. "I'm sure Gran will shred it when she sees it."

"I'm thinking to take her to a different doctor."

"Oh? Your wife's idea, I assume? Like the dress?"

"Doesn't matter, does it? What do you think?"

"This one isn't doing much for her, so it won't hurt." He stops, turns to me. "I don't think she's grown an inch in over a year."

I nod, worry and guilt making it hard to swallow.

He pats my back. "It's not your fault. You know that, right?"

I press my lips together and nod again in a way that is not convincing to either of us.

"I gotta go," he says.

"Be careful, brother. The Disciples are zealots, and no matter what we think of their archaic way of thinking, they are dangerous."

"So am I, brother." He turns and walks out the door, not waiting for me to follow as he heads down the street in the direction of the Wildblood house.

I head to my own vehicle, my mind racing with all this new information—with all the old.

Willow may be in danger, but I firmly believe the safest place for her is at the house.

Bec is sick, very sick, and not a single doctor can figure out what is wrong with her.

And this curse is hanging over our heads, a dark and flimsy promise of hope for my sister. But the cost it will demand, The Tithe that must be paid, is Willow's life.

I meant what I said to her. I'd give my life to save Rébecca's. I can't take Willow's, though.

I drive in a fog of thoughts and when I get home, the sun is beginning to rise. I head upstairs to my bedroom, where I'm glad to see Willow is still asleep. She hasn't even moved. The cat is asleep on my pillow, probably leaving a mountain of fur for me to clean up.

She opens one eyelid then closes it again. I guess she's getting used to me.

Quietly, I open the door that connects my room to Willow's, enter and close it behind me. I switch on the light and scan the place. The first thing I notice is that the frame holding Elizabeth's portrait is cracked. I wonder if she dropped it, but she'd be too careful for that.

I walk through, looking at the familiar piles, and go into her closet when I don't find anything other than what I already saw in her room. I open a few drawers to search but don't come across anything. I do recognize the black tank top her sisters had given her and unfold it to read what's on the front in rhinestones: *Hi, this is my resting witch face.*

It's from her life before me, before The Tithing—although when she was born with the crescent moon on her breast, her family knew her life was already forfeit. Like mine. Like Abacus's, when we were born with the scars where the wings of the angels who displeased God would have been torn from their bodies. Hell, maybe this whole generation is lost.

I push the drawer halfway closed but it sticks. I bend to look at what is obstructing it, seeing the corner of an envelope sticking out underneath it. I pull the drawer all the way out and turn it over. There I find the same letters she'd quickly hidden from me the other day.

I peel the tape off the drawer, collect the yellowed envelopes, and look at the first one. It's addressed to

Willow Wildblood, her name a deep, angry scrawl. No return address. No stamp. It must have been hand delivered to her house.

All the envelopes have been opened, and I reach into the first of the five and take out the sheet of paper that's folded in half. The fold is sharp, as if someone went over it again and again and again, and both paper and envelope are expensive. Made to look old, the letter page itself is embossed with a cross I recognize. It's the same one that is carved into the forehead of every woman The Disciples kill. My jaw clenches, every muscle tightening as I read the few words on the page:

We're coming for you, witch.

It's unsigned. Well, unless you count the cross at the bottom right hand corner a signature.

I open the others, all are similar. Cryptic threats by an anonymous stalker.

You can't hide forever, witch.

You will submit to baptism or you will die, witch.

You will repent for your sins, witch.

Then there's the final one, the one that has blood rushing through my veins, pounding against my ears—the one that has me crushing the page in my fist.

You belong to me, witch.

25

WILLOW

When I open my eyes to find sunlight streaming through the window, it disorients me. I blink several times, glancing around the bed, noting I'm back in Azrael's room. I don't remember walking up here last night.

Did he carry me?

"You're awake." His voice startles me.

I lean up on my elbows, meeting his gaze from across the room.

"What are you doing?" I ask him.

He's just... sitting there like a sentry. It looks like he's been watching me, and judging by the tension in his jaw, something has shifted since last night.

"I could ask you the same question." He rises to his full height, stalking over to the bed to dump a stack of familiar letters onto the sheet beside me. "When were you planning to tell me about these?"

I swallow, dread curdling anything sweet we may

have had between us last night. Whatever that moment was, it was clearly fleeting, and now it's been swept away by his anger. It has the immediate effect of putting me on guard as I sit up.

"It's my business," I tell him. "Not yours."

"I'm your goddamned husband," he growls. "I have a right to know. I can't protect you if you aren't honest with me."

His words soften me, but that feeling is snatched away a moment later when he continues.

"You aren't just putting yourself in danger. You're exposing any vulnerable member of this house. What if they came here? What if they saw Bec on the grounds? Did you ever think of that?"

"They don't know where I am," I choke out. "And it's me they're after."

The muscles in his neck strain as he tries to calm himself, and I can't help my reaction. I shrink into myself, going back to what I know. Closing myself off. Burying the pain and refusing to let it come out.

Last night, Azrael told me I could trust him. But right now, all I feel is the sting of his words and the heat of his scathing gaze.

"Tell me why," he grits out. "I need to know how this happened. How long has it been going on?"

I tear my gaze from his, tension coiling in my body as I stare out the window. There's no way I could possibly be vulnerable with him right now. Not when he's like this.

"Tell me," he barks. "I'm done playing games with you, Willow."

"It's not a fucking game to me." My voice wavers, despite my efforts to keep my emotions in check. The fact that he would think so hurts more than anything.

"Then tell me the truth. How do you know The Disciples? How did you end up on their radar?"

"Haven't you heard?" I toss my angry words back at him. "I'm a fucking witch, Azrael. That's how I'm on their radar."

He considers it for a moment before he shakes his head. "No, there's more to it than that. They don't leave letters like this. Something had to have happened to provoke them."

I stare at him, empty. That word, *provoke*, feels like a blade to the heart. He couldn't know what he's saying, that I somehow *provoked* Caleb Church into trying to rape and murder me. That, in some way... this is my fault.

I can't bring myself to tell him the truth. Maybe he does deserve it, but I can't handle the possibility of opening up to him only for him to cast blame on me. He knows I was supposed to stay pure for him. He wouldn't understand why I ever thought it was okay to sneak around with a boy when I was sixteen. Even if nothing happened, despite Caleb's attempt, would Azrael believe me? Or would he see that as a provocation too?

I can't take the chance of him lobbing more accusations at me. My heart can't weather that. So, I do the only thing I've ever known how to do. I keep my mouth shut.

"Goddammit, Willow," he snarls. "You will tell me—"

A sharp knock on the door interrupts him, and he casts a murderous glare in that direction before he sighs. "What is it?" he calls out.

"It's Bec," Emmanuel responds from behind the door. "You need to come now."

"WHAT'S WRONG WITH HER?" PANIC BLEEDS INTO Azrael's voice as he joins Emmanuel in the hallway, me trailing behind in my nightgown.

"She took a turn this morning," Emmanuel says. "The doctor's here with her now." He pauses to look back at his brother. "It's not good, Azrael."

They quicken their pace, and I follow in their wake, my bare feet slapping against the floor as I try to keep up. Azrael doesn't look at me, and I'm glad for it. I couldn't bear it if he told me not to come along, and there's no way I could abide by it either.

A strange feeling settles in my gut as I think of Bec, and I know it's related to her illness. It isn't right what I'm feeling, and Elizabeth's whispering voice confirms it.

Protect her.

I nearly stop cold at that, but I catch myself and

keep going, straggling after the brothers as Emmanuel leads us downstairs.

"She was at breakfast when it happened," he explains.

It's all he manages to get out before the sitting room comes into view, and we see the chaos unfolding before us. A doctor and several nurses are working frantically around Bec, one checking her vitals while the other shines a light into her eyes. She looks halfway catatonic, and it sends a cascade of fear through me.

"We need to get her to a hospital," I tell them.

Salomé glowers at me from her position above the sofa. "We have everything we need here. This is none of your business."

I stare at Azrael in disbelief. He shifts, the muscles in his throat working as Salomé meets his gaze in challenge. She wants him to choose between us right now of all times. But it's about Bec, and I can't believe they'd even consider letting her stay here when she's in this state.

"You don't understand our ways," Azrael says, barely sparing me a glance. "We have everything we need at our disposal and the finest doctors money can buy. All the medical equipment Bec requires is upstairs."

"Then let's get her up there," Emmanuel interjects.

I want to scream out my frustration, but I can only watch in a daze as the two men lift Bec from the couch and carry her slight frame toward the stairs. I move to follow when Salomé wraps her claws around my arm, trying to halt me.

"This doesn't concern you, witch."

"Fuck you," I snap at her as I yank away. "Don't ever touch me again."

Mocking laughter echoes behind me as I dart after Azrael, Emmanuel, and Bec's medical team. Not only is it wildly inappropriate at a time like this, but it makes me wonder if Salomé even cares how ill Bec is.

Everyone filters into one of the spare rooms upstairs, and I almost stop short when I see all the medical equipment there. Azrael wasn't lying about that. But still, I can't help feeling this isn't right. That Bec shouldn't be in this house. That, in fact, she needs to be far, far away from here.

I don't always understand these feelings when I get them, but right now, it's more potent than ever. I can't help myself. I know Azrael doesn't understand it. He couldn't possibly feel the same sense of desperation clawing at my insides. The warning bells are going off in my head. My intuition has never led me astray, even when I chose to ignore it.

"Azrael." I grab him by the arm, glancing up at him with the hope that I can still appeal to him. "Please, you have to take her to a hospital. I know you think this is the best place for her, but I'm telling you, something isn't right in this house. I can feel it. I can sense it—"

"Enough." He shrugs me off with a glare colder than I've ever seen from him. "You want me to listen to you now? You made it clear where the lines were drawn this morning, and this doesn't concern you."

"This isn't about that." My voice cracks. "It's about Bec."

"Yes, and she's my family," he snarls. "Not yours."

His words are meant to wound, and they do. But it isn't even the final blow.

"Go back to the room," he orders. "As of now, you are on lockdown in this house."

Horror washes over me as I shake my head. "No, you can't do that. I have to see my sisters. We have to do a binding spell for Bec. Please, Azrael, I'm begging you to listen—"

"Fuck your spells!" he roars. "They have no meaning here."

I know his words come from a place of helplessness and rage over Bec's illness, but it doesn't make them any less painful when he inflicts them. I can see that hope is lost in his eyes, and it guts me all the same. But whoever my husband was last night when he held me in his arms, that man has disappeared. He's going to remove me from the room, shut me away from Bec—and I don't know how to stop it.

So, with one last desperate effort, I hurl myself toward the bed, nearly knocking the nurse out of the way as I grab Bec's hand.

She blinks up at me, her eyes at half-mast, and I don't know if she can even understand what's happening right now. But I have to do the only thing I can at this point.

"Mother Goddess, please protect her," I whisper. "Stop the evil in this house from bringing further harm to her. Bless her body with your healing powers. Bind the evil, bind the evil, bind the evil."

"Enough," Azrael bites out, his arm latching around mine.

"Wait!" I meet Bec's gaze, my voice panicked. "Your protection stone."

"I... have it," she answers, her voice barely a whisper. "It was working. It was. And then..." Her words drift off, her mouth too dry to speak.

"Bec," I choke out.

Azrael yanks me back, effectively separating us when his arm bands around my waist, and he begins to haul me from the room.

"You can't do this!" I scream at him. "Something evil is working here. I'm telling you, it's not natural!"

Azrael doesn't respond, making it clear he won't listen to what I say right now.

But it doesn't stop me from trying again. "Salomé was in Bec's room last night," I blurt out.

He pauses at the door to his bedroom, his fingers wrapping around my jaw. "What are you trying to say?"

His question isn't a question. It's a challenge. He's daring me to speak ill of Salomé, to cast the accusation he can feel brewing beneath the surface.

"I'm saying Bec has been okay all week," I clip out. "And after Salomé snuck into her room in the middle of the night while she was sleeping, she's not okay anymore. You figure it out, Azrael. Your loyalty to that horrible woman has skewed your perception. She's fucking deranged—"

His eyes flash, and before I can even make sense of it, he shoves me inside the room and slams the door in my face. A second later, a lock engages, and when I rattle the door handle, terror claws its way through me.

My first instinct is to run through the connecting door to my room, but the moment I do, I hear another lock engaging on the main door.

"Azrael, please!" I beat my fists against the wood. "You have to listen to me!"

The echo of his footsteps drifts away and leaves me colder and more shattered than I ever thought I could be.

He told me I could trust him.

Now I know that was a lie.

26

AZRAEL

I return to Bec's room.

No, not her room, I remind myself. This is the one we had set up just like a hospital room in the best of Society hospitals with all the best possible equipment. We keep it separate of Bec's actual bedroom because I want her to have some sense of normalcy. Her illness, this mysterious, tricky thing that has her by the throat, is a part of her life right now. It cannot—I will not allow it—to become the whole of her life.

To steal that life.

My brother is at my side at the bottom of the bed. He is massaging her foot, wanting to make sure she knows we're here with her, that she's not alone as we try to keep out of the way of the doctors and nurses.

Bec lies there motionless, her eyes closed, looking so small, so fucking fragile.

"She was better," Emmanuel says. "I swear, last night, she was better."

Don't terminal patients have a last surge of energy before the end? But no, she's not terminal. She's too young, not quite sixteen. She is not terminal.

I squeeze Emmanuel's shoulder and watch his face in profile, his eyes not once leaving our sister. I don't give voice to the words my mind conjured.

One of the machines finally makes a noise that isn't an alarm, and the doctor working on her exhales. He looks visibly relieved, his flushed face beaded with sweat. He's in his thirties, and I've seen him a few times even though he's not her main doctor.

He looks up at his team and nods. "Let's give her some space," he says, drawing the blanket up to Bec's narrow shoulders. A child's shoulders.

"What happened?" I ask the doctor as we step away from the bed. Emmanuel goes to Bec and takes her hand in his. She doesn't move. "She was good last night."

"Azrael," he says, shaking his head, very clearly perplexed. "I don't know. Very honestly, I simply do not know. I've ordered more tests, but the poor girl has been through them all before and the vitamins and supplements we've prescribed... she's been taking them in varying dosages for more than half a year. They wouldn't cause this."

"Vitamins and supplements? She was complaining her medication hurt her stomach."

His forehead furrows. "They shouldn't have."

"Doctor," one of the nurse's calls.

"Excuse me," he says to me and turns to answer the woman's question.

I move to the other side of my sister's bed. I can't help but think of the timing of this.

In two days, it will be the first anniversary of Abacus's death.

I squeeze Bec's small, too-cold hand, my throat closing in that way it does. I say a mental prayer, something I haven't done in a very, very long time. I'm not even sure to whom I'm praying. But I ask whoever is listening to please spare her. Spare Bec.

Don't make me bury two siblings only a year apart.

"Azrael," Salomé calls from the doorway. She glances at Bec, and I recall what Willow said, that she'd been in Bec's room.

What was she accusing our grandmother of? She may hate Salomé, and with good reason, but to suggest she was the cause of Bec's sudden turn for the worse is inexcusable.

"Will you stay with her?" I ask Emmanuel.

His face is ashen as he glances at our grandmother and nods to me, pulling a chair closer and sitting down beside Bec's bed.

"We need to talk," Salomé says.

"Now isn't a good time."

"I think it's exactly the right time," she says with a glance at Bec. "I'd think you'd agree."

I study her, see the hollows around her eyes, the shadows of a woman who rarely sleeps. She looks more gaunt than usual. The incident must be weighing on her even if she doesn't want to show it.

"Was she up last night? Did you hear something?" I ask.

"What?"

"Willow mentioned she thought you'd gone to Bec's room."

Her gaze narrows on me, and she tilts her head back, cocking it to the side. "That witch was roaming free in our house? No, I shouldn't be surprised. But do tell. What was she accusing me of exactly?"

"I'm just trying to understand, Grandmother."

"Well, I am insulted you even bring it up, but I'll set your mind at ease since it seems your loyalties are shifting."

"My loyalties—"

"Rébecca was restless, as she often is," she says, cutting me off. "I told you all that junk food would be bad for her."

"I don't think popcorn and M&Ms caused this."

"Like I said, the child was restless. I went to soothe her, as I often do, I might add, while you and your brother are out devil knows where doing devil knows what." She glances over my shoulder. I guess that with her raised voice, the nurses took notice because she speaks the next part more quietly, "There is another matter we need to discuss. A private one."

"It can't wait?" I run my hands through my hair. I'm fucking exhausted.

"No, it can't."

Without needing a reply, she turns on her heel and walks toward the stairs, her long, heavy black skirt swishing behind her.

Although reluctant, I follow her down the stairs, glancing at my closed bedroom door. I know Willow cares about Bec, but accusing Salomé of doing real harm to her own granddaughter is unacceptable.

I don't let my mind wander to those letters as I follow Grandmother down the stairs and out the French doors that will lead to the backyard. I'll find whoever is threatening Willow and deal with them later. For now, locked in that room is the safest place for her.

The day is dark and damp, and the ground is wet and muddy beneath my feet. I don't have to wonder where Grandmother is headed. I know. She disappears under the cover of trees and just before I follow, I turn back to glance up at the house, at my bedroom window. There, standing against the glass is Willow. She rests her hand against the window, and even from here I can see the concern on her face.

But now is not the time.

I turn away and head toward the churchyard where Shemhazai's statue looms seemingly taller than ever. The cracked stone altar lays in two slabs at his feet, the offerings Bec made just days ago a muddy, sodden mess. I stop a few feet from Salomé, who bows her head, puts her hands together and mutters a prayer declaring her undying and unquestioning loyalty to this demon-angel. This dark guardian who supposedly shields us from the Wildblood curse, but not for nothing and not out of any goodwill.

No, Shemhazai is not a benevolent being. He demands a high price for his *blessings,* a word Salomé uses. For centuries, we've paid what he has required, and we've prospered. Our fortunes grew, our line continued healthy and strong, and our family remains powerful.

But Shemhazai's Tithe is paid in blood. Mine and Willow's. Delacroix and Wildblood.

Has every Penitent before me come to the same crossroads as I? This hesitation, this moral dilemma? Or hell, is it pure selfishness on my part? Maybe I just don't want to die.

No, it's not that. I am not afraid of death. But Willow... What I am doing is condemning her to death. I knew that before I ever set foot in the Wildblood house, before The Tithing ceremony, yet I did it.

I walked in there, found the woman bearing the birthmark, and took her despite knowing all along exactly what I was doing even if they did not. Even if they knew the marked woman's life would end tragically within a year of being taken, the Wildbloods do not know that that tragedy is brought down by us. The blood of their daughters, their sisters, very firmly stains our hands.

"You have angered him," Grandmother says without looking at me.

I don't speak. What can I say, that it was a bolt of

lightning? It's the truth, yes, but that will only support her argument.

And what do I believe? Am I a hypocrite?

She turns her head to look at me over her shoulder, but I keep my sight on the altar. "In two days' time, we will mark the anniversary of your brother's passing," she says, as if his death was in any way gentle, but I bite my tongue. "Will we bury your sister on the same day, Azrael?"

I meet her eyes. "Don't say that."

"Isn't it the truth?"

"Do not say it."

"As you wish," she answers, having hit her mark and made her point despite having heard the warning in my voice. She walks toward me. "It is up to you. Your sister's life is in your hands. The Sacrifice must be made, Azrael. And if you refuse it, for now, then as you wrestle yourself to come to terms with what must be, make an offering to him. Appease him, or he will take your sister. Does a Wildblood witch mean more to you than your own flesh and blood?"

"Grandmother, taking one life will not heal another. Bec's illness is not Shemhazai's doing."

She steps closer to me, so close I smell her acrid breath. "Then explain what happened to your sister," she hisses. "Make it make sense when not a single doctor can."

My jaw tightens and my gaze moves over her shoulder. I can't explain it, and she knows it.

"Medical miracles happen every day, don't they?"

she asks using a falsely sweet voice, one too young for her. Too unnatural. "It is not too late to reverse this. This..." She gestures to the altar. "This is a sign, a warning for you to act. It is a second chance. I won't allow you to waste it."

"What does that mean?" I ask, meeting her pale eyes, seeing the sheen almost like tears, but not tears. Never tears with my grandmother.

"It means what I said. I will not allow you to waste this second chance Shemhazai has given us."

With those words, she turns and walks away, leaving me standing in the shadow of the demon-angel.

27

AZRAEL

I don't sleep that night. Nor do I return to my bedroom.

I will not allow you to waste this second chance.

My migraine has returned with a vengeance.

The chords of the piano sound eerie in this abandoned room, this hollow, forgotten part of the house. I play louder, one eye on the ancient grandfather clock even though I don't need to watch to know what is coming. To hear every tick of every second that passes, time creeping along forgetful of our tragedies. Oblivious to our marking of them.

As the second hand crosses the twelve-o'clock mark, the minute hand follows. A door opens on the clock face where a small bird should emerge to announce the new day. But the mechanism is old, and I don't remember the bird ever having done its work. Instead, there's a black hole and a creaking of sorts before the door closes and the clock carries on keeping time, neither knowing nor caring what day this is.

I continue playing, closing my eyes, my song a lament with too much grief, too much loss, too much sadness. But even if I pour everything I have into the music, the pain never lessens.

And now, Bec lies barely conscious in the hospital bed upstairs. My wife is locked in my bedroom, and I don't know when I can unlock that door and face her —when and if I can set her free.

I recall our conversation just before I learned that Bec had fallen ill. Me telling her I can't protect her if she's not honest with me. That I have a right to know. What a hypocrite I am.

I will not allow you to waste this second chance.

Grandmother's words repeat in my mind. I stand, slamming the piano lid down so hard the keys scream, shrill and final. I blow the candles out, eight of them dripping wax from the candelabra onto the piano, and stalk out of that room in near solid darkness. Memory guides me down the corridor away from the main part of the house toward the door that will lead me outside. I don't want to run into Grandmother. I couldn't stand it.

I will not allow you to waste this second chance.

I hear her words again as I step out into the night. The air is humid and heavy, and I walk to the lake, to that tree. Time may not care, but I will mark my brother's death.

Did Willow understand when I told her how I'd

found him? Butchered. It's the only word to describe the sight I came upon when I got to the clearing that night. He was naked, having stripped off his clothes and left them in a neat pile nearby. Which somehow makes it all worse. He'd calculated it all. Planned it. Thought it through. He'd have carried both rope and dagger to the tree. He'd have to have chosen the place and the time so as not to be interrupted.

The fact that he did it here, not at Shemhazai's altar, means something, doesn't it? Or maybe it's what Willow said, that he sought the comfort of memories of happier times. Of our mother.

If she were here, what would she make of us now? Me, a man who has locked his wife away to await... what exactly? Her execution?

Am I a liar? Will this curse make a liar of me as well as a murderer?

What would my father think of me? Of us?

I can tell you they would not be proud. But there is one thing I am certain of. They'd send Salomé packing. They'd tear down the statue of Shemhazai.

But at that thought, I stop. Would they? They had years to do it. We lived on this property for almost a decade before they disappeared. We were away from Grandmother's ever-watchful eye, away from scripture as she sees it, yet Shemhazai stands tall and angry and blood-thirsty as ever. The demon-angel will never have his fill.

Why didn't my parents tear down the statue that stands as an icon?

When I get to the clearing, I slow my steps. In the distance, I hear Benedict whine, and guilt gnaws at me. I should have brought him. I'm sure Grandmother has him tethered to the pole outside the kitchen door.

I just want to be alone with my thoughts and my misery, though. I don't deserve the happiness he brings.

I move toward Abacus's tree. Once I'm near enough, I search the ground for a sharp stone and, in lieu of a proper memorial, I carve a line into the trunk of the tree to mark the first anniversary.

The dagger he used to cut out the birthmarks on his shoulder blades was an antique dating centuries back. Its place sits empty in the library still. For those Penitents who chose to shave the head of their sacrifice, inflicting yet another humiliation on the condemned woman, that was the blade they used. No scissors; that hadn't been barbaric enough. The significance of it all, the butchering of the hair that is so much a part of the Wildblood identity, Abacus having chosen that particular knife to slice the mark of our ancestry off his back, it is not lost on me.

That knife, worth a fortune once, now rusts in the bottom of the lake—and good riddance to it. If Grandmother knew, I'm sure she'd send a diving party to retrieve it.

Willow's face in the window last night comes to mind. The way she looked at me when I dragged her from Bec's bedside and locked her away is burned into my mind. Her concern for my sister. Her disbelief. Her desperation.

Then Grandmother's warning.

I will not allow you to waste this second chance.

I turn from the tree, that rock clenched in my fist and with a scream, I send it crashing into the water. I push my hands into my hair, pulling at it, the pain of the migraine almost unbearable. When Willow and I stood under this tree just a few nights ago, she set the tips of her fingers on my temples and, as if by some witchcraft, banished the pain. The way my head feels now, it's like someone's pushing pins into an effigy of me. Dozens of them. Hundreds.

I walk back toward the house, but veer off toward the chapel when I get to the crossroads. Anger carries me toward the statue. I find my hands are fists and my jaw is set tight with rage.

I don't plan on paying any attention to it, but I am going to do what my brother would have wanted me to do: light a candle for him inside the chapel. Abacus, for all our Grandmother's teaching, still believed in a good god. A benevolent one. He was terrified of Shemhazai's wrath. As much as Grandmother had tried to beat into him that Shemhazai *was* his god, he'd resisted. He was stronger than she wanted to believe.

In the end, not strong enough, but not in any way weak.

The red light of the tabernacle lamp comes into view first, and I don't mean to pause at the broken altar. I don't mean to pay the demon-angel any mind, but my eye catches on something glinting around his sword hand and I stop. Because there, since my visit with Grandmother, someone has hung a crucifix.

Is it a mockery of the angel? Surely it could not be Grandmother. She would not affix a crucifix to his wrist. Not Bec, obviously. The staff wouldn't come here. I hear their whispers. They're certain the thing is haunted. Willow is locked away. It's not her. Was it Emmanuel? An effort to temper Shemhazai's power? His grip on us?

It's strange, out of character.

I leave it alone. I'll ask Emmanuel about it later. Instead, I go into the chapel, which always feels cold no matter the outside temperature, and light two candles. One for Abacus and one for Bec. Because it can't hurt, can it?

My cell phone rings. I lift it out of my pocket to find it's Emmanuel.

"Where are you?" he asks, sounding urgent, his voice echoing as if off empty halls.

"Out at the chapel. Where are you?"

"I came to find you in your usual place. Heading back now. You need to meet me out front now."

"Why? Is Bec—"

"Bec's stable. She woke up a little while ago and managed to have a few sips of broth. Larissa just called."

"Larissa?" The hair on the back of my neck stands on end, and I make my way out of the chapel and back toward the house.

"There's been an attempt on another woman."

I hurry my steps. "What?"

"Disciples. She's alive. Badly hurt but alive. And we need to meet Larissa."

"Why?'

"They were interrupted. A neighbor was walking her dog and the thing went batshit apparently. Neighbor knew something was off at the house, and when she set the dog loose, it went bolting for the back door. Must have scared them, and three men fled, one of them injured."

"Still not processing why we need to meet with Larissa. I don't want to leave Bec and I need to talk to Willow." I see my grandmother in the living room and decide to take the long way around to the front of the house.

"You will. They abandoned a car. There's apparently photos inside. Photos of our house."

My blood runs cold.

"What?" I ask as I come around the corner just as Emmanuel steps out of the front door. He disconnects the call and tosses the phone to me.

"Scroll through the photos. That's just a few, apparently. I'll drive."

I catch his phone before he slides into the driver's seat of the Jaguar and open the photos. What I see there has me stopping. It's a series of shots and they're recent. I guess they're from the day the Wildblood sisters came to visit Willow because there they all are as I scroll through. Whoever took the pictures must have been following them.

"Get in," Emmanuel calls, leaning across the front seat to push the passenger side door open.

"What the hell?" I shake my head.

"There's more on the scene. The back seat of the car is apparently littered with photos of one particular redhead, not all recent, but documenting fucking years."

I get in, close my door and turn to him. "Christ."

He starts the engine, revs it, puts the car into first gear as I scroll to the last photo—one of my wife.

My wife, floating naked in a swimming pool, her eyes closed.

"What the hell is this?"

"The pool is at their house, in the backyard."

I zoom in on Willow's face in the photo and what I see there has me horrified and sickened at once. Because someone has taken a pen or hell, could be the point of a dagger, and carved a cross into her forehead. It looks like it's been done repeatedly, angrily. Across the top, written in furious red sharpie, are the words: *for the wages of sin is death.*

28

WILLOW

An entire day passes with no sign of Azrael. He doesn't come to the room. He doesn't bother to give me an update on Bec. When the housekeeper delivers my meals, she informs me she's been instructed not to provide any information. Whether those are Salomé's directives or my husband's, I don't know.

The only thing left to do is sit with my thoughts and come to grips with the harsh reality of my circumstances. Is this what's to become of me? Will he keep me locked in this room like a prisoner until I die?

Tears fall, and I swipe them away, but they return until, eventually, I stop caring and let them go unchecked.

I pass the time texting my sisters and parents, staring out the window, and pacing the room. Fiona watches in concern, never far from my side. She senses my despair and tries to provide comfort, but it does little to soothe either of us.

"I don't know what we're going to do, Fi," I whisper as I stare into her eyes.

She nudges my hand, showing me that I'm not alone, whatever it is that may come.

A little while later, I hear a car in the drive, and when I glance out the window, Azrael is climbing inside to join his brother. They're going somewhere.

He hesitates before he closes the door, and I hold my breath, waiting for him to look up. To meet my gaze and show me that he hasn't shut me out completely. But he just shakes his head and slams the door before the car disappears down the driveway.

Another wave of emotion catches me by the throat as I stand there, feeling his loss. The delicate threads of whatever connection we may have had are fraying, ripping, as if to prove the curse would always destroy us this way.

I fear this is only the beginning of the end.

I'm trapped in those thoughts, equally terrified and depressed, when the sound of the lock disengaging on the door startles me. I step back on instinct, knowing it can't be the housekeeper. I've already had my dinner. Sure enough, when the door creaks open, it isn't a friendly face staring back at me. It's Salomé.

"What do you want?" I snap at her, eyes narrowing on the tome in her hands.

"You've made a grave mistake," she informs me with a smug sense of satisfaction. "Did you really think you could undo the curse? That you could rewrite what has been done for centuries?"

"Leave me alone." I turn to face the window again so she can't see my vulnerability, though I'm sure she senses it. She wouldn't be here otherwise.

A moment passes, but she doesn't go. She allows the silence to bloom, filling up the space between us.

"I was foolish like you once," she says. "I had to learn the hard way too. Azrael is made of greater things than you could ever even imagine. But he is still a man, and mortal men have their faults. He thought it would be best to lie to you, to keep you complacent until it was time. And I suppose it worked because I've seen the way you look at him. You are falling for him. Perhaps you already have. But I know you aren't the sort of woman to hide from the truth. I think you'd rather know exactly what it is you're facing. Exactly what he has planned for you."

Her words prickle, and I don't want to turn around, but I can't help myself. When I meet her gaze, she knows she has me.

"Do you want to know the truth, Willow?" She glances at the tome in her hands before extending it in offer. "Do you want to know how Azrael feels about you? There was only ever one way this could end. It's written in these pages."

"And what will it cost me?" I narrow my eyes at her. "Clearly, you want something. So just spit it out."

She smiles, and I don't know how she manages it,

but the woman looks downright sinister every time she does that.

"A lock of your hair will suffice."

"For your God?" I snort.

Her eyes flash. "For Shemhazai. The Sacrifice must be offered."

There are no two ways about it. She's delusional. Insane, probably. But even so, I'm not above temptation. I don't know what's in that tome, but I do know that Azrael is a liar. He's proven I can't trust his assurances. If I am to go to my death, I don't want to go naively. I want to know exactly how the man I married has betrayed me.

Salomé waits for my decision, already knowing I will make a deal with the devil. She sees that weakness in me, and I hate her for it. But it doesn't stop me from walking into the bathroom and retrieving a pair of scissors.

I can barely meet my gaze in the mirror's reflection as I degrade myself by snipping off a lock of what feels like part of my soul. When I deliver it back to her, I wonder if I'm making a terrible mistake by negotiating with an emotional terrorist. But the truth is, she's right. I opened myself up to Azrael. I have feelings for him I never wanted or expected. I have to know if he's been manipulating me this entire time. I have to know what he's been hiding from me.

"Happy?" I hold the hair out for Salomé, and a wicked gleam reflects in her eyes.

"Very." She snatches the lock from my fingers and

hands me the tome. "You aren't half as stupid as I thought you might be."

I won't dignify her with a response, and I'm glad when she returns to the door without waiting for one.

"Enjoy your reading. There's quite a lot there."

She takes her leave, and it doesn't register in my mind until a moment later, as her shoes echo down the hall, that she didn't lock the door.

I glance down at the tome in my hands, torn between two options. I don't know how much time I'll have before Azrael returns. If I'm going to read it, it has to be now. But I also know Bec is just down the hall, and I want to check on her while I have the opportunity.

I crack open the tome, deciding I'll just have to be quick. But as I begin flipping through the pages, reading through the documented history of the first Delacroix and Wildblood marriage, my stomach revolts.

There are pages upon pages documenting their time together.

There is no other way to describe what's written in these passages: Ophelia Wildblood was tortured until the very day she was executed by her husband. The graphic descriptions of her punishments include whippings, beatings, and humiliation in the form of shaving her head and parading her around naked before leading her to the very spot where she was stoned to death.

A tear splashes onto the page before me, and my

eyes blur as I flip through more pages until I reach the next couple. And the next. And slowly, an undeniable pattern emerges.

While every Wildblood woman who had the ill fate of marrying a Delacroix dies, it was not fate who delivered the blow. It was their husbands who took their lives.

They were all murdered.

A silent sob wrenches from my throat as I try to keep myself in check, forcing my attention back to the last remaining pages, to the sections that detail the curse. The Delacroixes believe that sacrificing a Wildblood with each new generation will curb the tragedies that have plagued their lineage for so long.

To solidify their argument, there are well-documented examples of how the tides turned with every Sacrifice. And at the end are the contracts signed by each of the Delacroix men vowing to carry the torch to protect their bloodline.

When I see Azrael's signature on the last contract, my blood runs cold.

He never intended to protect me.

You have my word, Willow. As long as I live and breathe, I will protect you. I will keep you safe.

Betrayal like I've never known pierces my heart as I recall those words, those lies from his lips. He never meant any of it.

And now, there's only one thing I can do.

"Willow?" Bec croaks when she sees me standing above her bed.

"Hi." I offer her a soft smile as I take a seat beside her. "How are you feeling?"

Fear streaks through her eyes, and she averts her gaze. "I... don't know. I'm scared."

"It's okay." I squeeze her hand, even though, truthfully, I don't know if anything will be okay.

She's quiet while I take in the room around her, noting all the supplements stacked on her nightstand next to a case of nutritional shakes. My eyes linger on the open vanilla shake at her bedside. I don't know what prompts me to pick it up, but when I do, it's still full.

"Not hungry?" I ask.

She shakes her head. "I hate those things. They taste so awful. Gran makes me drink them."

I allow that to digest for a moment before I venture down a path of questioning that we might not be able to come back from. "What do they taste like?"

Bec wrinkles her nose. "There are different flavors, but they aren't even sweet. They're all too bitter."

I straighten my spine, regarding her with concern. "And what about the pills? How are they?"

She glances at the supplements and shrugs. "Those aren't bad, I guess. But the ones Gran makes me take hurt my stomach."

Terror wraps its ugly claws around me as I process the full meaning of her words. I didn't want to be right about this, but there's no way I can dismiss it. Maybe Azrael can't see the truth, but I can.

"Bec, I have to tell you something," I whisper, sneaking a glance at the time on my phone. It's been fifteen minutes since I called Raven already.

"What is it?" she asks.

"I have to leave," I choke out. "Because it isn't safe for me here. And I don't think it's safe for you either. I want you to come with me so I can take you to a real hospital. You can see a different doctor and get the treatment you need. Would you be willing to do that?"

A frown tugs at her lips as she considers it. "What about my brothers? Won't they be mad if we go?"

"I'll make them understand once you're safe," I assure her. "They won't be mad at you, I promise."

She bites her lip, anxiety creeping into her features. "How will we get out of the house with Gran here, though?"

"Don't worry. I have a plan."

Bec mulls it over, struggling to decide on her own while I wait with bated breath. I don't want to leave her here. I don't think I can, and this is the only chance we'll probably get to leave.

"Okay," she says finally. "I trust you."

Relief swells inside me as I nod, helping her pull back the bedcovers. "Okay. We're going to have to be very quiet. You wait here. I'm just going to grab Fi's crate."

I return to my room to gather the hobo bag I already packed, slinging it over my shoulder before I stoop to pick up Fiona's carrier. It's all that I'm taking. I don't care about anything else right now.

When I get back to Bec's room, I'm glad to see she's sitting up on her own, but she's still very weak. It will be a process getting both of us out of the house.

"Just one second," I tell her, eyeing the shake. "Let me take a couple of these."

Bec watches me curiously as I secure a latex glove from the nightstand over the open shake and stuff it into my bag, along with an unopened one.

"I don't need them," she tells me.

"I know." I give her a strained smile. "I'll explain later."

I help her from the bed, giving her a minute to adjust to being on her feet again. Ten minutes and one very careful walk later, Bec, Fiona, and I make it down the stairs and into the library unseen. Just that amount of exertion nearly drains Bec, and helping her while I carry Fiona's crate is no easy feat, but we manage somehow.

The house is mostly quiet, and I have no idea where Salomé is, but I'm hoping she'll stay gone long enough for us to get out. When I open the secret door to the dark wing, Bec stiffens.

"We're going through there?" she asks.

"It's okay," I assure her. "It's safe. I was just in here the other day, and Azrael does this all the time."

She still looks uncertain, but she puts her trust in me as I lead her down the dark corridor. With only the light from my phone to guide us, it's difficult to see, but

I already know where we're going. I've seen the door from outside the house, and I'm just hoping it's not barricaded shut.

It takes us an additional five minutes to get there, and when we do, I have to settle Bec on an old rickety chair while I muscle open the ancient locks. With a lot of creaking and groaning, the door finally opens, and I steel myself with another breath. I'm exhausted, and we still have to get down the driveway.

"Not long now," I tell Bec, helping her out the door as I clutch Fi's crate in my other hand.

My phone chimes, and I stop to look at it. Raven sent me a message informing me she arrived and asking if she should come inside. I pause to read her question in confusion before calling her and wedging the phone against my ear.

"Yeah?" she answers.

"The gate is locked from the inside," I tell her. "You'll have to wait for us down there."

"It's open," she says.

The hair on the back of my neck prickles with alarm as I consider that. I know they don't leave the gate open. Does that mean Azrael is on his way back, or did they just forget?

"Do you see anyone?" I ask Raven.

"No, it's all clear."

Her words should reassure me, but something about this feels too easy. Regardless, there isn't anything I can do about it. I just have to focus on getting us out of here.

"Walk down to meet us," I tell my sister. "You can help us back to the car. I don't want Salomé to hear you pull up."

"Okay, I'll be right there."

The line goes dead, and Bec's breathing becomes strained as we continue, even with me supporting her. She doesn't weigh much, but the journey is taking a toll on both of us.

When we finally see Raven, I feel the weight of relief as she takes over without question, helping Bec along while I carry Fi.

None of us talk, but Raven and I glance at each other, both of us worried. I don't know if we're actually going to make it out of here. I still have that terrible feeling Azrael will show up at any moment if Salomé doesn't find us first. To make things worse, Elizabeth's voice is notably absent to warn me like she usually does.

Regardless, I can still rely on my senses, and as we approach Raven's purple Volkswagen Beetle, I can't ignore the sludgy feeling in my gut. Something isn't right.

"We have to get out of here," I tell the girls as I shove Fi's crate into the backseat. "Hurry."

A scream behind me pierces the night air, and I whip around to see Raven being yanked back by her hair and Bec crashing to the ground. Two dark figures emerge from behind them, followed by three more from the other side of the road. It isn't until I feel the blade of a knife against my throat and smell the sickly cloying scent of a man I'll never forget that true terror settles over me.

"Hi, Willow." Caleb drags his nose along my neck, inhaling me. "Did you miss me?"

My body quakes, knees nearly buckling as I turn to meet his gaze. The scar slashed across his face, right through his eye, is confirmation that my mind isn't playing tricks on me. He's back with the disfigurement I gave him, and I have no doubt he'll kill me this time.

He's going to kill us all.

"I can smell your fear," he growls, his lips hovering over my ear. "And I can't tell you how long I've thought about this. You and I are going to have so much fun together, baby."

"Leave them," I croak. "Please. They have nothing to do with this."

A dark chuckle blows across my cheek as he shakes his head behind me. "Load them all into the van. It's time for the Wildbloods to learn about the wages of sin."

THANK YOU

Thanks for reading The Tithing, Book 1 of The Sacrifice Duet. We hope you are enjoying Willow and Azrael's story.

Their story concludes in The Penitent.

MORE BOOKS BY A. ZAVARELLI & NATASHA KNIGHT

Want more books set in the world of The Society? You can find them below!

The Sacrifice Duet

By A. Zavarelli & Natasha Knight

The Tithing

The Penitent

The Society Trilogy

By A. Zavarelli & Natasha Knight

Requiem of the Soul

Reparation of Sin

Resurrection of the Heart

The Rite Trilogy

By A. Zavarelli & Natasha Knight

His Rule

Her Rebellion

Their Reign

Kingdom Fall

By A. Zavarelli

A Sovereign Sons Novel

The Devil's Pawn Duet

By Natasha Knight

Devil's Pawn

Devil's Redemption

The Ties That Bind Duet is a Bratva Secret Baby Romance set in its own world.

By A. Zavarelli & Natasha Knight

Mine

His

ALSO BY A. ZAVARELLI

Kingdom Fall

A Sovereign Sons Novel

The Society Trilogy

Requiem of the Soul

Reparation of Sin

Resurrection of the Heart

Ties that Bind Duet

Mine

His

Boston Underworld Series

Crow

Reaper

Ghost

Saint

Thief

Conor

Sin City Salvation Series

Confess

Convict

Bleeding Hearts Series

Echo

Stutter

Standalones

Stealing Cinderella

Beast

Pretty When She Cries

Tap Left

Hate Crush

For a complete list of books and audios, visit http://www.azavarelli.com/books

Requiem of the Soul

Reparation of Sin

Resurrection of the Heart

The Rite Trilogy

His Rule

Her Rebellion

Their Reign

Dark Legacy Trilogy

Taken (Dark Legacy, Book 1)

Torn (Dark Legacy, Book 2)

Twisted (Dark Legacy, Book 3)

Unholy Union Duet

Unholy Union

Unholy Intent

Collateral Damage Duet

Collateral: an Arranged Marriage Mafia Romance

Damage: an Arranged Marriage Mafia Romance

Ties that Bind Duet

Mine

His

ALSO BY NATASHA KNIGHT

The Sacrifice Duet
The Tithing
The Penitent

The Augustine Brothers
Forgive Me My Sins
Deliver Me From Evil

Ruined Kingdom Duet
Ruined Kingdom
Broken Queen

The Devil's Pawn Duet
Devil's Pawn
Devil's Redemption

To Have and To Hold
With This Ring
I Thee Take
Stolen: Dante's Vow

The Society Trilogy

MacLeod Brothers

Devil's Bargain

Benedetti Mafia World

Salvatore: a Dark Mafia Romance

Dominic: a Dark Mafia Romance

Sergio: a Dark Mafia Romance

The Benedetti Brothers Box Set (Contains Salvatore, Dominic and Sergio)

Killian: a Dark Mafia Romance

Giovanni: a Dark Mafia Romance

The Amado Brothers

Dishonorable

Disgraced

Unhinged

Standalone Dark Romance

Descent

Deviant

Beautiful Liar

Retribution

Theirs To Take

Captive, Mine

Alpha

Given to the Savage

Taken by the Beast

Claimed by the Beast

Captive's Desire

Protective Custody

Amy's Strict Doctor

Taming Emma

Taming Megan

Taming Naia

Reclaiming Sophie

The Firefighter's Girl

Dangerous Defiance

Her Rogue Knight

Taught To Kneel

Tamed: the Roark Brothers Trilogy

ABOUT NATASHA KNIGHT

Natasha Knight is the *USA Today* Bestselling author of Romantic Suspense and Dark Romance Novels. She has sold over a million books and is translated into six languages. She currently lives in The Netherlands with her husband and two daughters and when she's not writing, she's walking in the woods listening to a book, sitting in a corner reading or off exploring the world as often as she can get away.

Write Natasha here: natasha@natasha-knight.com

NATASHA KNIGHT
sexy dark romance with heart

www.natasha-knight.com

ABOUT A. ZAVARELLI

A. Zavarelli is a USA Today and Amazon bestselling author of dark and contemporary romance.

When she's not putting her characters through hell, she can usually be found watching bizarre and twisted documentaries in the name of research.

She currently lives in the Northwest with her lumberjack and an entire brood of fur babies.

Want to stay up to date on Ashleigh and Natasha's releases? Sign up for our newsletters here.

Made in the USA
Las Vegas, NV
26 September 2023